WHAT THEY CHOOSE

Cora Baker

What They Choose

ISBN: 978-1-945994-80-7 Paperback
ISBN: 978-1-945994-81-4 Hardback

Cover created by: miblart.com
Edited by: Donna Royston

Published by Tannhauser Press

First Edition

www.tannhauserpress.com

For my ancestors who watch over me,
shaking their heads...

Table of Contents

WHAT
THEY
CHOOSE

Arrival

Felix was not the largest of the silent black cat colony, but he had the gift. He knew it. So he sat vigil until the day he watched the car pass by, knowing it was the one he had been waiting for.

***

"I remember the house from my childhood being isolated, but this is crazy," Eleanore Wright said to her best friend Emma over the speakerphone on the dash of her Ford Flex. "The road just became one lane on this side of a single-lane bridge."

"El, are you sure the GPS is working?" Emma asked over the car speakers.

"Yes. This actually looks familiar," El said as she drove by a gothic iron gate on her right with moss-covered granite pillars that looked rusted closed. "I remember the switchbacks, too."

"I was looking at the Seven Bends region of Virginia on Google Earth, and it looks beautiful,"

Emma said. "What do you remember?"

"I know what you're doing, Emma," El said. "Getting my mind off everything. I appreciate it. I'm OK. Really. My state of mind has gotten better since his funeral."

"So… What do you remember?" Emma deflected.

"My grandmother used to take us tubing in the river," El said, slowing a bit more. "My brothers and me and a crowd of cousins. All floating down the Shenandoah with a tube that had a cooler full of sodas and Boone's Farm wine. She'd always give me a sip."

"What did the parents do while she was corrupting you?" Emma asked.

"They would stay at the house, drink bourbon, smoke cigars, and cook giant briskets in the smoker," El said. "My uncles would hunt deer if it was Thanksgiving. Or work on old cars in the carriage house."

"When did you stop going?" Emma asked. "I didn't know you even had aunts or uncles."

"I was twelve the last time I was here. That was the last time I saw my gramma," El said. "I can't believe it was twenty-five years ago. That was Thanksgiving of 1992. She was 70 then. We were going to go back for Christmas that year, but Dad got that job in Texas."

"Why did you never go back?" Emma asked.

"Both my aunts died that year," El said. "Then my Dad died the following year—car accident in Texas. After that, something drove a wedge between my mom and gramma. The funeral for my dad was the last time I saw her."

"You're breaking up, El. I'm losing you," Emma said. "If I lose you, call me when you settle in, and we can…."

The call dropped.

The remaining drive was through dense woods. It was dark under the thick canopy above, but it had gotten much cooler. August in Virginia can be brutal. The winding road narrowed and turned into a single-lane dirt road.

She couldn't stream her favorite music without cell service, so she tried the radio. Options were slim, but she found a local radio station and was amused at the local commercials for a bowling alley, a subs and pizza shop, and a funeral home. When the music finally came on, it was 80s classic rock.

Eleanore's lights came on at one point. The forest was so dark. The headlights showed eyes reflecting from a black cat sitting on a rock outcropping. The rock had ancient graffiti that said KILROY WAS HERE, and she remembered that her Dad always called it Kilroy's Rock.

It meant she was close.

A view opened briefly on her left, and she stopped to look. She could see one of the Seven Bends and a town below. She remembered this view as well. She remembered walking to it from the house. She glanced at the GPS, and it was only half a mile to her destination.

Glancing up, a rusty sign said END STATE MAINTENANCE. Another faded sign said, "NO HUNTING," was nailed to the same signpost.

There were a couple of paths that led into the forest. No more street signs. There were more rusted metal "No Hunting" signs nailed to trees. The undergrowth in the woods here looked odd. It seemed to be trimmed clean to seven feet up. It allowed views into the woods where it was level.

Stone outcroppings looked like broken teeth flanking the road. Another black cat sat on one of these, watching her pass.

That can't be the same black cat.

The GPS announced her arrival. There was nothing here. El kept going because it all looked familiar. Like déjà vu.

Two pillars rose up on her left, and she remembered the lions on top of them. They were still there but no longer white. Instead, they were completely covered in moss, and the pine branches here now arched entirely over the road creating a tunnel that obscured most of the daylight.

Two massive stone-block columns flanked the road. Heavy iron gates were open and covered in vines. The house number engraved in a white marble block was barely visible: 137. These columns were covered in fine lichen on one side.

The massive iron gates were wide open, so she drove through without stopping. It was another 400 yards to the house. Tall grass to either side brushed her car. Giant oaks and pines surrounded the house. She remembered the expansive lawns from childhood that were now overgrown with waist-high grass and weeds. The house rose up from the gloom and broke

Eleanore's heart. She remembered it being alive, bright, beautiful, and full of light, love, and family.

It felt like a corpse of its former self.

The large wrap-around porch had out-of-control vines on its roof and a broken-down trellis. El's favorite porch swing was gone, but the rusting chains remained. A bare light bulb flickered as it hung from the wires. The front door was wide open, and the old familiar screen door hung by the bottom hinge.

Even though it was only 3:30 pm, it seemed like perpetual twilight.

Eleanore parked and quietly got out.

She could see immediately that a third of the porch planks were missing. Rotting timbers were visible and added to the mess. In addition, the granite steps that led up to the porch were no longer level.

She climbed them anyway.

She paused at the top step. El was reluctant to walk on the decking. Paint peeled everywhere on the siding.

Movement caught her eye.

It was another black cat.

How many of those cats are there around here?

She tried to recall what it had been like in her youth. She knew that beyond the yard was the foundation of the old church that had burned down a long time ago. She could only see the bell tower ruins because everything had grown out of control.

The cemetery on the other side was equally in disrepair. The tall grasses hid most of the monuments. The cat, another cat, sat on the arm of a cross, a tombstone.

Then she noticed what was wrong.

All the beautiful monuments above the grasses were vandalized and overgrown. They were all missing their heads.

***

It was unnerving standing before the open front door. El had the impression that the house was screaming. It gave her a chill that she had to shake off physically.

Each step was careful as she entered, feeling the floor with each step to make sure it was sound. She expected each step to creak on old floorboards, but her Converse Allstar sneakers were silent on the floor. That was even creepier.

Stop it, El. Grow up. It's just a house. Your house.

The foyer was expansive. It was flanked on each side with large antique furniture. To the right were a combination bench, coatrack, and umbrella stand. She recognized her gramma's coats: fox collars on wool peacoats. On the left was a narrow table about six feet long. It had a dusty Tiffany lamp and a vase full of dead roses. The lace doilies were covered in dust. A hat rack was in the corner with several hats. Dust and cobwebs covered most of the classic hats, fedoras, lady's hats, and an incongruous worn Buffalo Bills baseball cap.

Above the table was a large mirror. El startled. The opposite wall also had a mirror that created a kind of infinite tunnel that faded into the darkness.

Was that footsteps?

She listened closer. It was so quiet. Wind in the trees. Her own heartbeat. A few dry leaves blew in from the porch. She closed the door expecting the hinges to creak. They were also silent despite being old.

The latch sounded loud in the hush.

This is not a haunted house, El. Get a grip.

A staircase on the right side of the hall wound around and up. The runner was threadbare. It was as she remembered. She remembered being scolded for sliding down the massive oak railing by her mother as her gramma smiled and looked away, trying not to laugh.

To the right and left, there were regular oak columns and arches. To the right was the parlor. Sheets and dust covered the furniture. All the dark oak woodwork was covered in dust and cobwebs. It was obvious that this room had not been used in decades.

To the left was the dining room, in the same condition but worse. The dust seemed thicker. The cobwebs in the chandelier made her throat clench. Memories of this room returned: large family gatherings around that table, Christmas trees in the bay windows.

What happened to stop such joy?

El wiped away a tear.

Damn it's dusty in here…

She blamed all the dust.

Quietly she moved into the house. The hallway widened past the stairs. It was darker deeper into the house. As she moved through, she noticed things she didn't remember. The hall walls were covered with antique mirrors, beautiful in their placement and various sizes and shapes. As she moved down the hall, she got a fun-house mirror vibe. Mirrors faced more mirrors, and El's image was echoed.

She saw movement in one.

Was it her?

The closed double pocket doors she knew led to the library were to her right.

Using both hands, she used too much force to open them. When she was twelve, they always were difficult to open. They flew open on silent tracks, and she almost fell forward into a man that stood there silhouetted and motionless with a hammer in his right hand.

El screamed and fell backward. He reached for her, and she crab-walked backward to the opposite wall.

A deep gravelly voice demanded, "Who are you?"

El was trying to scramble to her feet in a panic. The top of her head hit the ornate frame of an oval mirror as she stumbled, and it crashed to the floor, shattering the mirror. Glass exploded in the hall. Before she got to her feet, she grabbed a long curved broken shard and pointed it at the man as he slowly entered the hall.

"Stay back." She pointed the improvised weapon at his face.

"Are you all right?" he asked. Concern was evident in his voice.

"Stay back."

"Calm down. Careful. Don't bump any more of the

mirrors."

"Who the fuck are you, and why are you in my house?"

"Your house?" He side-stepped into the hall and pressed a button on the wall, and ceiling lights came on.

"Answer the question and get out." She crunched on the glass.

"My name is Jake. You must be Eleanore." He put the hammer in a loop on his tool belt. He held out both hands, palm up. "I am a… was a friend of Lillian, your grandmother."

"What are you doing here?"

"Joyce Jacobs, your grandmother's attorney, said you would not arrive for another month. Lillian hired me to do a ton of repairs. Call Joyce. My name is Jake Harris. I'm sorry I scared you." He bent to pick up the ornate oval frame. "I may need CPR myself, to be honest."

The last piece of beveled glass fell from the frame as he lifted it and also shattered on the floor.

El dropped the piece she had held too tight. The adrenaline was fading, and she noticed the blood on her palm.

Jake was offering a perfectly folded handkerchief to her. He did not come any closer.

"I'm sorry about your grandmother," Jake said.

She took the handkerchief and choked out, "Thanks," then turned away. She was going to start crying. She didn't understand why.

After all, that had happened. Am I going to cry now?

"I'll just go." He leaned the ornate frame on the wall. "Call Joyce. I'll come back when you're ready."

El made no reply. She stood in the hall, holding it in until the door closed behind him. Sobs broke over her like a wave.

Jake Starts

From the shadows of the overgrown shrubs, the cat watched him go. He could smell the inner turmoil within him. It was better than fear. That would come soon enough.

***

Jake quietly closed the front door behind him, stepped off the porch, and walked around to the carriage house where his truck was parked. He took off his toolbelt and angrily tossed it into the back of his 1970 Chevy C-10. He consciously slowed himself as he drove down the long lane off the mountain.

Once he reached the paved road, he pulled out his cell phone and placed a call.

"Jacobs and Associates," a cheerful voice answered.

"Hi, Joyce." Jake let a bit of anger slip into his tone. "She's here, Joyce. I almost brained her with a hammer."

"What?" Joyce Jacobs abandoned her professional phone voice through the static.

"Yes." Jake said, "Jesus, I had just finished repairing that last window in the library when I heard someone in the house. You said I had four more weeks."

"Are you sure it's her?" Joyce asked.

"Yes. Lillian talked about her so much and had photos of her by her bed. It's her." Jake was venting. "She almost stabbed me, for God's sake."

"Did you say she stabbed you?" Static rose.

"With a broken piece of mirror," Jake said. "I'll probably be fired. She's going to call you. I hope."

"I'll take care of it, Jake," Joyce said. "Did you at least get that haircut and shave? The scary hobo look has got to go."

"You said I had another month."

"Is the house safe at least?"

"The roof is done. All the foundation repairs are done. All the windows and doors are repaired. The half bath on the main level and the master bath on the second level work but none of the others. And even those are scheduled for renovations."

"Bedrooms? Kitchen?" Joyce asked.

"Just the small one I had been sleeping in and Lillian's master bedroom. The kitchen's fine, but the place has not even been cleaned yet. I'm still planning a cleaning crew."

"I guess I will have to discuss it with Ms. Wright," Joyce said.

"Dammit. I just wasn't ready," Jake said.

"I know what you meant to her, Jake."

"Don't you start being nice to me now," Jake said. "Not happening."

"It's your fresh baked bread and that lasagna I miss, Jake," Joyce said.

"Don't say it."

"Any time you want to make lasagna and chill…."

"You said it."

"I just wish I could see your face blushing," Joyce said. "Did I distract you at least? I know you're upset."

"You did," Jake said, smiling at the memories.

"Gotta go. I think it's her on the other line," Joyce said quickly. "Bye, Jake."

***

Jake had turned right at the end of the long driveway, heading up the mountain. The rain had stopped. He tried to concentrate on the road and not think. The list of things he didn't want to think about was getting longer, not shorter.

Lasagna nights with Joyce and her amazing lingerie.

Finding Lillian Wright dead on the floor in the library.

The engagement ring was in his glove compartment.

Guilt for frightening Eleanore Wright.

Letting Lillian down.

Night raids and IEDs in Iraq.

So Jake did what he always did. He drove up the mountain.

The road got worse and worse until he pulled into the last driveway on the road. His driveway. It was unmarked, and a Quonset hut came into view around a bend, its old gray overhead door already opening. He pulled his truck inside onto the rough cement floor. The garage had a half loft above. He parked and got out.

The garage was big enough to hold four of his pickups if he wanted. All it had besides his truck was several tall tool chests, a washer and dryer, a single eight-foot-long folding table, and one overstuffed chair. A minifridge served as a side table to hold the stack of books.

His table saw was still set up on the right side.

His four-wheel ATV had its trailer attached. Jake unlocked the wheels and checked the fuel level.

He took two coolers out of the truck bed and placed them in the tiny trailer. Next, he opened the dryer, took a load of jeans and t-shirts, and folded them on the table. Each article of clothing was folded neatly and added to a sizeable rubberized tub.

Jake's phone rang as he loaded the tub into the small trailer.

The caller ID showed: Samantha Goodwin.

He stared at it while it rang. He knew if he pressed the ignore button, it would send it directly to voicemail, but Sam would know he did it. So he switched it to airplane mode, knowing it would act like he was already in a dead zone.

Talking to Sam was another thing to add to the list of things he didn't want to think about.

Eleanore Wright is nothing like Sam.

Why did I think that?

Jake started the ATV and drove it out as the overhead door closed. The garage door fob was affixed to his handlebars. He wound his way further up the mountain through groves of pines and narrow passes between rock outcroppings. He paused where he always did at a switchback that opened to a spectacular view across the Shenandoah Valley. Above, he could see his cabin. That view always made him feel better.

The trail wound around through the dense forest again and followed the ridge to the entrance. He parked the ATV at its usual stop under the corrugated tin roof shelter.

One day I will put on the walls. He mentally promised his ATV.

Grabbing one of the coolers, he walked the ten yards to his wide, hand-made door and entered The Cabin. It was not locked. It never was locked.

He liked to think of it as The Cabin. It was nothing like a cabin. It was a cross between Frank Lloyd Wright and Bag End.

I wonder if Lillian was related to Frank Lloyd…

He remembered she was gone. How often would that image of her on the floor in the library haunt him?

He put the groceries away. The large pantry was only about half full. He'd keep bringing an extra cooler of canned and dried goods until it was packed full. The fresh foods went into the propane fridge.

The rubberized tub went into the bedroom, and his clothes were put away.

Jake was never home this early. He checked the propane supply, water supply, filters, and solar panels.

The Cabin was all good to go, as usual.

Jake opened a Killian's Red from the fridge and went out through the twelve-foot-high window wall on the balcony. It was the only part of The Cabin that was not made of salvaged or local materials. Black iron frames held 4x4-foot triple-pane windows.

He stood by the stone wall and gazed at the view that never got old. Then, he turned his phone back on as he expected an important call from Joyce.

His phone rang again. He didn't even look this time.

Jake walked to the right and lit the stainless steel gas grill.

***

It was about 7:45 pm, and Jake was relaxing on the balcony with another beer and a full belly. Music drifted in the air as the solar lights came on in the planters and pots on the flagstone patio, one by one.

The phone rang again. He knew that Joyce Jacobs was on her landline by the wind chime ring tone.

"Why are you still in the office?" Jake asked without greeting.

"Saving your ass is why," she said.

"So I'm not fired?" Jake watched a bald eagle drift by as it looked for squirrels.

"I'll tell you, but you have to tell me what you made

for dinner first," Joyce demanded.

"If I had known food was a fetish, I would have only fed you PB&J sandwiches."

"Tell me or no details." Joyce was serious.

"OK, OK… Grilled salmon, braised mushrooms in a red wine sauce, and grilled asparagus seasoned with shallot salt. Garlic bread sticks as well. The last of them," Jake said. "Killian's Red beer instead of wine."

"Jesus, Jake," she sighed. "You could drown a toddler in my panties right now."

"When can't you?" he answered, amused.

"True."

"OK, details, dammit," Jake laughed.

"Well, I'm wearing the deep green emerald set, the lace ones," she began.

"About the Wright project!" he said.

"Oh, yeah, sorry," Joyce said. "Where are you?"

"I'm at The Cabin," he said. "The update? Please."

"Are you saying that because you know I hate roughing it?"

"For you, roughing it is staying in a hotel without 24/7 room service," Jake said.

"You know me so well."

"Joyce, for fuck's sake."

"OK. I talked her down. She knew she should have called." Joyce got serious. Jake knew the tone. "You need to know that her husband was just recently killed in a car crash. That's why she was early."

"Oh, no…" Jake said. "Now I feel worse. She was a mess."

"Jake." Joyce hesitated. "She said, for an instant, in

the shadows, she thought you looked exactly like him. After that, she said she was a little freaked out."

"A little?"

"She said you can come back tomorrow and give her an overview of the project. What's done, what's left," Joyce said. "I have to stop by there tomorrow to get her to sign some documents and give her keys. I hope to see you there."

"Please, behave."

"I will make no mention of lasagna or toddlers."

ELEANORE

From the windowsill, Felix watched. He could smell her blood from there. It was her. Absolutely her.

***

El sobbed for a long time after the door closed behind Jake, leaning against the wall in the hall. When she began to collect herself, she went to the kitchen and sat at the table. She wiped her eyes with the bloody handkerchief. As she wiped her nose, it smelled like cedar.

El looked at the cut on her hand. It wasn't bad. But it was her right hand. She got up and walked to the sink, and washed it. She tried to rinse the blood from the handkerchief with cold water. It mostly worked. There was a roll of paper towels on the counter next to a Mr. Coffee drip coffee maker. She folded a paper towel and held it in her hand.

The kitchen was huge and only partially renovated.

The black soapstone countertop was still in beautiful shape and had been recently scrubbed. The gas stove and large fridge were both obviously new, stainless steel models.

The Cabinets were dark stained with dated black handles and hinges. A large hole in the lower cabinets indicated where a dishwasher would likely go. There was an island that was new, but the countertop was a different stone. The cabinets below had the same style but were raw wood.

El took a deep breath. Then another.

This house will be a perfect distraction.

She pulled out her phone and found Joyce Jacobs was already in her contact list. She pressed call.

No Service.

"Dammit," she said out loud.

Looking up, she saw a phone on the wall. It was a rotary phone, but she tried it anyway.

There was a dial tone.

El held up the cell phone and pressed the receiver against her chin and shoulder as she literally dialed the number. It rang four times and was answered.

"Jacobs and Associates," a professional voice answered.

"May I speak to Joyce Jacobs, please?"

"Speaking."

"My name is Eleanore Wright. I believe we spoke once before."

"Yes, Ms. Wright," Joyce replied professionally. "I was planning to call you this week…."

"I am in town now at the house. I found a man

inside. He says he is a contractor. He scared the shit out of me." Eleanore was angry. "That was the last damn thing I needed today. And I broke a beautiful mirror and cut myself…."

El trailed off. She knew she was ranting and angry and needed to stop.

"I am sorry, Ms. Wright. That was likely to be Jake Harris. He is the contractor that Lillian hired. I helped your grandmother with the contract for that project. It was a big project. He was also a good friend to her," Joyce said. "If he had not been there… well." Joyce stopped. "In his defense, we were not expecting you until sometime in late September."

"I should have called. My husband was recently killed in a car crash. Honestly, I couldn't sleep in that bed anymore." El tried not to start crying again.

"I am so sorry. I was completely unaware," Joyce said. "Are you planning to stay in the house now, during the renovations? A cleaning crew was scheduled to give the entire house a once over in a couple of weeks after Jake was a bit farther along. It was part of the contract and already paid. I can reschedule them sooner."

"I don't know just now. I guess so. I have only seen part of the house. It needs a good cleaning. The kitchen is OK for now."

"The last status report I read said there were two serviceable bathrooms. In addition, the kitchen is usable, and the maid's quarters behind the kitchen were usable."

El let the phone come away from her ear, and she

listened. She thought it sounded like someone was crying.

Joyce had stopped talking.

"Ms. Wright?" Joyce said after a moment. "Is everything all right?"

"Not really." She sighed. "Please call me El or Eleanore. What's next?"

"And you can call me Joyce. If it's acceptable to you, I'd like to stop by tomorrow and have you sign some documents. I can also give you the keys I have."

"That's fine," El said.

"Do you have any other questions?" Joyce asked.

"Does anyone deliver pizza out here?"

"Ha!" A laugh slipped out. "I'm sorry. No. No one delivers that far out. I'm not even sure Amazon delivers up that far. Lillian kept a post office box."

"Do you know where my grandmother is buried?"

"I think she's in the cemetery below the Rectory. Jake would know where. He made the arrangements."

"I'll see you tomorrow," El said. "Can you tell Jake we can start over fresh tomorrow? I don't have his number. We can go over everything."

"Can do. See you tomorrow," Joyce said. "Bye."

"Bye."

***

El hung up the phone and glanced into the adjacent room. It was a huge butler's pantry. Built-in cabinets were on every wall. Directly opposite was a closed pocket door that likely led to the dining room. A commercial trash barrel stood in the center of the room. It was half full of old mason jars and expired canned goods.

The counters had canned goods that were not expired and various other items, including two new fire extinguishers and a dozen smoke detectors still new in the box.

There was also a new first aid kit.

She quickly found Neosporin and a wide selection of bandages.

She left the pantry and moved down the short hall at the far end of the kitchen. She remembered the maid's room. She could never get dibs on it when they visited there. It was right next to the kitchen and a half bath next door. Not sharing a bath with her brothers would have been great when she was twelve.

This room was pristine but tiny compared to the rest of the rooms in the house.

The room had a single bed, a bedside table and lamp, a dresser, and a leather armchair. On top of the dresser was a matching art deco Tiffany lamp and an old radio. The wainscoting was six feet tall and had a narrow shelf filled with old framed photos. She reached for one. It was grandma Lillian and her father and uncles.

They were standing in front of a new car. The frame smelled of Windex.

The bed was neatly made, so she decided to sleep in here tonight.

She didn't remember the radio. It was a Philco. She tried it and found that it was set to a classical station.

A sad piano echoed how she felt.

She heard it again.

Someone crying.

Did it come from the radio?

She turned it off, and silence descended again.

***

After El retrieved her luggage and unpacked it in the tiny room, she was surprised to find three t-shirts and three pairs of socks in the dresser already. There were even enough hangers in the closet.

She discovered she was hungry. El knew she had not eaten enough in the last month. She had not stopped anywhere on the way. She had a couple of candy bars and some beef jerky in the car that would do until tomorrow if need be. She opened the fridge and smiled. There was a package of Oscar Mayer bologna, half a loaf of white Wonder Bread, individually wrapped cheese slices, and Hellman's mayo in a squeeze bottle. The bottom shelf held an entire case of water, minus one bottle and an open 12-pack of Diet Coke.

She'd live.

She located a plate, and she quickly had two sandwiches. As she bit into the first one, she noticed another radio. This one was wood and cloth, just like the one her dad had, and it looked like someone had oiled the wood lately.

She turned it on.

The lights came on. El knew it had to warm up if

the tubes still worked. This one also had classical piano, and she tried to tune it to another station. There was a country and western station, a Christian station mid-sermon, and the classical one. She kept the classical one as she ate her bologna.

Crosstalk from somewhere bled into the music. Angry voices. She turned it to minimize the voices in favor of the piano. It helped for the moment. Then, as Moonlight Sonata concluded, she heard a distant voice in the station call out, "Noooo…" in the static.

She turned it off.

El finished her sandwich, trying not to think.

She pulled out her phone because of habit, and there was still no signal, no notifications. Nothing.

She pulled up her contact list.

It's crazy that I don't even know my best friend's number.

She went to the wall phone after she located Emma Coleman.

Just as she was reaching for the phone, it rang.

El almost jumped out of her skin. Then, collecting herself, she picked it up on the fourth ring. "Hello."

There was no one there. That cross talk again—distant voices in the static.

She hung up, lifted the receiver, and got the dial tone. It took forever for her to dial the number. It took forever for Emma to answer.

"Hello."

"Why do you have to have a number with so many nines in it, Em," Eleanore demanded.

"Because I KNEW it would bug you one day,"

Emma laughed. "So, is this the new number?"

"Yes, it is. Can you let me know what it is?" El asked.

"Just call yourself. Then you have it." Emma said.

"I have no signal," El said. "I'm calling from the wilderness."

"Just leave yourself a message."

"Will you just give me the damn number?" El demanded with a fake stern voice.

Emma laughed, "OK. Ready? 540-555-0666."

"Hang on. I guess I wasn't ready." El said as she found a pen on top of the phone. She grabbed a business card off the small bulletin board next to the phone and turned it over. "Now I'm ready."

"540-555-0666," Emma said. "You should answer it 'This is Hell, or Satan's secretary,' or something."

"Nice, Em," Eleanore replied. "I'm here less than a day, and I am already making friends and influencing people."

"What?"

"I threatened to stab the contractor renovating the house. I chewed out the lawyer taking care of all the shit I should be paying attention to. And I cried for a fucking hour."

"Don't you cry for that lying, cheating, bastard," Emma said.

"I saw a photo of her on Facebook. She had two small children," El said. "I wish I had never seen her. Or knew anything about her."

"Oh, honey. Want me to come out now? I can be

there in like three hours from DC."

"That's the last damn thing I need. I came here to get away from you and your wine drunk ass."

"I'll come. Right now." Emma was serious.

"Don't you be nice to me! That's what made me cry so hard earlier," El said. "That contractor being so nice to me after I threatened him almost broke me last time."

"What's he look like? I may be interested." Emma said. "Is he breathing? Is he cute?"

"I don't know. Maybe."

"I'll be right over." Emma was clearly joking.

"Thanks, Em," Eleanore said. "You always know how to make me feel better. I have bad news, though."

"You forgot your favorite sex toy?" Emma said, mock-serious.

"No, I remembered that. It's worse."

"What could possibly be worse?"

"There is no pizza delivery to this address," El said and heard a crash and curses under Em's breath. Then another crash. Eleanore's favorite gag that Emma performed on the phone was faking a fall.

"I'm never going there," Emma said deadpan.

"So… See you Saturday?" El replied.

Jake Googles Eleanore Wright

Felix sat on a tall tombstone and watched the black SUV briefly pulled up to the overgrown cemetery gate. A man climbed out and disappeared into the woods. He was quiet for a human.

***

Jake decided he should know a bit more about Eleanore. Curious, he did a simple search on the Internet.

Search: +"Eleanore Wright."
The first hit was an obituary.

RYAN McKINLEY 1976-2016
Ryan McKinley, a long-time Washington resident and lawyer, passed away on July 24, 2016. He is survived by his wife, Eleanore Wright; a sister, Ruth

McKinley; a niece, Rebecca Weston; nephews James Gilbert and Gerald Brown; and many friends and extended family. On Monday, August 8, 2016, funeral services will be held at St. Luke's Episcopal Church located at 1514 15th Street NW, Washington, DC, with visitation at 10 a.m. and Service at 11 a.m. In place of flowers, please make a donation in his name to St. Jude Children's Research Hospital.

The second hit was about a gospel singer of the same name, as were several other links. Then he saw an article about the automobile accident. It said drugs and alcohol were involved. A client of the law firm was with him. No other cars were involved. It occurred on Rt. 66 at 3:12 AM. Eleanore Wright owned the vehicle and was thought initially to be the second victim.

Was this her husband? Who was the woman? Drugs? 3:12 AM?

Jake stopped looking. Now he felt worse for prying. He knew he could not say anything about it or sound like a stalker.

You are a stalker, dumb ass.

He watched the sunset in the west. The clouds were lit this evening. It was a cool evening for August in Virginia. The Cabin was designed to be comfortable for two. It would have been the best wedding gift ever.

As if thinking of Sam invoked a spell, Jake's phone rang. It was Samantha.

Jake sighed, took a deep breath, and answered.

"Hey, Sam," Jake said, smiling as he talked. He'd heard people could hear you smiling. "What's up."

"Why don't you answer my calls? Why don't you call me back?" was Sam's greeting.

"This is why," Jake said. "So now we will fight about calling you back? Or will we fight about how we fight? Will we even glance at the elephant in the room tonight?"

Sam ignored the comment. "Where are you?"

"What difference does it make?" Jake could not help the sadness from leaking into his voice.

"What is the deal with the boxes you left for me at my mom's? Are you trying to embarrass me?" Sam accused.

"Sam." Jake got up and walked inside. "I thought it was obvious. The boxes are just punctuation."

"Where are you?" Sam demanded.

"I'm at The Cabin."

"Just what you always do. Run and hide in your dirt floor fort in the woods like a little boy that doesn't get what he wants."

"What is it you think I want?" Jake asked. He was serious and sincere.

"To grow the hell up," she said.

You don't know me at all.

Jake let the silence stretch. He waited for where these always went.

And there it was, the pouting sing-song voice he hated. "Come home, baby. I'll give you a massage and the thing you like."

"Sam, you can't always get what you want with hot oil and blow jobs." Jake was angry. "We are done. This isn't a tiff and a two-week cooldown. This is not me picking a fight to get great make-up sex. This is the whole relationship in a nutshell. You are not hearing me. You are lying to me to get what you want. Manipulation and gaslighting, and narcissistic bullshit. We. Are. Done."

"OK, baby. You win. Whatever it is, you can do it. Have it. Bondage. Anal. A three-way with Joyce."

"I want you to hear me clearly," Jake spoke in no uncertain terms. "Our relationship is over. Stop calling me. Please, never call me again."

"Is this about the hysterectomy?"

"Goodbye, Sam. I hope you find someone right for you." Jake hung up and blocked Sam's number.

***

Jake tried to read. His mind would not let him. He needed some mindless distraction. He pulled down a projection screen that was concealed behind a valence over the fireplace. He turned on the projector that was on the opposite wall, hidden among the books. DirectTV Sat television had 400 channels of things that didn't interest him tonight.

Barnwood Builders on Discovery+ didn't have any new episodes. So he channel surfed—something he never did.

A show he had never seen caught his eye. Stargate Universe. An actress on that show looked precisely like Eleanore Wright.

Jake fell asleep watching it. Watching 2nd Lt. Vanessa James.

He woke as his phone rang. The sky was beginning to brighten. His watch said 6:35 AM. Another night on the large sectional sofa. He loved that sofa.

Grabbing his phone from the coffee table, he saw a number he didn't recognize.

Who the hell would call this early?

"Hello," Jake said sleepily.

"You blocked me? You win, baby. I give…" Jake hung up on Sam without saying a word. He activated 'Do Not Disturb' on his phone.

Jake set up the French press for coffee and went to take a shower. He tossed his dirty clothes in the hamper where the washer should have been. The power draw of the thing was one of his biggest design failures. The solar bank of salvaged golf cart batteries just could not keep up. So he settled for propane and 12 volts for The Cabin and laundry at the bottom of the mountain in the garage.

Looking at himself in the mirror, he decided to trim his beard back to a civilized level at least. Maybe even get a haircut soon.

Lillian used to nag me to get a haircut.

Her "damn hippie" comments had always amused Jake.

He took a shower longer than usual. He was scrubbed until his skin was red.

A clean t-shirt and jeans were Jake's standard uniform. Today it was a black Molly Hatchet tour shirt. He actively avoided thinking of Sam's disdain for his t-shirts. He didn't know how many she had tossed out before he noticed she was doing it.

This morning, the coffee was strong as he stepped up to the glass wall.

Rocky, the squirrel, was out by the feeder, pretending not to be waiting for him.

Jake reached into one of the urns and drew out another coffee mug. Except this one was half full of walnuts.

Now carrying two mugs, he walked out to the short wall. He stood by the squirrel, and they both looked out at the view. When he looked down at Rocky, the squirrel stood up on its hind legs and looked up at him with a Good-Morning face.

Just beyond Rocky was a miniature picnic table and a miniature rain barrel. There was plenty of water from the rain yesterday, so Jake poured the walnuts onto the small table. Rocky sat on the bench and started to eat.

Jake finished his coffee, watching the view and giving Rocky an ear scratch now and then.

"Have a great day, Rocky," Jake said. He could swear Rocky waved goodbye over his shoulder.

***

Jake poured a second cup and cleaned the French press.

With practiced ease, he made a quick three-egg omelet with fresh salsa and pepper jack cheese. He almost texted a photo of his plate to Joyce to exact vengeance for the teasing. How she stayed so fit was beyond him.

With breakfast cleaned up, he put the now-empty

coolers back in the small trailer.

He made it down the trail in the usual time. In the garage, he transferred the coolers into the back of the truck and checked his phone for the time.

Six voice messages. He pressed play.

"Jake…" It was Sam, delete.

"Jake…" delete.

"Come on, baby…" delete.

"Baby…" delete.

"OK, I give…" delete.

The next one gave Jake a chill. The caller ID said, 'Lillian.'

"Hi." This was not Sam. "My name is Eleanore Wright. I talked to Joyce Jacobs, and she explained everything. I owe you an apology. Can we get together tomorrow morning and start over? I was having a bad day. Joyce said you were a morning person. Anyway, is 8:30 OK? I think I ate some of your bologna. I will replace it." After an awkward pause, she said, "Bye."

"Shit. I am already fucking late!" Jake said to the inside of his truck. His phone said it was 8:47 AM.

It was 9:05 when he pulled up next to her Ford Flex. He didn't bother parking in his usual spot in the carriage house. He rushed onto the porch and found the front door was wide open.

"Hello, Ms. Wright?" he called into the empty house, knocking on the open door frame. He could not explain it. It never felt this empty. "Hello?" he said a bit louder.

He stepped in and softly moved up the hall. The floor was creaking loudly under his feet. "Hello? Ms.

Wright?" a bit louder.

The glass was still on the floor in the hall from the broken mirror. It crunched under his boots. The library doors were open, but no lights were on.

"It's Jake Harris, contractor guy." Louder still. The kitchen was the same except for a single plate in the sink. Memories of finding Lillian ignited adrenaline and a rapid pounding heart. He searched the butler's pantry and the dining room beyond. Jake circled around the parlor and back into the library. He paused to stare at the spot where he had found Lillian.

Then the kitchen again, calling her name in an urgent shout that could have been heard outside. He glanced into the half bath and then glanced into the maid's room.

Jake froze. All he saw in the dim light was disheveled hair and red splatter patterns on the bed. Jake couldn't breathe.

Breaking the vapor lock, he knelt beside the narrow bed he had slept in a hundred times and gently moved the hair from her face. She was lying face down. Her head was angled toward the wall. The red splatters were the design on the t-shirt she wore.

"Eleanore? Eleanore Wright?" he said in a hoarse whisper. He placed two fingers on her neck to check her pulse. Her heartbeat was as strong as her skin was soft.

Then she woke with a start and screamed. Jake fell back onto his ass. She tried to retreat into the corner by the headboard and wall, uncovering her long bare legs. She wore black panties with Champion on the waistband.

She also wore one of his t-shirts.

They both sat there gasping for a minute, staring at each other.

"That t-shirt looks better on you than me," Jake said conversationally.

"What?" Eleanore said.

"My Chemical Romance. Great concert. My t-shirt." Jake pointed but made no move to get up.

"What is happening?" Eleanore said as she hugged her knees to her chest.

"Our appointment. You said 8:30 AM. It's now about 9:15. I called out, but I ended up searching the house. I thought something had… happened."

Eleanore reached over, turned on the lamp, and looked at her phone. Then back at Jake.

"Are you OK?" Jake asked, moving a little to sit up against the wall.

She dropped the phone on her lap and scrubbed her face with both hands.

"Please, don't be nice to me," Eleanore said. "I'll just start crying again."

"OK. There is no way you're keeping my favorite t-shirt," Jake said in a mock stern tone. "MCR broke up after that tour."

She smiled.

"I'm really sorry. I have not slept like that in months." Eleanore said. "Something about this bed. This place."

"It's the magic t-shirt. That's why you can't keep it, dammit."

"I had a dream about this t-shirt," she said. "My gramma was calling my name. I couldn't find her. I looked and looked. She was lying on the floor in the library. She was following me with her eyes. When I looked where she was looking, I looked down, and it was this t-shirt, old jeans with a hole in the knee, and work boots…."

The image of Lillian dead on the floor, white film over open eyes. My god. I was wearing that shirt.

"I'll go make coffee. I need more coffee. I will let you get dressed." Jake averted his eyes, got up, and made a rapid exit.

Rounding the corner into the kitchen, Jake stopped in his tracks.

Joyce Jacobs was leaning against the counter, sipping from a Starbucks cup.

Jake went to the coffee pot without a word, shaking his head.

"It was always my favorite t-shirt, too," she whispered. "I like her already. It took me six solid months of flirting before I got to wear that shirt."

"It's not like that," Jake said.

"It never is. What did you make for breakfast?"

"Joyce, dammit." Jake smiled as he started the coffee maker.

"Remember that lamp we broke?" She smiled into her coffee, looking at the shards in the hall.

They heard the toilet flush and the faucet start. Then, there was an unmistakable sound of teeth being brushed.

"Joyce, behave. Nothing happened," Jake said.

"Some people's definition of nothing is why I make so much money as a lawyer."

"Who are you talking to?" Eleanore called from the hall as her footsteps returned to the bedroom.

Jake raised his voice. "Joyce Jacobs is here."

"Let me brush my hair, and I'll be right out," she said.

"Was it an omelet?" Joyce whispered. "One of those three-cheese masterpieces?" She sipped her coffee with her eyes closed.

"Joyce, you know I love you, but you are impossible," Jake said as the coffee maker beeped.

"Fill me up, Jake? Please?" Joyce said innocently as Eleanore entered the kitchen.

Jake topped off her cup as Joyce extended her right hand to Eleanore. "So happy to meet you finally." Joyce gave a firm professional shake. "How do you like your coffee? Jake makes the best coffee."

"Just black, please," El replied.

Coffee with El and Joyce

The cat listened from under her bed, wondering if they could hear the screaming, alone in the dark.

***

After Jake rose and left the bedroom to make coffee, El realized how she was dressed. She keeled over, hugged a big armful of pillows and blankets, and breathed it in. El allowed herself a minute and then jumped up. She had not felt this rested for months. Maybe the quiet here was just what she needed.

She pulled on clean socks and the jeans she had worn yesterday. Before taking her shirt off, she closed the door and heard Jake speaking to someone but not the words. Closing it, she quickly took off the MCR t-shirt, folded it, and returned it to the dresser.

As she folded, El noticed how many mirrors were in the room. Feeling a bit self-conscious about being topless, she put on her favorite Under Armour sports bra, jeans, and a black tank top.

She had to pee and brush her teeth.

Why do I feel so good?

After brushing her teeth, she glanced into the single mirror and saw how wild her dark hair was. She heard voices again as she returned to the bedroom to retrieve a hairbrush from her bag.

"Who are you talking to?" Eleanore called from the hall as she returned to the bedroom.

Jake raised his voice. "Joyce Jacobs is here."

"Let me brush my hair, and I'll be right out," she said.

El attacked her hair quickly to put it into some order.

She stood too close to the mirror. She was punished with a close look at the scar that went through her left eyebrow.

She shook it off and went in search of coffee.

As she entered the kitchen, El saw Jake was refilling the Starbucks cup of an attractive woman in a black form-fitting business suit with a pencil skirt. She was fit and about 40 years old. Joyce had dark hair with just a few perfect highlights and a genuine friendly smile. She wore that expensive-looking black outfit easily. The charcoal gray silk blouse revealed just a whisper of black lace beneath. It was a look El would love to pull off but never would because of the shoes. El was doomed to wear sneakers.

"So happy to meet you finally." Joyce gave a firm professional shake. "How do you like your coffee? Jake makes the best coffee."

"Just black, please."

"A purist. A woman after my own heart," Joyce said.

Jake handed El a black ceramic mug filled with steaming coffee. She hesitated only an instant. Her hand went to the scar on her brow.

"Let's sit." Joyce gestured to the kitchen table where her briefcase was. Moving around to the far side with El, Joyce continued. "Did you and Jake get the schedule and task list sorted out?"

"No. We didn't get a chance to discuss it yet." El looked at Jake's jeans, the hole in the knee, and Jake's boots.

The dream replayed in her head.

She shook it off and saw Joyce raise an eyebrow at Jake.

Opening her briefcase, she said, "I have a copy of the last status report and the original proposal, estimate, and current actuals. The timetable is three weeks old. But Jake can fill you in on the rest."

El raised her head and looked at the ceiling. "Is someone else here?"

"No. Not as far as I know," Jake replied, and then he heard footsteps above.

They all looked up.

"I'll be right back," Jake said, moved into the hall and beyond, and found nothing.

***

Joyce reviewed the scope of work for the

construction project with El. Jake had been paid in advance, and no hard deadlines were in the contract. However, the most important items had been completed over the last six months. Most notable was the new roof on the main house and all the outbuildings of consequence.

They heard more footsteps upstairs. Jake must be searching every room.

"That is a lot of money." El was looking at the estimates. "And my gramma paid it all in advance. All of it? What's to keep Jake from just walking away with the cash?"

"Jake," Joyce said. "Jake will keep Jake from walking away."

"Have you known him long?" El asked.

"We went to the same high school, but he was four years behind me." She smiled. "I didn't get to know Jake until I got back from law school. I had been gone eight years, and that little kid I remembered was now the area's best restoration craftsmen. We became friends when I acquired a historic storefront in Covington, and he renovated my first-level storefront office and designed the loft above. He is a good man. And a good friend. And an excellent chef, by the way. I will never understand why he wastes his talent swinging a hammer."

The paperwork for the estate was way more complicated. El had a tough time with all of it.

"The estate assets are entirely held within a durable trust," Joyce said. "They are all owned by the trust, and you are the sole member of the board of trustees. It's a common model, nothing fancy. Your grandmother was just smart. This was set up decades ago."

A flurry of signatures and explanations followed.

"What is this part?" El asked.

Joyce went through her notes and files and found a large survey map, unfolded and spread it out on the table.

Footsteps were heavy upstairs. It sounded like Jake was moving something.

"This is the Wright Family Trust property holdings. Everything within these lines is part of the trust."

"But this says 2,167 acres?" El looked at the map. It was the side of an entire mountain.

"Yes. But as you can see, access is limited. Just this road to this house. Then the road along the ridge, way up here."

"What is this?" El pointed to a label that said 'The Rectory.' "Is that this house?"

"Yes. And here is the carriage house, the barn, and a few other structures."

"And this?" She pointed to a shape close to the house.

This is the old church that burned down in the fifties and was never rebuilt. I think the foundation is still out there. Jake would know; you should have him show you. For safety, if nothing else. I believe this is an ice well. Very deep, I understand, and dangerous."

"I remember. And this is the cemetery? All this is a cemetery?" El said.

"Yes, there was a time in the 70s when they tried to make it a historic site. The local boy scout troop was trying to clean it up, and a couple of scouts wandered off, got lost, and died. No one has brought it up since."

"Where are all the heads?" El asked.

"Heads?"

"All the statues are missing heads."

"I have no idea. That is creepy as fuck, though," Joyce said. "Sorry, I didn't mean to curse."

"What kind of law do you do?" El asked in a non sequitur.

"Mostly contracts, wills, divorces, real estate stuff," Joyce replied. "I like small towns for that. Plus, the Internet allows me to work on things in Richmond. Why?"

"My husband died." She swallowed hard. "He was a lawyer in DC. A good one. He was a big-time asshole lawyer. A partner in a firm of assholes. He had a will. I have a copy, but the partners won't… they are not helpful."

"I can look into it if you like. What is it you want?"

"Just want out of it. The business, the DC brownstone. All of it. Nothing managed by the firm. Liquidated."

"Got any cash?" Joyce asked. "A dollar will do."

El found seven dollars in her jeans. Joyce pulled a one-page document from her briefcase, filled in Eleanore's name, and plucked the dollar out of her hand. "Here, sign this. It says I am now your lawyer, and I am on retainer."

She signed and then got up, went to the bedroom, and returned with a thick envelope. "This is Ryan's will. Let me know what you think."

Static burst from the radio, like voices of a station too far away.

Joyce began to load the signed docs into her briefcase.

El was looking at the map again.

"Joyce, what's this square marked South Trust?" Eleanore asked.

"Wow. I never noticed that," Joyce said. "That's Jake's cabin. I never knew where it was. I hate camping."

"But this says the parcel is 404 acres," El said.

"Good guy to have as a neighbor. Even though it's miles away."

"Can I keep this? It says it's a copy."

"Sure. It's yours, anyway."

As El walked Joyce to her car, neither noticed the shards of glass in the hall were gone.

***

"You drove a Jaguar F-Type Coupe up this road? I'm impressed," El said.

"My weakness. Cars, shoes, and food," Joyce said as she climbed in. "I'll be in touch. But, as your attorney, I advise you to get a damn answering machine. I never could talk Lillian into one."

El waved as she drove off.

The map was still in her hand. She looked at it again and oriented it to match how she was standing. Situated between the church and the house was the ice well. It turned out to be about a football field away, at least. She walked up to the edge of it slowly. She could smell the rotting carcasses before they could be seen. She only remembered a fence around this and the church.

The grass all around it was hip-tall. The ice well was a 20-foot diameter hole in the stone-lined earth and went straight down 50 feet.

The bottom of the well was filled with skeletons in various stages of decomposition. Most were deer. There was evidence of the rusty wire fence around it.

Beyond that was the foundation of the old burned church. Half of it was filled with water. The other half, including the bell tower, on the left, was overgrown with vines.

"2100 acres? I wonder what the taxes are on it," she said aloud.

Looking back toward the house, trees were so dense and the sky so overcast that she could see the lights on upstairs—even a single light on the third floor, despite the overgrown plants.

The new roof could be easily seen at this time of day. It was in high contrast to all the peeling paint. Some of the clapboards that had already been replaced would disappear with the new exterior paint.

Turning to the west, she could see into the overgrown cemetery. In this light, she could trace the vine-covered cast iron fence. She sat down on a flat rock and breathed in through her nose and out through her mouth several times as she tried to focus and empty her mind.

You really need to start up yoga again.

Movement caught her eye. A black cat had jumped

up onto an arm of a heavy thick cross. The cat watched her as closely as El watched the cat.

Her eyebrow itched, and when she reached up to scratch it, she happened to look down and to the right. A black ceramic coffee mug sat on the rock near her.

She snatched it as if it was a bomb and threw it into the basement foundation with a splash.

That bastard will never throw another mug of hot coffee at my face again.

At the same time, she noticed that it wasn't a rock. It was a granite tombstone that had toppled over.

She knew without brushing off the stone that it must have once said, WRIGHT. Unfortunately, only the GHT letters were visible under moss and vines.

How had her life gotten so toppled over?
Maybe quitting the meds was a bad idea.
Why did I start flushing them every night?
When clarity emerged, my mind started racing.
But I wasn't paranoid because it was all true.
Sleep evaded without them until today.

El thought about Gramma. Life in this house, the loss of her husband, and all three of her children. Children are not supposed to die before you.

It was the thought of children that brought on the tears again. She held her face in her hands, and with her elbows on her knees, she let herself cry.

She heard someone approaching through the tall grass. When she had gotten herself under control, she wiped her eyes on her sleeves. Jake had walked right by her to the overgrown fence. He stood by a granite post. He didn't say a word to her.

He clicked his tongue.

The black cat appeared out of nowhere on top of the post and demanded a thorough ear scratching.

"Does he have a name? Is it a he?" Eleanore asked.

"Felix," Jake said, and the cat looked up. "No idea the gender. It doesn't matter."

"Why Felix?" For some reason, she wasn't self-conscious.

"I have been seeing this cat my whole life," Jake said. "Can't be the same cat."

Felix was watching the house now.

"You grew up around here?" she asked.

"Yes. Right here in Covington. Well, just outside."

"How long did you know Lillian?" El asked. She didn't know why she felt like she could ask.

"Over twenty years, I guess." Jake turned toward her only then. "You need to know. She loved you."

"How would you know? I haven't seen her since I was twelve," Eleanore said.

"Did you know she came to your graduation from high school? College too." Jake paused. "She was even at your wedding."

"How do you know this?" El asked, knowing inside it felt like the truth.

"When you go upstairs and see the master bedroom. Look at the photos on the mantle."

Jake turned around to gaze across the cemetery. In a single leap, Felix jumped to his shoulder. Without looking at her, he said clearly, "Until I get to this, please never come out here at night. Better still, never come out here without me."

Both Jake and the cat turned to look at her over their shoulders.

"Promise me?"

Handkerchiefs

Felix watched the ruined church and was now certain these humans could not hear the screams.

*****

Jake needed to get back to work.

Felix bumped his head into the side of Jake's face. This was the fattest feral cat he had ever seen. He focused on the cat as he talked.

"Can I ask a personal question, Eleanore?" Jake turned as Felix jumped down from his shoulder.

"Sure, why not?" Her nose was red, and her eyes puffy. She wasn't trying to hide it.

Jake walked over and casually handed another handkerchief to her.

"Why didn't you visit Lillian?" He sat next to her on the toppled tombstone, but not too close.

"I thought she… I don't know. My life had become complicated. After my dad passed away. Family ties

51

got thinner or disappeared. My mom went soon after, and her family was all in DC. I even lost touch with them. Especially after I got married."

"You were married?" Jake asked. It was a natural question. He looked at her bare ring finger.

"I WAS married. He died in a car crash six weeks ago." She stared off into the cemetery.

"I am so sorry. I didn't know any of this," Jake said.

Eleanore did a sloppy nose blow just then.

"Who carries hankies anymore?" She offered it back to Jake. An obvious joke.

Jake smiled and waved it off.

"Lillian always said, 'A gentleman always carries a handkerchief.' She gifted me with many white ones after she saw I started carrying blue and red bandannas. She said she saw on TV that those were some kind of gay dog whistles. She was always trying to find a 'nice girl.' for me. She was so cute about it." Jake shook his head. "Not googling that again."

"Lillian knew that?" Eleanore added. "That's funny. She was a proper little old lady even 23 years ago."

"I'm really sorry about yesterday and this morning," Jake apologized again. I was trying to get back on track.

"I'm keeping the shirt."

"Nope. You're not," he said flatly, trying to fake super serious.

"I will make you a deal." She stuffed the soaked hanky into her back pocket. "I will return your shirt and hankies, freshly laundered, when the project is complete."

"We have a hostage situation then?" Jake was feeling better. As he turned to face her, he saw she was staring into the cemetery. There was a black cat sitting on each of at least a dozen tombstones.

"That's why they are all named Felix." Jake thought the comment had been amusing. It didn't land as he had hoped.

"Why is this tombstone on this side of the fence?" Eleanore asked, still looking at the cats watching her. "I don't remember it as a kid. I remember the ice well had a plywood cover and a fence, but not this monument."

"Must have been no room in there." Jake lied to her for the first time. He knew why.

***

They walked back to the house, and Jake gave an overview of the work that had been completed. "I did the roof first. It was a way bigger project than I thought in the beginning. Bats, squirrels, and honey bees had all moved in, and Lillian wanted them all out with none being harmed. It took twice as long, but we managed. I had to build hives in the orchard, bat houses on the far side of the carriage house."

"What about the squirrels?" she asked.

"They were the worst," Jake said. "I trapped a half dozen Felixes. Then let them loose in the attic. The squirrels fled in less than an hour. After I closed up the access points, the cats came out. Food bribes made it easy."

"Do you feed all those cats? How many are there?" Eleanore could see where the eaves were repaired and tree branches artfully trimmed away.

"Lillian had the policy never to feed the cats," Jake said as they walked around the outside of the house. "It makes them dependent. Cat food outside attracts rats and mice. They do a great job at control."

"Why didn't she hire a big crew or company? No offense." She was looking at the small amount of lawn mowed just next to the house.

"Honestly, I don't know." It took a year just to close it all properly. "Most of the work was done first to just keep the house from rotting and falling in on itself."

A gust of wind came through the upper leaves of the trees. An odd crying sound came through on the wind. It sounded like a scream.

Eleanore stopped in her tracks. "What the hell is that?"

"It was probably a fox or an owl. Maybe even a coyote. I worry about Felix sometimes," Jake said. "But he is a bad-ass."

They rounded some overgrown foundation planting that encroached on the back porch— shredded screens waved in the wind. The covered walkway between the porch and the carriage house was almost done. New decking was going in. A new green metal roof covered it.

"You can park in the carriage house and come in through here. Damn handy in the rain." Jake said, moving up two steps onto the covered walk. "Lillian's car is still in there. And my truck." There was lots of room in there. The cement floor was old but well swept. New overhead lights all throughout made it bright. Behind Jake's truck were air compressors and various tools. Jake hadn't realized how many until now. Beyond was a large car under a canvas tarp. The substantial barn doors were open on tracks slid to the side outside.

"Do you leave the door open all the time?" Eleanore looked from the tools to the vast opening. "Don't you worry about your tools getting stolen?"

"No one ever comes up this far," Jake said. "Ever."

I am not the one that is going to tell her.

"What's upstairs? That's big enough for an apartment," Eleanore asked, seeing the stairs directly to her left. Unfortunately, dozens of paint cans blocked them.

"It's full of junk—trunks and dust and cobwebs. The only time I ever went up there was to inspect the windows and look to see if there were signs of squirrels. Thankfully I never went back up. I looked like a coal miner when I finally got out. I was so dirty."

Two disembodied cat eyes stared down at them from the top of the stairs in the shadows. Eleanore didn't show any indication of seeing Felix there.

"Are you planning to stay here while the work is finished? Or will you stay in town?" Jake asked as they moved back toward the house.

"I think it's far enough along that I can stay here," Eleanore said. "I always did like camping. Joyce said something about a cleaning crew."

"Yes. Mabel's Mops. It's a small army. I will get them in ASAP," Jake said. "The only working shower is on the second floor. They will also clean out the master bedroom for you. The bath is the new on-suite for that bedroom. Lillian never really got to use it." Jake sighed.

"You were sleeping in the maid's quarters, weren't you?" Eleanore asked honestly, unperturbed.

"Sometimes," Jake admitted. "Especially when it rained. It was easier than just coming back in the morning. It was Lillian's idea, actually. She liked having someone around. I liked being that someone."

"Do you live at that cabin?" Eleanore asked.

Jake opened the ragged screen door to the back porch when she asked this. He hoped she didn't see his face.

"Sometimes," Jake said. "That is even a slower work in progress than this. It's totally off-grid. Remote. Not even 4x4 accessible. How'd you know about that?" He tried hard not to sound pissed off that she knew.

"Here, I'll show you." Eleanore ignored the condition of the porch and went straight for the back door. It opened into a mudroom with a washer and dryer and a large concrete farm sink. A long bench ran along one wall with coat hooks above—lots of coats for various weather.

Past that was another door to the inner hall— maid's quarters to the right and a big, mostly empty pantry to the left. The short hall opened into the kitchen, and the map of the property was flat on the table.

"This was in the deeds and stuff Joyce had. See, it's marked." Jake knew this map. He had a copy artfully framed over the fieldstone fireplace in The Cabin.

"It's got a nice view. Great hunting." Jake tried to change the subject. "I'll finish off the covered walk, the porch, then the hall bath upstairs next. Mabel's crew will make this level more livable. But I do still need to plaster and paint. The cosmetic stuff is always last. At least the new breaker box is in. So is the new forced air heat and AC. The plaster and drywall are still a mess. Sorry."

"Stop apologizing," Eleanore said. "I am amazed. I don't know how you do it."

"I usually come in the back door. The wrap-around porch has a huge hole and rotten decking. So I put in temporary decking just from the door to the steps. I recommend the back door."

"I can do that."

"OK. I will call Mabel's Mops now," Jake said, walking to the wall phone. "I'll install the cordless phones today. Right now, these are the only two phones in the house."

"I love these old phones," Eleanore said.

While calling the cleaning company, he was about to warn them about the broken mirror. Looking into the hallway, he saw that it was already cleaned up. The frame was also gone.

Jake put his hand over the receiver. "Is tomorrow OK?" he stage whispered. She gave a thumbs up.

Then, placing the receiver to his ear, there was a wave of static and distant arguing voices. "Tomorrow is good."

The distant voices silenced.

***

After the plan for the next few days was detailed, Jake walked her out to her car. He tried not to stare at her ass, but he lost that battle between the faded jeans and that form-fitting tank top.

"Need anything from town?" Eleanore asked. "Beside replacement bologna and cheese?"

She smiled then. The first full wattage smile he'd never forget.

"I'm good," he choked out. "Thanks."

Her smile faded as she looked up and beyond Jake at the house. She shook her head.

"What? Squirrels?" Jake asked lightly.

"Oh, nothing." She got into her Ford Flex and pulled out through the gate—another thing Jake had to fix.

Jake looked up at the house in the direction she had looked—the third-floor turret room. Sheer curtains moved there.

I thought I tossed all those old curtains when I inspected the windows.

The phone started ringing in the house. He jogged his way into the kitchen. "Hello."

"You're late, fuckface." That was all the voice said.

"Oh shit, I'm sorry, man." It was Jake's friend, Rob

Jensen. Jake went to adjust a baseball cap that wasn't there. "The new owner showed up a month early and tossed the apple cart. Sorry, man."

"Are you canceling to just get out of buying lunch? I skipped breakfast, you bucket of puke, betrayer of my need for bacon-cheeseburgers."

"I'm on my way. Thirty minutes, old man." Jake knew his smile could be heard through this time.

"Good. This load of lumber is over-compressing my delicate leaf springs," Rob complained.

"Well, if you had a real truck, you could have driven it all the way up here."

"And miss lunch? Screw that," Rob said. "The bitch is not going to be there again, is she?"

"Sam and I are quits," Jake said flatly.

"Does she know this?" Rob was laughing like it was the funniest joke ever spoken.

"You'd think a woman smart enough to go to college and become a pharmacist would hear me better."

Suddenly serious, Rob said, "That girl will be a problem."

"Yes. I know." Jake said. "We'll talk when I get there."

"Is this why I have not seen your ugly ass in town this week?" Rob asked. "You didn't give her that damn ring, did you? No amount of BJ's is worth putting up with that bullshit."

"I also have the receipt. I just haven't been back to Front Royal yet." Jake couldn't keep the anger from slipping into his voice.

"Get down here, shit stain. After lunch, I am buying you a top-shelf Scotch to celebrate," Rob said.

"Rob," Jake said in a serious tone.

"Yes?"

"Fuck you, ass-wipe," Jake said deadpan.

"I love you too, man."

***

Jake took the coolers out of his truck and checked for tie-down straps behind the seat. Then, he shut off the lights and headed down the mountain. He ignored the sound of a baby crying coming from the cemetery.

Stop Thinking

Felix watched her go from Kilroy's rock. The cat wasn't the only one…

***

El drove down the mountain for about fifteen minutes before she got to the paved road. She thought about the need for a four-wheel drive. But, first, she'd ask Jake where she should look.

I think he trimmed his beard.

She was distracted by a small crack in the dash. Ryan had been driving. He had pounded the dash with his fist and threatened to do it to her face. That crack was why he bought her the Audi she didn't want. The car he died in.

Stop thinking about that stuff.

Her phone started lighting up with notifications. There were voice mails, texts, and emails coming in. She dreaded the voice mails most.

She turned on the highway and pulled into the first gas station on the way into town. It only had two pumps and big hand-painted signs touted FULL SERVICE. An antique Texaco sign was on the gable end of the roof above the old pumps. There were two garage bays with both doors down. It was cute in a retro kind of way. Benches and folding chairs were out front. It was a Mayberry RFD vibe. She liked it. A large-bellied black man with mirrored sunglasses sat by the entrance door to the tiny convenience store. A stub of a cigar was in his mouth but not lit. He was mid-conversation with a thin, bug-eyed man with a graying goatee.

"You don't HAVE a soul. You ARE a soul," the man said around his cigar. "You HAVE a body…"

The man with the goatee rushed over and around to her window as it powered down. He wore classic blue coveralls and had a patch on them that said 'ED.'

"Mornin', what can I do you for?" he chirped.

"Ed, how many times I gotta tell you you can't say that to the ladies," said the man with the cigar.

"Sorry, ma'am. How can I help you?" He was literally blushing.

"It's all right, Ed. Fill it up with regular, please," she said as she opened the door and got out.

"Ain't no 5G round here yet. You're safe," Ed said as he began pumping gas. He grabbed the squeegee and began cleaning all her windows. "Check your oil?"

"Yes, please," Eleanore replied. She was looking up from her phone.

"5G ain't controlling the birds, Ed. Or people," the

man said, shaking his head.

"Not yet, Hector. Cause we ain't got any." Their voices faded as the door closed behind her.

It was a tiny convenience store—fifteen feet on each side square. A teenage girl with brown hair in a tight ponytail and no makeup sat behind the small counter, reading an US magazine from the small magazine rack.

El thought about another coffee, but it smelled burned.

She opted for a Diet Coke from the wall of glass-doored coolers. Only one of the doors had food items, like milk and OJ, eggs, and bacon. And Oscar Mayer bologna and Kraft cheese slices. Even the squeeze mayo. Wonder bread was the only kind they carried, and only three loaves were there.

The girl rang El up as she heard the hood shut on her Flex. The conversation outside escalated. The only word she understood was "Chemtrails."

"Don't mind, my dad. He's not really crazy." She handed El her change. "He just likes arguing with Hector."

El reached out her hand to shake. "You'll probably see me a lot." The teen shook her hand immediately. "My name is Eleanore Wright. Lillian Wright was my grandmother."

The girl froze mid-shake.

"You live up there?" she asked. "I thought… Miss Lily was always nice to me. I'm sorry she died."

"Me, too," El moved to the door. "Nice meeting you, Ed's Daughter."

"I'm Olivia. Olivia Barns. Nice meeting you, too."

She kept the credit card out, not knowing how the full-service thing worked here yet.

"Them birds ain't real, man. I seen them killing the real ones." Ed was pointing a finger at Hector. "$22.50, ma'am, your oil's good. Nice car. Never seen one of these before. Took me a minute to find the dipstick."

"You are a dipstick," Hector added.

She handed the card to Ed, and he gave a formal bow over it and moved to the door where Olivia was already pushing it open. "Papa, this is Miss Eleanore Wright, Miss Lily's granddaughter. She came from up the mountain."

Ed's eyes seemed to bug a bit wider as he looked at El again. "$22.50" was all he said to Olivia. "Nice meeting you, Miss Wright. You staying or visiting?"

Small towns were like this.

"I will be staying for a while. For now."

"Hey, you gonna see Jake?" Before she could answer, he said, "I found that big bottle jack he wanted to borrow."

"Sure thing, I'll tell him, Ed. Thanks," she replied as she got in her car. Olivia came out with a small clipboard. El signed and put her card back in her wallet.

"Piece of advice, Miss Wright." El could see white all around Ed's irises. "Don't wander outside at night. Just sayin'."

"OK, Ed. Jake said the same thing." As she started the car, she noticed Hector slowly nodded his head in agreement.

All three were waving as she pulled away.

***

El had vivid memories of the village of Covington, Virginia, from her childhood.

To her surprise, the trees still lined the street. But they were now huge. Cars still angled in to park. The main road through the village still had only one traffic light.

To orient herself, she drove all the way through town. It took less than a minute. She turned around at the feed store on the west end of town. Going back, she parked at the diner on the opposite end. As she passed it, she saw the Jacobs and Associates sign. The store fronts were beautiful in the tiny village.

There was a bank on one corner at the only light, the post office on another, a small 7-11, and the Covington Funeral Home on the final corner. In addition, she noted a drug store, a hardware store, a bakery/coffee-shop/Internet cafe, and a small bar.

She got out of her car and looked up at the diner. The place was the same as she remembered, all-glass block, stainless steel, and 1940s look. The sign was neon and, in large letters, just said DINER. Above it, in small letters, it said EAT. Below on a separate sign, it bragged AIR CONDITIONED.

She loved it. *Ryan would have hated this.*

She entered, and a short, busty waitress said from behind the counter as she drew a key lime pie out of a glass case, "Sit where you like, darlin'. Be right with you."

It was exactly the same as she remembered. Half the booths were already occupied. Besides, she loved sitting at the counter when she was a kid. She went all the way to the right and sat on the stool, second from the end. The last stool had no counter space due to the baked goods case filled with pies, muffins, and banana bread.

Laminated menus were stuck in the back of the napkin holder. There was also salt and pepper. The red and yellow squeeze bottles for the ketchup and mustard were also the same. The only thing different was two small bottles of hot sauce: Franks and Brenda's Booty Burner.

"Know what you want, darlin', or you need a minute?" the waitress asked as more people filed in, laughing.

"Do you still have grilled cheese and tomato soup?" El was hopeful.

"It's today's special." She pointed over her shoulder at a chalkboard.

El looked at it on the chalkboard, and below the daily special was an algebraic formula that said, "Solve for X, and your meal is free."

"137," El said casually.

"What's that you say?" the waitress looked up from her pad.

"And a Diet Coke. X=137," El said now with confidence.

"That's right." The waitress laughed. She winked

and said, "I'll pretend you ordered pie as well!" She walked away.

"Well done. That one's been up there almost a month." A man with an impressively dense, full beard said from two stools away. "Mike's going to be impressed."

"Who's Mike?" El asked.

"Mike, the owner. This is Mike's Diner. Mike Brewer. His wife runs the bakery across the street. And the rest of us try not to get fat."

"Why the formula?" El asked, looking up as the waitress wrote X=137!

"Mike used to be a math teacher in Front Royal. He is a whiz at tests that can't be googled or solved with a phone. Well done."

A man dressed in white came from the back and rang a bell on the wall with a giant smile. The waitress pointed to El. His t-shirt strained on his massive arms and even more on his cauldron-sized belly. He was wiping his hands on his white apron as he walked over.

He reached out to shake with a hand the size of a baseball mitt. "Congrats. Did you guess or solve it? The rest of these pork chops just guess every day. But they can't show their work."

"It's a prime. Knowing that, it was easy."

"May I have your name for the wall of fame?" he pointed to a small white board to the right of the door into the kitchen that had a list of about 15 first names and dates.

"Eleanore," she said. "Nice meeting you, Mike."

The waitress set two plates down in front of the

bearded man. He had breakfast for lunch—eggs, sausage links, hash browns, and Wonder bread white toast with OJ.

"Eleanore?" he squinted his eyes at her. "Eleanore Wright?"

"Yes." She looked closer at him now.

"I'm Alex Fischer. I remember you. My parents were friends with your parents!" He leaned back and pointed at her. "You were great at softball. We used to play summer pickup games with you and your cousins! It was the only time we could field two whole teams. How are you?"

"I'm fine," she lied. "What about you? You stayed."

"I own the Ace Hardware on Main. I like it here."

"It seems like it."

"Oh, I was really sorry to hear about your grandmother," Alex said. "How's Jake holding up?"

"Jake? He's fine too." *What the hell?*

"He was distraught. She was 95 years old. Even if he had been there…" Alex must have seen her expression. "He found her. I'm sorry, I'm gossiping." Alex went back to his lunch.

El dipped her triangle of grilled cheese on Wonder bread in her bowl of Campbell's tomato soup and was in heaven.

Ryan would have walked out of here.

"It's OK, Alex. I'm going to have to cultivate my own spy network here if I'm going to stay. I'll need the gossip," she said as her lunch was delivered.

"Stay?" He paused with a sausage halfway to his mouth. "Stay? At the Rectory?"

"Lillian left me the house. Jake's restoring it," El said. "What's wrong? You are not the first person that looked like they smelled a fart when they heard that news."

Alex dug back into his lunch as he said. "Well, it's haunted. They say it is. Even the teens won't go there anymore. Not on a dare."

***

Eleanore and Alex chatted until he had to get back. El promised to stop by the store and see him sometime.

El had coffee and key lime pie as she reviewed her messages. Fourteen of fifteen voice mails were from the law firm Thompson, McKinley, Jones, and Levi. She didn't even listen to them. The last one was from Emma. She complained she never answered the phone. She also was amazed at the time she got a busy signal. A real busy signal. It had been more than a decade since she had heard one.

All the rest of the texts and emails were from the TMJL firm as well. El decided to drop in and see Joyce up the street. She took her car even though it was only a hundred yards. She didn't want to take up parking at Mike's Diner.

She pulled in a spot right in front of Jacobs and Associates.

She walked in, and it was a beautiful, though small, space. The walls on both sides were covered in floor-to-ceiling bookcases, packed with leather-bound legal volumes with impressive names. A mahogany table for four was to the left, and a leather sofa and armchairs were to the right. It looked more like a living room than a law office. Even the ceiling was tin squares painted a deep green.

Behind a tall counter making copies, a young girl said, "May I help you?"

"Yes. I'd like to see Joyce if she's available," El said.

There was a single door behind the girl in the middle of the wall of bookcases. Joyce appeared there. "Amy, this is Eleanore Wright. Our newest client. Come on back."

El walked around the counter to the left. It concealed computers, phones, copiers, and printers.

"Well, Ms. Wright, I have so far this morning managed to confirm that Thompson, McKinley, Jones, and Levi are, in fact, major league assholes." She sat behind a large desk with papers stacked in piles. A massive computer monitor was on the side desk.

"That's why I am here. They're basically harassing me," El said, sliding her unlocked phone across the desk.

"May I?" Joyce asked before she touched it.

"Please do."

"I have never been called "Sugar" before in my life," Joyce said. "If I'm sugar, I am giving these chauvinists diabetes!"

"Michelle Levi is a woman. She's the worst one."

"Thompson called me Sugar."

Joyce paused and was thumb-typing faster than El had ever seen. When she finished, Joyce spun it around so she could read what Joyce had typed. It basically instructed them that any further communications should be directed to her lawyer. It also informed them that her lawyer was already in possession of an original copy of Ryan's will and would be executing some of the time-sensitive issues soon.

"What does that mean?" El asked with her finger poised over SEND.

"It means your husband, as one of the two founding partners and biggest asshole in a kingdom of assholes had written this will to nuke the firm if they aren't careful. My god, I have never seen this level of assholery. It's truly epic. It was like an attempt to keep them from murdering him."

El pressed send.

"I already forwarded myself all their emails. I set up a rule to copy me on ALL communication from them, except voice mail. They shouldn't leave another message. Evidence."

"They have been trying to get you to sign away your rights since the day after his death." Joyce leaned across the desk. "The day after. You were smart not to sign a single thing."

"They had me come into the office. The woman he was with was the wife of their biggest client. Two kids." El knew her eyes were getting misty. "Those bastards tried to blame me for what happened. If I had been a better wife, none of this would have happened kinda thing. Like losing their biggest client was more important."

"Ass-wipes."

"Shit-stains."

"Motherfuckers."

"Puss-buckets."

"Did we just become best friends?" Joyce said. "Don't tell Jake."

"I love that movie."

"We used to fuck. A lot," Joyce said. "Just disclosing now, so you are not surprised later."

"You dated Jake?"

"There was no dating involved," Joyce said. "Cooking but no dating."

"Any other disclosures I should know?"

"Do you know about Sam?" Joyce asked.

"Who is Sam?"

"Sam is the pharmacist at the drugstore. She thinks she is Jake's fiancée."

"We shouldn't gossip about Jake."

"Normally, you'd be right. But Jake just dumped her, and she's not having it." She opened a drawer and pulled out a folder. "This is a restraining order I have already drafted. Jake's too nice. I only tell you this because it's only a matter of time before she comes to look for him at the Rectory. Your home."

"Oh, now I get it." El nodded. "Thanks for the heads up."

"When she sees you, she will likely fly off the handle in a jealous rant."

"Can you draft one of those for me?" She pointed to the folder with her chin.

Joyce reached into the drawer, pulled out a second folder, and opened it. It was another restraining order. An arrow marked SIGN HERE. El signed.

"Don't file that until something happens. We did just become best friends." El smiled.

Jake and Rob

Felix sat on the ruined wall of the burned church. The black water below buried the secrets and muffled the screams. A waterfall spilled out what was once a basement window. No animals drank from that water…

***

Jake pulled into Rob Jensen's driveway and backed up to his Ford Ranger. It was full of pressure-treated lumber and a dozen bags of cement. His suspension was so low that Jake was amazed the back tires were not scraping.

Rob came out of the house wearing a dirty white tank top. He was 60 years old, but he was fit, and his arms were heavily muscled.

How long before he asks if I like his wife beater.

"Rob, sorry it took so long. The new owner arrived a month early. It's been a bit of chaos."

"I figured you were hiding from Sam like a pussy.

She's been here twice looking for you. God only knows how many times she has driven by looking for your truck."

"Sorry about that," Jake said as they hit a rhythm, sliding and stacking lumber. "Hopefully, it will stop now. I was clear. No uncertain terms."

"I hear the new owner is hot. If Sam sees her, she will go ballistic," Rob said seriously but added, "Don't wear a wife beater. Too sexy. If Sam sees it, she'll just murder you."

"Damn, I had not thought of that," Jake said. "I already seem too high maintenance. Too slow on the work. Fuck. And I already spent all the money. My profits anyway."

"You gotta be shitting me," Rob said. "Need me to come up and help speed things along? Just say the word, man."

"I may take you up on that." They slid the last of the lumber over. "There is a lot of stuff that needs doing outside, like the initial mowing. I'm tied up in the bathrooms. But if you do… You gotta understand that the new owner is having a tough go."

"Does she know about all the deaths?" Rob asked, jumping down. "All that still creeps me out."

A Prius pulled into Rob's driveway, blocking Jake's truck.

Sam's Prius.

Oh shit.

She got out. Rob leaned back against the side of Jake's truck and crossed his arms over his chest, showing off his biceps.

"Hello, Sam," Rob said politely before anyone else.

"Love those shoes. Are they Bruno Magli? The color is perfect with that sundress." The dress was pale sunflowers on white. Halter spaghetti straps left most of her back bare, in addition to the plunging neckline. The sun shining behind her made it clear the only other thing she wore was a thong.

Jake silently blessed Rob and his ways. Instead of the rant she had queued up, he made her think of that.

"You have a good eye." She looked down at them, revealing her already deep cleavage that much more. "Yes. They are Bruno Magli."

"Don't step off the driveway. The ground is still soft from the rain," Rob added as he stepped away from Jake's truck. "I'll leave you to it. Always nice to see you, Sam. I have an errand to run. Ciao!" And he pulled out his keys, got into his now-empty truck, and drove away.

You bastard.

Jake stood in the back of the truck, the pile of lumber between them.

"Why won't you return my calls?" She had her hands on her hips. She wanted to fight about the lack of communication. Jake had had this conversation with her a hundred times.

"I thought I was clear as to why." Jake was calm, and he knew she hated that.

"We need to talk this out," she said.

"There is no WE anymore," Jake said. "I know this is hard for you to understand. You always bragged to me that no one had EVER broken up with you. You always did the breaking. That streak is over."

"You are not thinking this through. I had already

told my parents we were planning to get married. They love you. My mother has already picked out a dress. My dad is paying for the whole thing," she said. "Come down from there."

"Sam. You're not hearing me." Jake was getting louder. "We are DONE. I do NOT want to see you anymore." He tried not to raise his voice. Tried.

Cue the waterworks.

"Why are you yelling at me? You don't need to be so violent."

In a calm, quiet voice, he said, "Repeat what I just said to you. Please. So that I know you understand."

And the tears began to fall. She always let the first few fall into her cleavage for dramatic effect. "Why are you so mean?"

I feel nothing. I'm free.

He looked away from her as she covered her face with her hands and her shoulders started to shake with her sobs.

That is the cue to go to her and console her.

That's when he saw why Rob left. Jake could back his truck out that way. He wasn't trapped here. He lightly hopped down and slid through the open driver's door behind the wheel. He slammed the door and started the truck at the same time.

Her hands snapped down to her sides as fists. Fury was in her face.

"Goodbye, Sam." He backed out onto the road and headed for the mountain, wondering if she would follow.

***

Jake watched the rear view as he said, "Siri, call Rob, mobile."

He answered, "That was fast."

"Thanks, man," Jake said. "I thought you just ran when you could. Thanks for the exit."

"She's got really nice tits," Rob said amusedly. "Really nice. You sure about this?"

"I am sure. Really sure now," Jake said.

"You tie down the load?"

"What?"

"The load, dumb ass. You're going to drive up that grade and lose the load."

"Oh shit!" Jake laughed. "You are the man. Thanks."

"Fuck you, dip shit," Rob said in a ritual goodbye.

"You too, old man." Jake hung up.

He pulled over into Ed's filling station to secure the load. Ed came skipping out and was at the window before Jake could even open the door.

"Jake, you're alive!" Ed barked. "I was trying to work up the nerve to bring you the bottle jack. Did she tell you? That was fast. I like her."

"Who?" Jake said as he pushed open the door and retrieved the tie-down straps from behind the seat.

"Miss Wright," Ed said. "Met her this morning. Does she know about the Wright House, Jake? Anyone tell her about the house—the cemetery? Remember the time we went up there as kids, Jake? Did you tell her that story?"

"No, I did not," Jake said. "You mentioned the

bottle jack."

Ed moved quickly into the closest garage bay. He came back as Jake secured the first strap. He placed a large jack shaped like a fire hydrant in the back of the truck.

"Go ahead and fill it up. The oil's fine but check the tires. I've been moving loads like this a lot."

"Will do, Jake. Did I say I like her?"

"How you doing, Hector," Jake said. There was no reply. He was sleeping in the chair again.

The load was secured, and the cement bags moved to the front. Jake hopped down and handed Ed his credit card.

Ed asked as he walked to the door, "Nice frame. What you doin' with it?"

Jake looked inside the cab to see what he was talking about.

The oval mirror frame was leaning against the passenger seat on the floor.

How did I not notice that?

"Is that gold leaf? Nice. Nice frame," Ed said.

Yes, it was.

✳✳✳

Jake put Sam out of his mind by working. He had finished the decking and railings for the breezeway to the carriage house in just a couple of hours. The following job he had been dreading, but the lumber was already on the truck, so he would do it.

Lunch first. Two sandwiches and a glass of milk

were consumed in ten minutes. Eleanore had raided his supplies. He'd use the small fridge in the carriage house after this.

Flashlight and tape measure in hand, he lowered himself down through a hole he had opened in the wrap-around porch. Grabbing the broom he had laid down, he began clearing cobwebs. There was not quite enough room in the space to stand upright. It was also filled with those half spider and half cricket bugs. They always seemed to jump at his face.

It was dry down there because the wrap-around porch roof had covered it, but the house was old, and a few joists had rotted. Jake measured twice and then climbed out with more difficulty than he expected. In short order, he had a ladder, bright work lights, his boom box, tools, and screws. He was finishing up the fourth sister joist to Pink Floyd when he felt a strange vibration under his boots.

He turned off the radio.

That weird screaming sound that foxes made echoed faintly in the space. Timed perfectly with the vibration in his boot.

I have not had that much coffee.

The dry dirt floor was lit super bright with the halogen work lights he had in there on stands.

Taking the broom, he swept the floor, revealing large stone blocks. Jake imagined he could hear words in that faint scream.

"Help us…"

"Hello there," echoed loud in the space, startling Jake, causing him to bash his head hard enough to bring a rain of dirt and dust from above.

"I am so sorry. I didn't mean to sneak up on you." It was Eleanore peeking down the hole.

"It's OK. I have been bashing my head down here all day," Jake said.

"Better you than me. I hate jumping spiders! I'm afraid I'll need to burn the house down now," she joked.

"At least you wouldn't bash your head down here," Jake said, surveying the work. He looked at his watch. "Two more, and I'll be out of your hair. For tonight."

"I grocery shopped," she said down the hole. "Got dinner plans? We can chat over food. Besides, I eat alone too often. I have a rotisserie chicken, salad, and some potatoes. How long until you're done?"

"Twenty minutes or so. I am filthy, though." Jake came back to the hole to stand up straight and roll his neck. "How do you know I don't have a hot date?"

"Joyce and I are now best friends, and she told me about Sam. And the two of you. Did I mention we're best friends now?"

Jake must have frozen at the comment. He coughed, looking up.

"I'm sorry, I shouldn't joke," she said.

"Joyce told me about your husband, so I guess we're even," Jake said.

Now it was Eleanore's turn to freeze up.

"Dinner is a good idea," Jake said, looking at the work to finish. "I'll update you on a few things you need to know."

The phone began to ring inside.

Eleanore's face disappeared as the vibration returned to Jake's boots.

****

It took longer than he had thought to do the last few joists. Around this end, leaves had blown in and rotted for years, and the stone was not underfoot here. By the time he turned off the work lights and climbed out, a light August rain had started about an hour later.

There was a bowl of water, a washcloth, a towel, and one of his clean t-shirts neatly folded there on a plank between two sawhorses. Jake looked down at himself. Filthy.

He stepped off the porch and took off his shirt, and used it to scrub most of the dirt off his jeans and out of his hair.

He returned to the porch and took off his boots, and left them by the door. He scrubbed his face and arms as best he could and put on the clean t-shirt, a Rolling Stones concert t-shirt he didn't like because it was kind of short for his torso. But at least it was clean.

He walked in and wondered if he should start knocking. He opted for just announcing himself.

"Hey… Thanks for the t-shirt." Jake walked through to the kitchen, and Eleanore looked up from a massive pile of papers at the far end. The near-end had two place settings on woven straw mats that Lillian used all the time. They were set with her favorite colorful plates as well. It tugged at Jake's heart. "I still need to wash up a bit." He moved to the bathroom as Eleanore got up.

"I'll set up."

Soap and water were a must. The water ran black in the sink. All the mirrors in there kept sending him back to the sink to get the black from behind his ear or the back of his neck.

By the time he emerged, the table was set. The chicken had been quartered, the bagged salad was in a bowl, and some cherry tomatoes were added. Each plate had a steaming microwaved potato.

"So, to eliminate the suspense, am I fired?" Jake asked before he sat.

"Fired?" she said, genuinely surprised. "You're not getting out of this that easy."

"Decide after I tell you a few things." Jake sat and cut his potato open. "You mentioned Samantha Goodwin. I hate even bringing up my drama, but we recently broke up, and she isn't taking it well. She may at some point come up here."

"You think she is the one who called and hung up?" Eleanore said as she filled her plate. "Someone called. No one there, just weird static. It's weird having no cell service or Wi-Fi. On the other hand, I sorta like it."

"I'm with you on that. If you need the Internet, you can use the connection at the bakery-cafe in town," Jake said before digging in. "Anyway, please let me know if she stops in."

"Was there anything else?"

"Everyone thinks the place is haunted. You probably already know that. Even when I was coming here as a kid, it's gotten worse since the house fell into disrepair, and those kids died."

"Kids died?" she echoed.

Jake sighed. "Just the facts. Kids used to dare each other to come up here. About ten or fifteen years ago, three kids came up. The dare was that on a full moon, they had to walk the entire length of the cemetery, with no flashlights. Then spit into the pool at the bottom of the old church."

"What happened?" Eleanore asked.

"Something spooked the kids. They ran in the dark. Two of them fell into the ice well. They were both impaled on deer antlers."

"What happened to the third one?"

"He ran full tilt into that tombstone we were sitting on. Hard enough to knock it over. Lillian heard them. It wasn't the first kids fucking around out there. But it was the last." Jake swallowed. "The one that lived was in a coma for a couple of months because of head trauma. The cops investigated it. They said the surviving kid was lying."

"About what? Why would he lie?"

"It was the fence. It was intact. Plus, the gate at this end of the cemetery was closed and latched." Jake said. "As you can imagine, the story got bigger with each telling. Soon the story became that Lillian was a witch, and she murdered them."

"Oh no."

"It broke her heart," Jake said as he stared at a cherry tomato impaled on his fork. "The real ones to blame were all the kids that came before them. Made the midnight run. That includes almost everyone that grew up here. Including me."

They ate in silence for a while. Then, when he looked up, Eleanore's face was drained of color.

"Eleanore, what's wrong? It's just a story."

"My friends call me El."

"What's wrong?" Jake asked.

"Do you know Alex Fischer?"

"Yes, of course, my favorite hardware guy."

She looked Jake right in the eyes and held him there as she said, "He and I made the first Midnight Run."

Silence stretched out for a minute, maybe two, or an hour, before Jake spoke again.

"Other than that, Mrs. Lincoln, how was the play?" He was deadpan.

"Now, you can't call me El. And you are FIRED." She laughed like it was just what she needed.

The phone rang.

They both jumped, and with perfect clown timing, Jake even fell out of his chair.

He and Emma would get along…

Laughing, she answered the phone. "Hello."

Jake could hear it was only a burst of static and distant whispers of voices from his place on the floor.…

Felix watched them through the window. The screams were louder when the female picked up the phone. They didn't notice the burning eyes in the shadowed corner behind them.

***

El almost jumped out of her skin when the phone rang. Jake's genuine jump turned into comic gold as he disappeared onto the floor, his stocking feet suddenly appearing. His socks didn't match, and one was half off his foot.

"Hello…"

The burst of static was louder than last time. She held the receiver out to Jake.

Neither of them saw the face of the cat Felix in the window.

She hung up the phone.

"I know it's safety first. But can we do something about these phones soon?" She walked to the fridge, and Jake saw it was now full. "I hope you are a dessert guy. I saw these at the bakery and had to have them. Keep your fork." She took the plates away.

She returned to the table with what looked like two tiny strawberry pies on small plates and a can of whipped cream tucked under her arm.

"We already have the cordless phones. I can install them tomorrow, but the base with the answering machine will have to be in the carriage house for now." Jake just nodded when she offered the whipped cream with a gesture. I'm sure the static is in the house lines. Out there, at least I can tie in straight from the pole."

After topping his, she did her own, then tilted her head back and filled her mouth straight from the can.

Through her full mouth, she mumbled, "Coffee?"

"Yes. Coffee, please." Jake was shaking his head at her clowning.

She set the whipped cream can on the table, retrieved two large colorful mugs and the carafe, and brought it all to the table, pouring while she took another comic hit of whipped cream.

"No. Really. I do not stress-eat from ghost stories, really." Then, with the exaggerated licking of her lips, she sat.

"New mugs. Nice," Jake said as he took a sip.

Ryan would have hated these mugs. And clowning. And me being myself.

A couple of hours ago, she collected all of the black ceramic mugs and threw each one into the ice well in a ritual breaking. She rubbed her eyebrow.

"After the porch, I want to cap the ice well," Jake

said as if he was reading her mind.

"Do we have to cap it? I don't want it to be ugly," El said.

"Lillian said the same. The plan was to use stone from the collapsed church chimneys to build a wall, so it's still there, still historical, but no more rotting deer."

"That's better," El said as she wiped her mouth.

"My friend Rob can help with that. He was already planning to come up and start mowing and general clean up outside."

"If you're not careful, you'll totally ruin the Munsters vibe I was hoping for."

"I was thinking more like the Addams Family motif."

Jake drained his coffee and wiped his mouth with the paper napkin as he pushed his chair back. "Thank you for dinner… El. Or am I still fired?"

"You're welcome. Not fired yet."

"I will probably be here around 8 am and start on the phones."

"I will be gone by then. I'm going to go to the Super Walmart in Front Royal to get some things. Need anything?" she asked.

"I'm all good." He headed down the hall.

Good thing he swept up the glass.

"Goodnight, Westley. Good work. Sleep well. I'll most likely kill you in the morning," El quoted the *Princess Bride*.

Ryan hated that movie. Especially all my favorites. Why does everything make me think of him?

"Inconceivable…" He waved as he made his way

back to his boots.

Why does that one word make me want to cry now?

***

"El… El wake up," she heard someone say. "Would you rather I let you sleep in?"

That wasn't Ryan. He'd never let me sleep in.

She opened her eyes. No one was there. At least she knew where she was this time. She was already on her back, and her arms stretched over her head. It was a warm morning. The MCR t-shirt was pulled up just below her breasts. One leg was sticking out from under the covers.

"You OK?" Jake said, peeking around the door.

El immediately pulled down the MCR t-shirt to cover her panties.

"I'm up. I'm up," she said to herself.

"Your phone alarm was going off in the kitchen. The alarm was going off in here, too," Jake said from the hall. "I made coffee. I'll be in the carriage house for a bit."

El heard his booted footsteps, and the door closed behind him. She hugged the pillow and breathed deep before she reluctantly got up and went to pee. She sneaked back into the tiny room and changed into shorts and her favorite Hawaiian shirt and sandals. She admired the new ankle bracelet and matching red peppers earrings she bought yesterday.

These are fun. This shirt is fun. This new bra is comfy. Ryan hated fun. Hated comfy. Fuck you, Ryan.

She grabbed her new small Coach bag from the

dresser. She liked it, too.

She moved into the kitchen and grabbed her fully charged phone from the counter. It said 8:36 am.

Man, I sleep good in this house.

She opened the cupboard and tore open a box of grape Pop-Tarts. She broke one in half the long way like she used to, and dipped it in her coffee. She devoured the first one right over the sink. She broke the second one in half the long way but was determined to enjoy it.

There were footsteps upstairs.

While she enjoyed her first cup, she decided to look at the completed breezeway in the daylight. She slowly looked at the old oak beams above, complemented by the new metal roof. The pressure-treated decking was not stained or painted but was still perfect.

The carriage house door was open at the far end. The transition had no steps up or down, and she liked that feature.

Jake was there just to the right.

I thought you were upstairs…

A large box was open with eight phones lined up on charger bases. Jake finished attaching a yellow box to the wall next to a box marked VA-Telecomm.

"Just in time. Want to record an answering machine message?" Jake said as he held the handset and finished dialing a number from memory. "Ron, you coming out today… Late? Slacker… Sure. I'll be here all day. Thanks, man. Later."

"Would you mind recording the message?" El

asked, "That whole woman all alone in an isolated house thing."

"Sure." Jake pressed and held a button until it said. "At the sound of the tone, please record your message."

"You've reached 540-555-0666. At the sound of the tone, please leave a detailed message." He hung up the receiver.

"Want to help me deploy and test these?" Jake asked as she popped the last of her Pop-Tart into her mouth.

"Sure." He was already piling three of the sets in her arms. "As long as it doesn't take all day."

***

El watched Jake make a pouch of his YES t-shirt and pile the other four handsets and bases in it. Then, they entered the house. He turned directly into the maid's bedroom.

Jake took the first one from her, set it directly on the bedside table, and plugged it into the same outlet as the lamp.

"It might take a bit for the phone to charge. Kitchen next." Jake followed her to the kitchen as she up-ended her coffee mug and put it in the sink.

Jake took the next one from her and plugged the charging base into an outlet next to the toaster. "By the way, they delivered the wrong dishwasher and will be delivering the new one, the right one, hopefully, this week."

"No worries," El said. She stepped closer to him, "Want me to take a couple of these so you don't stretch out the shirt too much?"

That smell is him. The bed. The pillow. The shirt I have been sleeping in.

"Library next," Jake said. "Can you get the door?"

It was two doors, actually—double pocket doors. El slid one open, then the other. But unfortunately, it was on the north side, and even though the window seat shutters were open, it was dim inside.

"Is there a light switch?" El asked as she felt the logical location.

"Yes. Over here and the table lamps as well." Jake said, trying the switch. Nothing happened.

El crossed the room and set the last handset she held down on the table next to the lamp. It was cold in here. This lamp didn't work either.

"Dammit, sorry," Jake said. "I don't come in here very often. So just plug it in there. Where the lamp is plugged in?"

"Why is all the furniture pushed over here?" El asked. She managed to plug in the phone base but could not help but notice Jake's hesitation.

"I had to take the rug out to get cleaned," he said.

El remembered the dream. Grandma was on her back, eyes milky, she was wearing jeans with a small hole in the left knee… boots. She looked over at Jake, and he was staring at the floor.

All the lights came on at once.

They were the same jeans. Jake is standing right

there. Her dream was Jake's memory.

"I hate power problems," she said, breaking the vapor lock. She walked out, and Jake followed. "I don't want a phone in the dining room. Parlor, maybe."

"Just plug this one in here. We can move it after the cleaning crew comes through." She put the set on the floor, just inside.

"These three will go upstairs. You can head out if you need to. I can handle these."

"I haven't been upstairs yet. A quick peek, and I'll go."

"Sounds good." Jake hit the switch at the bottom of the stairs, and a dim light came on. "The cleaning crew will clean all the lampshades and fixtures and replace all the bulbs with full-spectrum LEDs. Everything will be brighter. Hope you're not allergic to dust."

The hallway upstairs was the same width as the one below. Jake rounded the railing and went back toward the front of the house, entering the turret room. This was the first bright room El had been inside. The space was empty. The walls and trim were all freshly painted. The oak floor was refinished.

"I think this is the first room here with no mirrors."

As Jake plugged in the phone, he said. "This should give you a sense of how the rest of the rooms will be." Jake tried the phone. There was a loud dial tone. "Good. This is the one farthest from the base station in the carriage house."

"She died on that rug?"

Why did you ask him that?!

He looked out the window. "Yes. They came and got her. Good people. Kind. The rug…well, it smelled like urine. I did not want to leave it too long. I rolled it up that night and took it to a cleaner in Front Royal. Should be done soon."

Jake moved down the hall, opening each door for a dusty peak. "There are six bedrooms on this floor of various sizes, plus the turret." He opened a door at the bottom of the stairs that went up. "I think all the beds are OK, but the plan was to replace all the mattresses. The cleaning crew will handle the old ones. Another thirty-yard dumpster will be dropped off tomorrow."

"The antiques are lovely. Well, probably." Lots of furniture was covered in sheets and deep dust."

"There are two baths. Now anyway." He swung open a door. "I need to gut that one. It's rotted from leaking."

"I remember this bathroom. Is there any way we can save that old clawfoot tub?"

"Probably, it will need some work. And moving it…."

The other bedrooms had obviously been closed up for a long time.

The hallway was still lined with mirrors everywhere, all with beveled glass and beautiful frames. "She had quite the mirror collection," El said.

"The ones resting on the floor, leaning on the walls, were at risk of falling as the plaster and lath failed." Jaked pointed out. "It will all be fixed. You can keep or remove the mirrors. The walls should look perfect when I'm done."

El looked at the stained wall and the clean place where the mirror had hung. Glancing in the mirror that rested on the floor, angled up a bit, she thought she saw something move. She looked at the transoms window above the door.

Pointing at a door, she said, "I slept in that room."

"This is the master bedroom," Jake said. "The project started here. We added the master bath and this walk-in closet. Lillian thought she'd need a wheelchair-accessible bathroom one day when she got old."

El was amazed at the size of the flat-screen TV on the wall. On a shelf below it was a DVD collection of TV shows, including *Matlock*, *Murder She Wrote*, *The Rockford Files*, and one she didn't recognize called *Mannix*. Lots of classic Westerns and other black and white titles.

Then she saw the photos of herself. One was of the two of them on the porch swing. Her high school graduation, her college graduation, her wedding. And a few other random photos of her. They made her heart ache.

Jake seemed even taller in this room. El realized the counters were a few inches lower because her gramma was so short. Lillian's clothes still hung in the closet. Glancing around the bedroom, she realized it was all just as she had left it.

Jake plugged in the phone on a bedside table. The mattress was bare. The visible tag said it was not that old. It said, QUEEN.

"I'll get some new sheets and pillows to tide me over today at Walmart. That reminds me, you said this wouldn't take all day. I'm so late. I'll see you later."

She flew down the stairs holding in tears again, then out the back door and through the breezeway to the carriage house. She waved at the figure in the third-floor window.

She thought it was Jake.

Jake Gets Back to Work

Felix sighed. Sitting in the turret room, he watched. So easy to see them, if only they would simply be quiet, and look.

***

Jake had to get back to work. He set the last phone on the steps going up to the third level. Those steps were narrow, and he always wondered why. They could have easily made them full width. Furniture options would have been more accessible.

He had just turned on the flood lights on the front porch when Rob pulled up in his Ranger.

"Just in time," Jake said. "I need you to hand down this bottle jack to me. I figured out why this section settled so much."

"Dude!" Rob said in greeting. "Where the fuck did you get this, Jake?"

"Ed Barns loaned it to me," Jake said. "This whole side has a massive block foundation. This side doesn't, so that side settled, and this didn't."

"Did he mention chemtrails?" Rob asked.

"No. He didn't mention wife-beater tank tops, either," Jake teased.

"So you and Sam are over." It was a statement more than a question.

"Jesus, Rob, are you turning into a high school cheerleader gossip? Take that 4-foot level and put it over here. Let me know when you are ready."

"OK, go," Rob said as Jake pumped the big hydraulic jack.

"You know she will come at you a couple more times, right?"

"I know. She's not hearing me," Jake sighed. "I hope she doesn't slash my tires or key my truck."

"Or worse," Rob said.

The house gave a mighty creak.

"How's that?" Jake asked.

"It's good, Jake. Right there," Rob said. "Promise me you are done with Sam."

"Done. I think I was done when Lillian died," Jake said in realization. "She had no empathy. None. Didn't care at all about what happened. To Lillian or me."

"She fucked me," Rob yelled out. "Last night. Twice. And again this morning. It's why I was late. She thinks she is exacting vengeance upon you."

Jake burst out in uncontrollable laughter down in the hole.

"She's trying to destroy our friendship," Rob said, trying to see Jake laughing in the hole.

"She really doesn't know either of us at all." Rob

was laughing now. "She's supposed to be way smarter than me."

Jake's laughter suddenly stopped. "You know what this means, Rob?"

"No. What?" Rob answered. And Jake's head popped up over the edge.

"That she actually finally believes me!" Now Jake was making whooping sounds.

"Jake, can you do me a big favor and not tell her you know," Rob said sheepishly.

"Sure. Why?"

"Well, this vengeance thing is working out great for me. I'm 60 years old and, well, you know she still has a key to your place in town. She ransacked it looking for that ring already," Rob said as Jake started to laugh again. "Well, tonight she wants to go over there and fuck me in your bed, even film some of it. So email will be so NSFW. Just sayin'."

Jake almost pissed himself laughing this time.

***

Jake spent the rest of the day installing the new tongue and groove decking on the wrap-around porch. The pneumatic nail gun made it easy.

Rob spent the day clearing fallen branches and mowing. The baggers had to be emptied often onto the compost pile behind the old barn. It was slow going because the grass was so tall. If she kept up with it, it would be easier. Finally, the area between the porch and the driveway was mowed just in time for the dumpster to be delivered.

Mabel's Mops will be here tomorrow.

Jake stood back and looked at the house exterior. So much work to do. The peeling paint mocked him. The crappy storm windows had to all come off. The screens were all in tatters.

Something moved in the third-floor turret room window.

That room was empty. Jake looked to see if a large bird could have been a reflection in the glass. Nothing.

If I can finish the steps on this side, I will call it a day.

He heard the new phones ring.

The sound was odd in the old place. Incongruent. He let it ring. They either hung up, or the new answering machine had its first customer. Finally, it occurred to Jake that he could have a phone with him as he worked.

The old side steps were so rotted he pulled them all out with just his hammer. All the rotting wood went directly into the dumpster instead of the debris pile by the barn. He'd have a couple of days cleaning all that up as well.

Under the stairs, he found the original brick steps. The wooden ones had been built over them. They had settled and were eight inches out of level. Jake finished the new eight-foot wide set of steps in less than two hours.

Shadows were long when Rob returned to inspect his work. He went up and down them with ease. It was only three steps.

"What have you been doing all day, slacker?" Rob

said. "I ran out of fuel. All the cans in the carriage house are empty, so I put them in my truck. I'd stay longer, but I gotta take a shower. I got a hot date."

"I'll be at The Cabin if you need me." Jake smiled. "Be careful."

"Hey, I have had a vasectomy, she's had a hysterectomy, and I have fresh Viagra. So if I knock her up, we'll know it's Jesus!"

"You are so going to Hell."

"I'll be smiling, though." Rob combed out his gray beard as his eyebrows went up and down.

Jake followed Rob back to the carriage house and waved as he drove away. As he was putting his tools back into the tall tool chest, the phone on the shelf rang.

He picked it up. "Jake, speaking."

"Hi, Jake. It's me. Please don't hang up," Sam said.

"Sam, you have to stop," Jake said. There was no anger in his voice.

"I know, I will. I'm coming to terms with that." Sam sounded sincere. "I have two boxes of things for you. Those t-shirts you like. A winter coat. Some of your books."

"Thanks, Sam."

"You know that stained glass candle holder? Well, my mom made that. I'd like it back."

Jake knew the piece. It was beautiful.

"OK. No problem," Jake said. "I need to get it. It's at The Cabin."

"Can you meet me at your place in town around 7 pm?" Sam asked. "After my shift at the pharmacy?"

And there it was. She wanted Jake to walk in on them and make a scene.

"Sure. Just let yourself in. You can also leave the key. Make yourself at home. I'll be there anywhere between seven and nine."

Rob is going to owe me big time.

"OK, Jake," she said, calm as could be. "See you then." She hung up.

What a horrible person.

Jake saw there was a message on the machine. A bright LED read the number 1.

There was static in waves that sounded like popping fire, and then a distant scream seemed to come closer like a Doppler effect.

He hammered the delete button, and the display returned to zero. He pressed the call log button. The only number listed there was: 540-555-7734.

He pressed the dial button.

It never rang. It was like it was picked up instantly, and it was all static like a really loud campfire.

"Hello?" Jake said into the static.

A quiet whispering voice replied, almost too soft to be heard, "Kill her while she sleeps...."

"Not funny." Jake hung up and grabbed the phone's manual from the bench. He blocked that number.

EL Sleeps Hard

Felix watched it as it looked from the third-floor window. It was watching, waiting for something, someone…

***

"I'll get some new sheets and pillows to tide me over today at Walmart. That reminds me, you said this wouldn't take all day. I'm so late. I'll see you later."

She flew down the stairs and out the back door, and through the breezeway to the carriage house. She waved at the figure in the third-floor window as she drove past the house.

She thought it was Jake.

El had to pay close attention as she descended the mountain. She noticed that the graveyard was way bigger than she remembered. Moss-covered headstones peeked through the trees for what seemed like a mile. She even noticed three gates. All closed and locked with chains and padlocks.

Just like last time, as soon as her tires hit the paved road, her phone came alive. She stopped her car on the single-lane road. There was no traffic and no shoulders.

She looked at texts first. At the top was one from Joyce.

- Do NOT reply to them.
- I got this.
- If they send a courier, send them to me.
- SIGN NOTHING.

Her other texts were from Emma.

- Taking Friday off.
- Your housewarming gift is a blender.
- And Margarita mix.
- And Tequila.
- You better have ice girlfriend.

El added to her mental list to ensure she had enough beds by Friday. Sheets, towels, shampoo, and ice…

El didn't even open the emails, just marked them all as read.

She dialed Joyce on speakerphone and started moving again.

"Ms. Wright. My favorite client ever! How are you today? Ghosts keep you awake?" Joyce said.

"I am sleeping better than I have in weeks, to be honest. Do you need me to do anything today? I am coming down now but just passing through town to go shopping in Front Royal."

"No need to stop in today, but I need to update you on a couple of things." Joyce turned on her lawyer's voice. "Your husband must have hated these people. The will he made is rather bulletproof. He has basically cut a leg off a three-legged stool they are sitting on. That prick even owned the building the law office is in. Yesterday they received notice that the building is up for sale, and they have five business days to exercise the right of first refusal. After that, they have to buy it or get out in 30 days. This is on top of the shares you own in the law firm. They have to buy you out on-demand, or you become a silent partner and share in their profits, or they take you to court."

"What do you recommend I do? What will they do?"

"They will try to get you to sign several agreements. Not sell the building, not start charging them rent, not demand a buyout. Don't sign anything. I took the liberty to have all your postal mail forwarded here. You're going to get some checks, life insurance, stuff like that.

"Knowing these assholes, they might try to find a nitwit lawyer to buy into the firm with an existing client list. They are scrambling to secure your husband's clients, but they have all been notified of his demise and warned to go elsewhere.

"All I want is to liquidate it all, including the brownstone," said El.

"There may be mail at your home that is important.

I know it's three or four hours away, but can you get it?"

"I have a friend coming out on Friday. She can bring it," El replied.

"I expect it won't take them long to see the jam they are in. After that, they will likely write up a comprehensive offer. At that point, I will present it, and you can decide."

"Thanks, Joyce. I'm glad I met you."

"Happy to help."

***

El waved to Ed and Hector as she drove by Ed's Texaco.

"Siri, call Emma, mobile," El said to the air as she drove toward the village of Covington.

"Wassup, girl?" Emma answered.

"Aren't you at work?" El replied.

"I am, but these wildcats know me and the value of my ginormous brain. So I repeat, wassup, girl?" El could hear people laughing in the background of the cube farm.

"I need a favor," El said. "Do you still have the code for my garage?"

"Of course I do. I keep my scooter charged in there to scoot around Capital Hill. Plus, if I ever need a good bottle of wine, I help myself. By the way, you're running low on the Fox Den Chardonnay. That shit is good. Steams my panties thinking about it." More laughs.

"Must be nice to have your own studio audience,"

El said, slowly entering the village.

"The favor. Name it, and I shall make it so." Emma stated it as fact. Background laughs were replaced with rapid staccato typing as she multitasked.

"I need you to bring my mail this weekend," El said.

"Get your mail? That's all? I thought you'd want me to murder more people. I did such a good job last time." Emma played to her audience.

"Emma!" Eleanore laughed.

"OK, I'll do it. But I'm taking a boy toy to your place on Thursday night and leaving the blinds open," Emma said. "You're blushing right now. I know you are." The ambient sound changed as El heard a door click closed. "You sound good, El. How are you doing? Be honest. I was really worried about you."

"I am doing way better and sleeping way better. Keeping busy with good distractions. Being away from the Internet is helping, too, I think."

"Get laid yet?" Emma asked flat out.

"Emma!"

"Well, don't," Emma said. "Bet you never thought you'd hear me say that."

"That's an understatement."

"Seriously, the cops came by asking about you. I think those wankers at Ryan's firm put a bug in their ear."

"How do you know that?"

"That Thursday night boy-toy is my friend Steve. He's a cop and told me they are going over Ryan's car with a fine-tooth comb. Well, your car. The Cougar he died with had big money, and now the Metro Police are hoppin'."

"Thanks for letting me know," El said. "Tell Steve the Boy-Toy I said thanks."

"I will. Thursday is lady's night. It's all about me on Thursday."

"Thanks, Em. I love you."

"Love you too, El."

El pulled into a space in front of Jacobs and Associates and got out.

She walked in, and the bell chimed over the door.

Joyce looked out of the inner office door when the door closed, ringing the bell again.

"Didn't expect to see you so soon. Forget something?" Joyce asked. "Wanna come in? Coffee?"

"I called my friend Emma. She said she'd bring the mail in Friday," El said. "She also said the police were asking about me. She thinks the wankers at Ryan's law firm put a bug in their ear. They are looking very closely at the car. It was actually MY car."

"Those guys are some world-class douche-baguettes. Do you happen to have the police report number? Accident report number?" Joyce asked.

"I think I might." El did an email search on her phone and sent it to Joyce.

"How are you holding up?" Joyce asked sincerely.

"To be honest, really well. And I have no idea why." El tried to explain it again. "I am sleeping through the night—serious rest kinda sleep. Jake's coffee is like magic. I swear that having no Facebook or other social media and no broadcast news is healing me. I'm starting to feel like myself again for the first time in years."

"El, I think you have just been swimming in a toxic swamp for so long you can't help but feel better when the pollution dissipates." Joyce opened a desk drawer and drew out a stack of business cards. "Take these. They are the answer to EVERY question. Couriers, cops, insurance, everything."

"What if Ed asks me about chemtrails?" Joyce laughed.

"I went to high school with Ed Barns," Joyce said. "I love that guy."

"Really? He's a hoot," El said.

"He was my class's valedictorian."

***

El left the law office and looked up and down the street. She strolled down towards the diner. She passed the bakery/cafe and thought she'd stop on the way back and get some good stuff. The next was a beer/wine/liquor shop, and she'd need that when Emma got here. There was a real butcher, a drug store, a barbershop, a bank, and beyond that, the post office.

El walked in the large door. It was propped open. The walls were lined with classic brass post office boxes—the larger ones to the bottom. The marble floors matched the marble counter at the far end. A wrinkled little old lady was behind the counter.

"Can I help you?"

"My name is Eleanore Wright. My grandmother was Lillian Wright. I have recently moved into the house. How do I get mail? How did Lillian get mail?"

"Can I see your ID, dear?" The little old lady squinted at the ID, and then El. "Lily talked about you a lot. You should have visited."

She had no idea how her comment hurt.

"Did you know my Gramma?"

"We played bridge on Tuesdays. She had the touch. She had a reputation of being a witch cause of all the goings-on at the Rectory. I never believed it. Except for her cat. A familiar if ever there was one." She was writing a note on a Post-It. She handed it to El. "Wait here."

El looked at the Post-It, and it said, "PO Box 0666, Covington VA 22407". Then, "combo 12-5-19." Looking to her right, she saw box 666. Someone used a Sharpie to add an O to the medium-sized PO box number. El tried the combination, and it opened.

It was empty. She heard squeaking sneakers on the marble floor and saw the clerk appear behind the counter. She carried a laundry-basket-sized bin mounded high with mail.

She set the bin on a counter next to a large recycle can and said, "I'd sort through it here, dear. Dump the junk mail here."

It was good advice. Ninety percent of it was clearly junk and went straight into the barrel. She opened what looked like important or official mail, including two Social Security checks and some bank statements from the Covington Bank.

She returned the bin. The woman had taken off her sweater and put on her cat-rim glasses. Her name tag was now visible.

"Thank you, Ester," El said as she left.

She took out the phone and added to her list "Banking, Liquor." The list already had "Sheets, pillows, long phone charger, two-prong extension cords, ice."

Looking uphill past the funeral home on the other side of the street was a small garden center and greenhouse. Back the way she came, she also saw the Covington Hotel, which looked like a bar with pool tables if the neon sign were to be believed.

Ryan would have hated it. Sheep-pens, he called places like that. Like this whole village.

An Urgent Care was right next to the bar. Handy. Then there was a real estate office beyond that with accountants upstairs. There was a pet store, groomer, vet office, and a used bookstore. Across the street was the Ace hardware store. Alex was waving from the window. The hardware shared the parking lot with Alan's Alley, a bowling/pizza place.

The bell rang here as well when she entered the hardware. "Hi, Alex."

"Greetings, Ms. Wright. How are things at the end of the road? See any ghosts yet?" He smiled wide.

A middle-aged woman squeezed behind El as she replied, "Well, there are these two teenage boys I keep seeing sprinting in the fog…" Alex and Eleanore both looked at the wide eyes of the severe woman as the door closed behind her. "Too soon?"

"We used to do that run," Alex said. "I heard about your husband. I was sorry to hear that."

"Heard about it?" she said. "Where?"

"It's a small town. Don't you ever watch Hallmark movies? It's like that, except we don't have a cool town square, and we say Fuck a lot more."

"My friend Emma is visiting this weekend. Is there anything to do here so she won't drown me in Margaritas? Something that doesn't involve advanced math?"

"The Covington Hotel is social on Friday and Saturday. Alan's has great beer and pizza. League bowling." He took a deep breath as if to continue and paused. "And that's all I got."

"We could do a Midnight Run." Of course, El was kidding, but Alex's face drained of color, unable to hide it behind the beard.

"I guess it is too soon," Alex made light.

"Well, I'm off to buy stuff for the house at Walmart," El said.

"Depending on what you need, try to buy stuff in Covington. We are all trying to get by here."

"I know where to get screws," El said. "That did not come out right."

"That's what she said." Alex deadpanned.

***

Sheets, pillows, extension cords, charger cables, and two bales of TP were obtained from Walmart. El took her time and just wandered the store for ideas. By the time she was driving back through Covington, it was already 6 pm.

She stopped at Alan's Pizza Alley to get a pie to go.

The small four-lane alley still had that magical sound of artificial thunder and pins crashing. There was the smell of pizza and beer and more people there than she expected. More people were watching than bowling.

Without a word, the man behind the counter raised his chin to Eleanore and telepathically conveyed, *Can I help you?*

She raised her voice to be heard over the people, the lanes, and ZZ Top. "I'll have a large meat lovers pizza to go, please."

"Name?" He asked.

"Wright." She said loud so she would not need to repeat it or spell it. Having worked this kind of job in college, she knew speaking clearly was a kindness to the staff.

When she spoke her name, several heads turned her way.

"It'll be twelve minutes and $20. No tips in here." He added, pointing to the sign over the register that stated the same.

Then he surprised her by stripping off a latex glove, reaching across the bar, and offering his hand to shake. "You must be Eleanore. I'm Alan Price. Welcome to Covington and Alan's Alley specifically."

She shook his hand firmly, and she liked him immediately. "Nice to meet you."

He took the slip and passed it back to the kitchen via the stainless steel carousel. He started filling a pitcher of beer, saying, "Want a beer while you wait?

On me."

"Thanks."

Pitchers of beer. Ryan, You don't know what you missed.

Instantly, there was a beer in a frosted mug in front of her. She took it up and spun her stool to watch the bowling. It was on a lower level and easy to see, even with the tables and chairs and people in between.

The man sitting on the next stool over was watching her now, not the bowling. He looked like an old Wilford Brimley, right down to the glasses and cookie duster mustache. He held a chicken drumstick up in his right hand like a magic wand.

"Hello," El said and took a long pull on the excellent beer.

Wilford said nothing and just put the entire drumstick in his mouth, and when he pulled it out, the bone was absolutely clean of meat.

El just smiled.

In the crowded room, a buffer zone had appeared around her. People kept glancing at her. It didn't feel unwelcoming. Just curious.

Her beer was empty as the crowd cheered a strike by a girl in black jeans and a tight t-shirt with the sleeves cut off.

"Wright."

She turned as Alan set the pizza down on the bar. "Have a good evening."

He was gone.

A young man held the door open for her as she passed him. He touched the brim of his Yankees ball cap.

Yeah, Ryan would have hated this town. And they would have hated him.

***

The smell of the pizza was driving her mad by the time she reached the house. There was a lot of visible progress today. The massive dumpster couldn't hide all the new decking on the porch. A lot of mowing had been done along the road on each side and around the house.

Man, the house really does look haunted. Was the paint peeling that much this morning?

El decided that the light from the west was doing it. She pulled into the carriage house. Only one row of lights was on. Jake's truck was gone.

She grabbed the pizza and her purse and went in. She loved the breezeway more and more. It was now mowed on both sides.

The late afternoon light revealed how dirty the windows and curtains were.

She turned on all the lights she could find and then the oven on low. She put the pizza inside the oven, box and all. She made two more trips to the car to get everything in. She even slid the large carriage house door closed. She found the right light, so the only light was a single bulb over the workbench.

It was dark for 7 pm. There must be some weather brewing.

She dropped three rolls of Two-Ply in the bathroom and the rest in the pantry. She set the second bale at the foot of the stairs for the next time she went up.

El called Jake on the cordless kitchen phone. But while she was talking, she was distracted by sounds in the house.

"You were busy today…." she said. But she swore she could hear Jake walking upstairs.

It was chit-chat after that. She barely paid attention. She thought she heard Spanish… More footsteps. She carried the cordless phone to the other side of the kitchen and slid the butcher knife out of the block.

"Thanks, Jake," El said.

"For what?"

"We got off on the wrong foot. I was not in a good place. Between good sleep and the kindness of everyone…."

Lightning struck the house with a tremendous clap of thunder.

There was a loud crash upstairs, breaking glass, and the phone went dead as all the lights went out.

Jake's Ride

Felix and dozens of other cats sat on the tombstones waiting. Then, when it struck with a great explosion of screams and lightning, it began…

***

Jake stared at the phone.

He went to the call log and dialed her back. It was busy.

He hung up redialed. Busy signal again.

He was moving through The Cabin toward his motorcycle.

Busy again. Then it cut off. And the static was back.

As he climbed on the bike, his phone beeped—voice mail.

"Jake…" The static sounded like it was echoing from the bottom of the ice well.

"…broken." The voice cut off…

***

Jake didn't remember the ride down the mountain. He didn't dare look to see how fast he was going. He'd ridden the path a thousand times before. He should slow down. But it was like that Doppler scream was chasing him the entire way. Pine branches whipped his face. He'd forgotten his helmet and took a painful hit at one point on his head.

When he got to the road, he really opened it up. He'd never gone 100 mph on this motorcycle before. And never on any bike on a dirt road.

The scream of the engine added to the chorus of the Doppler scream.

Turning into the drive, the darkness seemed to gather ahead. It was resisting his headlight as he plummeted ahead. The house was a black silhouette in the gloom. He leaped from the motorcycle, and it dumped into the brambles.

The front doors were open wide in a toothless scream.

"EL!" he called into the black. "EL!"

No reply.

He skidded to a stop in the kitchen.

Empty.

He turned on his phone flashlight and began frantically searching the house.

"EL!"

He ran up the stairs. Shards of mirrored glass covered the entire hall. He crunched through it, calling her name.

He even searched the closed rooms.

Standing in the turret room on the third floor, he

saw outside the flickering glow of a fire.

Then he saw her.

The ice well was burning. It glowed from below like a window into Hell.

El was standing at the edge. She was looking into the pit, backlit by flames from below.

Jake barely touched the stairs as he flew down them. He shot out the door like a bullet from a muzzle.

He followed a single mowed path that went directly to the ice well. A circle of grass was cut all the way around it.

Jake now slowed.

El stood right at the edge. She was hugging herself and looking down into the burning pit.

"El, please step back from the edge," he said as calmly as he could.

She was startled at his voice but took a half step back and turned toward the sound of his words. He had been watching her feet, the edge, and when he looked at her face, it was pale and her eyes so wide he could see the white all around the pale blue.

They stumbled a step toward each other and fell into an embrace on their knees.

At the same time, they both said, "What happened?"

"It doesn't matter. You're OK. That's all that matters," Jake said, holding her so he could see her face.

She replied, "What happened to your face? This entire side is covered in blood." She pushed his hair back.

"I'm fine." Smoke drifted over them with a change in the breeze. It smelled horrible, like burning hair and rotten meat. "You're OK. That's the important part."

"There was a lightning strike. And a crash that shook the house. It was so loud. And it knocked mirrors off the walls. It must have hit this old tree. The huge one with the hollow trunk and it toppled as it burned right into the ice well."

He hugged her then. Closer. And she clung to him. Finally, she buried her face in his neck.

Jake had a rule. Always be the one to stop hugging last.

They stayed like that for one minute, then two. Jake sensed they both needed it for various reasons of their own.

The next wave of horrible smoke drove them to their feet and back up the path Rob had cut. She held his right hand in both of hers, and they moved toward the house.

"Let's have a look at that cut, you idiot," she said.

Jake's motorcycle was on its side, up against the dumpster, the headlight still on. There was a significant gouge in the lawn where its handlebar had dug in.

He felt her reluctantly let go of his hand, and she helped him stand it up. He turned off the key, extinguishing the headlight and plummeting them into darkness.

"I have flashlights and stuff in the carriage house." He lit his phone again and reached for her hand, and she took it instantly, again with both of hers. She clung to his arm as they walked along the house.

"You got here that fast from The Cabin?" El asked.

Jake kept forgetting that she knew where The Cabin was. No one else really did.

"I forgot to put on my helmet." He slid open the carriage house door enough to enter. A dim light shone beyond some of his tall tool chests at the far end.

An emergency flashlight was plugged into an outlet there. It came on when the power was out. Jake handed the phone to El, so he didn't have to release her hand. He grabbed the emergency light and turned it on.

"The cordless phone died when I lost power. The wall phone worked mostly, but I got your voice mail. I think you were probably calling me back."

"I was." They crossed the breezeway to the house. "I got here as fast as I could. I heard the crash. Scared the shit outta me."

"Me, too. I had never heard anything like that thunder followed by horrible slow motion crunching," El said.

"Why was the front door wide open?" he asked as they entered the kitchen.

"I was trying to let light in," El said. "Then I saw the fire. Fire scares me, especially in an old wooden house. Sit. Let me look at that cut."

"There is a box in that cupboard with a lantern, candles, matches, and other stuff in case we ever lost power." He pointed with the flashlight beam.

She grabbed the box. The small battery-operated

lantern was first. Then she started lighting all ten candles. They were the 100-hour kind in tall glass jars.

El left the kitchen to close the front doors. Jake retrieved the first aid kit from under the sink.

He felt something run down his neck. Absently, he wiped at it, and his fingers came away bloody.

Great.

He was sitting again before she was back. She went directly to the sink and grabbed a checkered kitchen towel, and wet half of it.

"Hold the lantern up," El said. "Jesus, Jake. You're a mess. Take this shirt off."

He did and used it as a rag for the initial wipe.

She scrubbed his face and neck and even halfway down his back. She could now feel the scratches on his face. She had to rinse the towel out twice before she was satisfied.

She repositioned his arm and finally opted for the flashlight.

Eventually, she said, "You'll live."

"Thank you, doctor." She stood *very* close. One of her legs was between his knees where he sat. She wore a tight black tank top. Her breasts were just a few inches from his face as she probed his scalp. Jake could smell the lightly scented soap on her skin.

"Don't thank me yet." She was pouring some rubbing alcohol on a thick square of gauze. "The cut is in one of your natural parts on your scalp, about two inches long."

She pressed the gauze down. Jake winced but didn't move. His intake of breath carried her scent. He took another deep breath, closed his eyes, and forgot the sting.

"Scalp cuts bleed a lot. But it's stopped now." She lifted the gauze and looked at the few dots of blood. She replaced it with another thick four-inch square. She took the lantern from his hand and set it on the table. Then she grabbed his hand and pressed it on the gauze.

Her right hand was resting absently on his bare shoulder.

"Now, just keep direct pressure there for two days, and I won't need to shave that spot."

He breathed her in one last time as she stepped back.

He opened his eyes, and she was cleaning up.

"You are really tough on your shirts. Where is the laundry in this house?" She dropped the bloody gauze in the trash can and added the bloody threadbare kitchen towel as well.

"Laundry…" Jake had an obvious realization. "Did I mention you were six weeks early?"

"No laundry?" She struck a pose for effect. "Didn't I see a mudroom back there?"

"Out of order. I thought you liked camping?" Jake said, and it was punctuated by a loud crunching crash. "Don't worry. That tree will continue to collapse in more as it burns."

"I'm not worried," El said as she started closing up the large first aid kit. "This isn't the first time this has been used. And I do love camping. Did love it. I've not gone since I moved to DC."

"We have options regarding the laundry," Jake said. "It was in the basement. But after Lillian… I resealed the foundation walls and perimeter drain piping and poured a concrete floor to stabilize the foundation. Even you might bump your head down there now. Also, the old boiler is gone, and I need to get the new forced air system installed...."

"Jake," she interrupted. "I can wait for the upstairs laundry. The plan said it was right after the hall bath on the schedule. That's fine. I don't mind laundromats for a few weeks. Camping. Bonus is that Ryan would have hated it."

"Ryan?"

"Sorry, did I say that out loud?" El said, closing up the kit. "My dead asshole husband."

"Sorry, I didn't mean to pry," Jake said.

"It's fine. He was a world-class douche-baguette," El said as she took one of the candles from the table and followed its glow into the maid's bedroom.

"I've only ever heard Joyce use that term."

From there, she said, "That's where I heard it. It fits perfectly. Plus, there is one thing I need to tell you. The police are still looking into his death. The car he was driving was registered to me. It was a single-car accident. So they may still want to talk to me."

"Jeeze, I thought my drama with Sam was bad." He laughed. "Did you piss on his grave?"

She came out of the bedroom with one of his clean t-shirts.

"No. But only because I don't like standing in lines."

***

El exited the bedroom with the t-shirt, and Jake

stood bare-chested in the candlelight, his hand on his head. The candlelight called out the muscle tone of his flat stomach and cut abs, his biceps and triceps, and even the veins in his neck and arms. It warmed her below. She had not felt that sensation in a long while.

"Has it been two days yet?" Jake joked.

"Ha!" El snorted. "Put this on. It's your last clean one here, by the way. I'm still holding the MCR t-shirt hostage, though."

Jake took the shirt and looked at the gauze. Just a few dots of red. He stood and slid the shirt carefully over his head.

El wanted to hug him again. Bury her face in his neck and let her senses flood again. She suddenly wanted to cry and choked it down. If he said one more kind thing to her, she was doomed.

Instead, she said, "Options for laundry? I didn't see a laundromat in town."

"The closest laundromat is in Front Royal. You can use mine, though," Jake said, replacing the first aid kit under the sink.

"You have laundry at your cabin?" She opened the fridge and took out two beers, and opened them. She handed Jake one and opened the oven. The smell of pizza filled the room.

"Was this all a clever ploy to get me to have a candle-lit pizza dinner with you?" Jake teased as he flipped open the warm box.

"Need a plate?" she asked, holding up one.

"Only if you do," he said as she put the plates back and brought a roll of paper towels instead.

"Meat lovers is my favorite. Did Alan tell you that?" Jake took a huge bite.

"No. It's my favorite too. That place was packed for a Wednesday." El took her own bite. It was amazing.

"It's a league night. It seems packed, but it's just small." Jake must have been hungry. "Friday's it's fish fry FRY-DAY. That's when it's packed."

"I saw Alex again today. He said to say hi," El added. "I love the small-town feel here. The people are so nice."

"There are two kinds of people that live in Covington. People who have lived here their whole lives, and people who came here and loved it, so they stayed."

"Which are you?"

"I'm a little of both. I grew up here in the county and thought I had escaped when I went to college. Then 9/11 happened, and I joined the army. So many lives changed then. After my dad died, my mom sold the house and moved to Manassas with her sister. That was 2005. I got out a year later and bought the building downtown that has Brian's Books now. I fixed the building up and moved into the apartment upstairs."

"I saw that place today. The building is nice."

"Joyce hired me next to redo her building." Jake sat back with his beer and dabbed his head with the gauze.

"I was in there today too. Great job," El said.

"Next thing I knew, Joyce had helped me get my contractor's license. People kept lining up for restoration work. The only buildings I haven't worked on in town are the bank and the funeral home. I even restored Ed's Texaco. Of course, it's not really a Texaco. He just loves the sign."

"What did you study in college?"

"Architecture," Jake said. "I keep thinking I'll go back, but I've been so busy."

"When did my grandmother hire you?"

"January of 2014. She wanted me to fix up her bathroom. The more I did, the more she wanted. Finally, she traded me the bathroom reno for The Cabin. I had no idea the size of the lot she included," Jake said. "I have worked for her almost exclusively for two and a half years. I miss her. It feels like she'll shuffle in here any minute and nag me to get a haircut."

"I'm glad you were here for her," El said. "I didn't even know she was still alive."

"She knew about my dream of being an architect. She had me draw up what I thought was needed to restore the Rectory. Including a full cost estimate. When I showed up the next day to install her new TV in her bedroom, she had a certified check waiting for the full amount with a full contract that Joyce had written up."

They sat in silence for a minute. The pizza was gone. They both drained their beers. Jake stood first. El followed.

"If the power is still off in the morning, I'll call Virginia Power. I know a guy," Jake said as he moved toward the front door. "You might consider the Hot Pockets for breakfast that are in the freezer. Don't forget Mabel's Mops."

They stopped on the porch. "Mabel's Mop, but don't vacuum yourself," said El.

In a gesture that seemed automatic and completely natural, they reached for each other and hugged in the dark of the porch. She buried her face in his neck again and clung to him.

She wanted it never to end. The pure joy of this feeling. She knew she was safe and wanted in her heart and that he'd hold her as long as she needed.

It stretched on for a minute.

"You OK?" he whispered. He didn't let go.

"No." Despite her best effort, a sob slipped out. She dropped the flashlight and burrowed deeper.

"You should know that was my best flashlight."

Was that a sob or a laugh?

The power came back on just then. As one, they both leaned their heads back and looked at the naked bulb and old fixture hanging by the wires above.

She then looked at his mouth and then his eyes.

El spoke first. "I guess your Hot Pockets are safe."

The moment passed, and Jake stepped back and picked up the flashlight, and with a click, it came back on. He handed it to El and stepped off the porch.

"Set your alarm."

"Already did. On my phone as well." El said. "Coffee will be ready when you get here."

Neither of them felt the eyes on them or the ill intent.

***

El was dreaming of coffee and hugging Jake.

"Wake up, sleepyhead," a voice said, a real voice, the same one from her dreams. "Wakie wakies."

She opened her eyes to a steamy fog and the smell of coffee. Then, as she became awake by stages, she knew she was in her new bed. She was face down, buried in antique quilts.

All was good so far.

Her face was at the edge of the bed. The coffee mug came into focus. She followed it to a hand, a Rolex wristwatch that said 7:49, a muscled arm, and a smiling Jake.

"Not again… Gimme that." She raised up and took the mug as if it was the elixir of life. Then, resting on both elbows, she sipped and sensed more than saw Jake sitting on the edge of the bed. His messy hair obscured his face.

She did have a direct view of her new classic wind-up clock. It was 7:50 am.

"You have ten minutes. You didn't even hear the phone when they called."

"Oh, shit. Sorry." She started struggling to get up. Jake stood and freed her.

"I'll meet them out front." He was laughing and shaking his head.

El sat up cross-legged and gave herself a minute, several sips, a few spine stretches, and neck rolls. Then, finally, she set her mug down in front of the clock and jumped up. She pulled on the jeans she'd worn yesterday, then dug out a clean sports bra and her own t-shirt that said: I LIKE COFFEE AND MAYBE THREE PEOPLE.

Another of Ryan's least favorites.

She heard voices and grabbed some clean white socks. She could not remember where her new Timberline boots were. Not in the kitchen or hall or on the front porch. The double doors were open to the dusty parlor, including the round turret room. It was wrapped in a window seat, covered in a dusty sheet. Felix, the black cat, sat on the window seat, looking out the window at a van and two large box trucks with about a dozen men and women moving around in a kind of choreographed dance unloading equipment.

Looking down, Felix was gone.

Cat prints in the parlor followed bare footprints that wandered the room. And even stood in the corner to the right of the fireplace. She lifted her foot to see, and the print she left was the same. Of course, they were the same, and her feet were filthy. A few blades of grass still clung to them.

The front door opened, and Jake came in with a burly Hispanic man.

"El, come and meet Mabel!" Jake saw her then. "El, this is Andrew Rodriguez. Everyone calls him Mabel." Pointing at her feet, he said, "You gotta wear shoes, and there is glass everywhere."

"I know. I was looking for my boots when...." El looked again at the footprints.

"By the breezeway bench. Passed them when I got here." He turned back to Rodriguez and kept pointing and talking.

The dining room doors were open. She could see footprints in the dust in there too.

She went straight to the breezeway and put on her boots. Once armored, she looked in the library. The floor had no dust in there, and she almost didn't look up. The mirrors were gone. She saw all six empty spaces where they had been. El ran up the stairs. All the doors were open.

Glass covered the hall floor. Jake and Mabel crunched through it.

ALL the mirrors were covered.

She looked in every dusty room

There were footprints, and all the mirrors were covered. Some were missing. Room after room was the same. Sheets taken from furniture and used, sometimes torn in half. Mirrors were gone or covered.

The third floor had no mirrors. No dust and no footprints.

She went down to the main level. She was passing Jake while they were in the master suite. She nearly ran to her bed and tore the quilts and blankets back. The sheet at the foot of the bed was muddy and covered with fresh grass clippings. She threw the quilts back as if to cover a snake. She staggered to the kitchen for more coffee, her mug now lost. Absently she opened the coffee mug cupboard.

It contained a single black ceramic mug.

***

El sat at the kitchen table, drinking coffee from a small mason jar listening to the organized chaos in the house. It was the laughter and even singing that helped clear her head. It was a couple of hours before Jake sought her out. She still had not brushed her hair.

"Hey, I've got to… What's wrong."

"Will you walk me out to the ice well? I want to see something," El asked calmly.

"Sure. I wanted to check on it before I ran to…"

El was trying to figure out what to say and was coming up empty. Then, halfway to the ice well down the newly mowed path, she realized she had taken Jake's hand in hers.

"You OK?" Jake said kindly… again.

"Last night, I… After you left. I…" They reached the ice well. She clung to Jake's arm.

"It's very fortunate the tree toppled directly down there," Jake said. El knew he was being intentionally cheerful. "Lucky, really."

"It didn't rain. Lightening with no rain," El said.

Rob drove down the path with the garden trailer piled high with branches and logs.

Rob stopped on the opposite side and started tossing the logs in. When he was finished, he climbed back on the tractor, and as Rob drove by, he said, "Great idea, Jake." He yelled over the engine noise. "How you got that whole tree in there is beyond me!"

To El Jake said, "I told him what happened. He's been busting my balls all morning."

"I would never have tossed those mirrors in there, though," Rob said, followed by, "Jake, you're late."

"Mirrors?" Jake looked closer. He could see shards now that he looked closer. Straight down by the wall, there was a partially charred frame.

"I did that," El said softly.

"Let's go back to the house and talk."

"You have to do the thing. We'll talk later," she said. "But come back tonight, and I'll make dinner."

"Tell you what. I'll bring dinner. But I won't be back before they are done in time to do the inspection. I am sure it will exceed expectations." They could see a small man was on the roof of the porch, taking off all the shredded screens and tossing them into the dumpster. Another man was washing the windows on the outside while a woman washed them on the inside.

"I'll be back." And he took off at a jog. He said something in Spanish to one of the men, and he piled in the truck and sent gravel flying as he accelerated down the drive.

Eleanore sighed deeply.

As soon as she entered the house, she was taken into the parlor and was amazed by the transformation, and they were not done yet.

One of the women held up a pile of dirty sheets and said, "Keep? Or trash?"

"Basura," El replied, and he gathered them all up and sent them to the dumpster with a smile.

It went on constantly like that for hours. It was a welcome distraction. They would pack the random tchotchkes into heavy-duty moving boxes, leaving choice antiques like the art deco clocks and lamps. El was restoring the rooms to the way she remembered them. They even found a revolver that Jake had mentioned. Like in the movies, it was a loaded stainless steel Smith and Wesson .38 snub nose. The woman set it on the table like she had a hundred little figurines in front of her. A box of bullets followed it. She stashed it all in a drawer in the butler's pantry.

When they were almost finished in the late afternoon, El had just come down from the third floor, where she realized they had washed all the walls and even the ceilings. She had watched all the old mattresses go into the dumpster. She had not seen the queen-size mattresses and box spring come up. Teresa had just finished putting on the new sheets as she smiled a toothy grin through the door.

The hall was scrubbed completely clean. She realized all the light fixtures were clean and new bulbs installed.

As she marveled at the progress, a man in a dark suit slowly came up the stairs. He was revealed a step at a time, and the look on his face was like dark threatening clouds.

She started down the hall to meet him, extending her hand in greeting. When he raised his hand, it held up a gold badge. Perfectly polished.

"Mrs. Eleanore Wright." It was a statement of fact, not a question. "My name is Frank Tate. I am a detective for Fairfax County. I'm looking into your husband's death. I was hoping we could chat for a few minutes."

"I'm sorry, detective Tate, but I am afraid I can't do that. My lawyer has advised me that all inquiries should be directed through her." El was surprised to find the stack of cards still in her pocket. She handed one to the man.

"Those suits in DC making the stink told me you were stupid." He held up the card. "Well done." He put the card in his jacket pocket. "You don't have to answer any of my questions. But I just want to leave something with you. We know you weren't involved even though it was your car. We know you were at home at the time. We know this because we have his phone and know he was watching you on a security camera in your living room as he was getting his… being entertained by the woman he was with. We also have the traffic cam footage of the man on a motorcycle that shot out their tire at 85mph."

He drew a photograph out of his pocket and held it up. It was a photo of Jake holding her on the porch, a silhouette of his motorcycle handlebars by the dumpster.

After half a minute, he put it back in his pocket. He was waiting for her to say something.

"We also know you had nothing to do with Lillian Wright's death," he said casually. "Despite what certain interested parties say."

He turned and started down the stairs. "Please let Ms. Jacobs know I am on my way to see her. Unfortunately, my cell doesn't work out here."

"Detective Tate?"

He paused, and when he looked up at her, El took his photo with her phone camera. "I will call her right away."

Sleep Walking

It's in the house, Jake. And they are outside—the quiet ones. The shoeless one grows stronger.

***

When Jake got to the breezeway door, it was locked. He transferred the bag of Chinese takeout to the other hand and dug out his key ring. The key was easy to find because it was the only skeleton key on his ring. He walked into the kitchen, and it gleamed. He loved the smell of bleach and Windex.

"El!" he called.

He could hear the TV on upstairs. As he moved in that direction, he glanced in the rooms as he went. Polished wood, bright lights, clean windows, tattered screens gone, and the western light streamed in.

The library, the butler's pantry, and the dining room were all buffed. Jake had never really seen the Craftsman-style dining room or parlor. The black iron

137

chandelier had never been lit.

Eleanore must be so happy.

The runner going up the stairs was so clean he paused to take his boots off before going up. He put them next to El's Timberlines beside the front door.

On that level, all the doors were closed. He glanced in a couple before announcing, "It's me. I'm back. I brought dinner!"

The room had never been so clean or decluttered. The bed was beautifully made. The mattress delivery was supposed to have been a surprise. The two overstuffed chairs looked like new. *Wheel of Fortune* was on the TV. El was in the far armchair, wearing comfy-looking dark gray sweat pants and his MCR t-shirt, hugging her knees. Her hair was wet from a shower.

"I figured out how to turn it on." That was all she said, faking a smile. Jake pretended he didn't notice her body language.

"I brought Chinese for dinner." He sat in the other chair and stretched out his legs. "I didn't know what you'd like, so I got a bit of everything." He wiggled his toes in his stocking feet.

"Your socks don't match," El observed in a monotone.

"They're not supposed to. This brand never does. Well, they kinda do, I mean," he replied smoothly.

"Jake, can you do me a big favor?"

"Sure, name it." Jake had never been so sure of anything in his life.

El stood up and came over to his chair, and paused. She curled up in his lap and buried her face in his neck without a word. Then, she gathered up two fists of his shirt and burrowed deeper.

He gently closed his arms around her. And he softly rubbed her back.

"How was your day?" he said in mock comedy.

El told him about the dust's footprints and her dirty feet in the bed. The missing and covered mirrors. Her certainty that she was sleepwalking to the edge of that burning pit, probably several times.

Jake let her talk. He held her. He didn't interrupt.

El told him about the detective.

"They had a photo of us on the porch last night?"

"Out in the dark. Watching."

"About the favor…." she said finally, lifting her head to see his eyes when he answered.

"Will you stay here with me tonight?" Her eyes were pleading.

"Sure. I can stay in the maid's room, and you can…."

"No. I mean in here, with me, to make sure I don't walk again in my sleep."

"OK, but you have to feed me first and let me take a shower."

"What brand are they?"

"What?"

"Your socks."

"Solmates."

There was a long pause before Jake continued.

"El, it will be OK in the end," Jake said as she shifted in preparation to rise.

"How do you know?"

"Because it's either OK, or it's not the end."

El's stomach growled comically loud.

"Food first?" she said and climbed off him sheepishly. But then he saw her stretch and roll her shoulders. "Did you see the results of Mabel's crew? Whatever they get paid, it's worth it."

Jake followed her into the hall and into the next bedroom. The room was bright, and dappled light came in through the leaves. The old curtains and blinds were gone. But it was spotless, and the cleaned lampshades and bulbs were terrific. The walls needed some patching and a new coat of paint, but that was it.

"I saw light bulbs with an inch of dust on top of them," said Jake. "The floors in the hall were washed but not waxed. A coat of wax and these floors don't even need to be refinished."

Back in the hall, Jake pointed to where the four broken mirrors had been. "Plaster repair and paint will be fast. Will you replace the mirrors or do something else? These mirrors that didn't fall will have more repairs if we take them down. Each has four screws holding them on."

The next room was the same. The antique sleigh bed frame was empty. The room was great. It had only one mirror over the dressing table like a normal room. All the lights on, even in the closet, made it cheerful.

"I have never seen all the lights on before. It's a different house," Jake said as he pulled the closet string and the new bulb clicked off. "It'll take an hour just to turn off the lights."

"Can we leave them on, Jake? Please, just tonight."

"Sure, it's your power bill," Jake smiled. "Sunset is in about a half-hour."

Jake followed El down the stairs, and instead of making a U-turn and heading up the hall, she turned right into the dining room.

"I want to eat in here tonight. I love this room." El ran a hand over the long polished mahogany table. It had a medieval vibe—dark wood furniture with black iron accents. It had a colossal sideboard buffet with massive legs and a tall china cabinet. "They even washed all the dishes, Jake."

Jake slid a wine bottle out of that rack in the center of the buffet. "You may want to hold off drinking these."

"They all turned to vinegar?" El said. "I don't really know much about wine. That was Ryan's thing. I just knew the brands I liked. He brought home a chardonnay named Ménage à Trois one night. I suspected he was throwing the idea against the wall to see if it stuck. It turned out to be my favorite wine, despite the name. He hated it because the price was too low, too common."

"These might probably now be vinegar. Let's just say your husband would balk at the price and love them."

"I don't want any wine or beer tonight…." El said. She took two fine china plates from the cabinet and placed them on the table. "Not tonight."

Jake went into the kitchen through the butler's pantry, retrieved the bag, and collected two Diet Cokes from the fridge, which was also super clean inside.

By the time he got back, two full formal place settings had been laid out. Dessert plates and all. Jake insisted she sit at the head of the table. He emptied the bag of its containers and set the empty bag on the floor. He opened all the containers and stabbed chopsticks into several.

He poured Diet Coke into each of their crystal goblets and then placed a plastic-wrapped fortune cookie on each of their dessert plates.

He sat and raised his glass. "What should we toast?"

El retrieved her glass and thought. It wasn't so much a toast. "Thanks, Jake, for putting up with all my bullshit."

"You are terrible at toasts," Jake said. "How about this? To Lillian Wright, the kindest woman I ever met." They both sipped and started filling their plates.

"You're good at that," El said. "You say the right things."

"What?" he smiled. "To be honest, I'm not good at interactions. I hate people."

"No, you don't. Look at this right here. Whatever it is you're doing right now makes me feel better. It gets me out of my own head."

"I spend a lot of time away from people. Hate is probably too strong a word. People… disappoint me, I guess." He silently ate before adding, "Lillian never disappointed me. I wish you had known her."

The house made a creaking groan sound that was loud enough to stop the chopstick full of lo mein on the way to El's mouth.

"Rob and I leveled up the porch. The house has to get used to it."

El swallowed the mouthful before, "Please keep reassuring me. I'm used to traffic sounds 24/7 in DC. I may never get used to foxes screaming like tortured children or the cats howling." Then, she stopped and pointed her chopsticks at Jake and said, "I found Felix in the house today. How many cats are there?"

"I have no idea how many cats are in that feral colony. I never feed them, and the population has been stable for a long while. So I have no idea how they get in the house. But I have not seen a rat or mouse here for years."

"We had to toss all the linens because of old mouse nests. Ruined everything. Table cloths, doilies, kitchen towels, napkins, everything." El got up and opened a drawer in the china cabinet. "I save two of these." They were napkins that were beautifully embroidered with an artful ELW. I know the order is wrong, but I have the same initials. I don't know what Lillian's middle name was."

"It was Eleanore, with three E's beginning-middle-end she'd say," Jake said. "She was so cute. What's your middle name?"

"Lily."

"That's what your grandfather called her."

"I didn't know. My parents never talked about them after we stopped coming to visit."

***

The sunset outside the picture window was nearly cloudless, clean, and significant with the curtains gone. They carried everything to the kitchen. There were a ton of leftovers.

"I'll clean this up. You go take a shower."

Jake grabbed his long-unused gym bag from the truck and headed up to the shower.

The only shampoo in the enormous master shower was Head & Shoulders, and it made Jake smile thinking of the hundred or so products Sam kept in her shower. Jake had a long hot scrub. The huge new hot water heater would never run out. The scratches on his face stung, so he was careful with washing his hair, not wanting to open the cut again. The new exhaust fan kept ahead of most of the steam. Finally, he dried off and put on clean boxers, a Firefly t-shirt that was a size too big, and dark blue sweat pants.

As he brushed his teeth, he realized he was nervous. Nevertheless, he was determined to be a gentleman. He hoped his body didn't embarrass him, especially in the morning.

He turned off the bathroom light and slid open the pocket door when he was done.

"Can you leave that light on? Just close the door," El asked. She was already in bed. It was warm, so the quilts and sheets were turned down.

Jake complied.

"I heard a loud sound. I think that tree collapsed down more," she said, trying to sound brave while in a mostly sitting up fetal position. Only her feet were under the quilt. "Could you check the doors are all locked? The keys are just there. It's the big one. I don't know what the other two are for."

The keys were on the bedside table at the base of the lamp. Jake opened the slim drawer and held up a Samsung remote control. He tossed it to her. "Not many channels. Over the air only."

"That's still a thing?"

He grabbed the keys and went downstairs. Both the front and back doors were unlocked and used the same key. Jake locked and tested them. Taking the key with him ensured she could not wander out even if she got up.

Jake then went into the butler pantry, and the last door in there was not a storage pantry. It was the stairs to the basement. He remembered that the basement access bulkhead had no lock. He made a mental note to get a hasp and padlock.

He opened the door, and the black below looked black as the void because the rest of the house was so bright. He closed the door to the basement and tried the other two keys on a whim, and one of them locked the door.

He went back up and left all the lights on against his nature. When he entered the master bedroom, the side table lights were already off. Just the overhead ceiling fan and the light were on. The volume was all the way down on the TV, and it was on the Home Shopping Network. The 55-inch TV gave off a lot of light.

She was asleep. The remote had slipped from her fingers. He closed the door, and the third key turned in the lock with a loud click. El stirred and rolled over but did not wake.

Jake turned off the overhead light. The six-foot-wide mirror over the headboard was tilted forward a bit, and El was reflected in it as he walked along the foot of the bed. Jake quietly placed the keys in the drawer and turned off the TV. He slid the drawer closed after adding the remote.

Jake slowly lay down and positioned himself, so only the small of their backs touched. Jake relaxed and wondered if he would sleep at all. The bedside table had a digital clock with six-inch tall numbers. He remembered buying it for Lillian so she could see it at night without glasses.

El stirred then. She rotated toward him to spoon him. Her left arm wrapped around his chest, and she burrowed in. She was good at that.

Just their feet were under the turned-down quilts. It was August in Virginia, and he was wearing sweatpants and a t-shirt. He wondered if he would be too warm when she started to snore lightly.

Yep. No sleep for me.

He stared at the light coming under the door from the bathroom. Then, finally, a great crunching sound of the tree settling in the ice well lulled Jake to sleep.

His dreams started with giant fire pits while camping. El in The Cabin and autumn leaves falling. Movement woke him, and he found himself spooning El. She held his right hand where it rested on her hip. He adjusted slightly to make sure nocturnal erections would not embarrass him.

Jake's left arm was under his pillow, and the old school glow-in-the-dark Timex told him it was 1:45 am. The wind in the trees and El's breathing lulled him back to sleep.

Jake's dreams were immediate.

Eleanore straddled him as he lay on his back. His palms were caressing the tops of her bare thighs as she rocked back and forth. She was sliding her sex back and forth on his hard cock. Her eyes were closed as she drew the MCR shirt over her head. She tossed the shirt on the floor as her rocking quickened.

She found his hands and directed them up to her amazing breasts. Her fingers guided his to squeeze her nipples.

She leaned forward to press harder on him.

This is too real to be a dream.

When her climax began, she opened her eyes and her mouth. Her eyes glowed like there was a fire inside her. She arched her back, sitting upright, facing the ceiling, and gasped and shuddered.

This is too real to be a dream.

Jake pulled his hands away. "Eleanore, wake up." He started to buck her off when he saw her see herself in the mirror. The light faded from her eyes. Her eyelids fluttered like they always did when she was waking. Jake could still feel her trembling from the orgasm. "Wake up, El."

"Jake?" she looked down at him. He was in shadow, and El could not see his face. She looked up and saw herself in the mirror. The bathroom light backlighting her was enough. Her head snapped down to see she was astride Jake. His arms were wide, palms up.

"El, please wake up."

She realized her breasts were bare. She covered up and collapsed next to Jake with her back to him. "Oh. My. God." Mortification dripped from those three words. She was still trembling.

"At least you weren't sleepwalking," he said casually.

It earned him an elbow in the ribs, hard.

"Jake. You couldn't wake me sooner?" she said. "Oh. My. God."

"I tried." He said, turning to face her. He could feel her heart pounding in her chest. "Weird thing is, I think the mirror woke you."

He rubbed her shoulder as she caught her breath. "It's OK, and you're OK."

"I'm so sorry. I'm so embarrassed."

"Don't be." Jake drew the sheet up over her and then bounced out of bed. "FINALLY! A chance to get my shirt back!" He scooped it up off the floor.

El watched him over her shoulder as he held it out to her. She took it, and Jake turned his back to her.

He realized too late another mirror framed her perfectly. Light from under the door lit her beautiful shape as she turned the shirt right side out and front. After she pulled it on, she held her arms out to him.

"Come here. Please."

Without turning, he sat and then lay down on his side. She was there in a few seconds, her arm wrapped around him.

"What's happening to me?" Her voice trembled this time.

Jake took a chance and turned onto his back and raised his left arm so she could rest her head on his chest.

They were both asleep in only a minute.

Black SUVs

I like this one. He never sees me.

***

El woke with a start at the sound of the phone ringing. She didn't want to wake. She was warm and comfy. There was that smell she loved. She felt him move and stretch to reach the phone.

Her back was to him. Her head pillowed on his shoulder. She hugged his arm like a drowning woman.

"Hello," he said sleepily.

El could hear the caller clear enough. She recognized Rob's voice, "Dude, where the hell are you? The house is locked, and I've been pounding on all the doors for like fifteen minutes. What the fuck are you doing?"

"Just start the mowing like we planned. I'll be out in a bit."

Oh my god. Can I do anything else to embarrass myself?

El realized she had been drooling on his shirt sleeve. It was as soaked as her panties.

Oh. My. God.

"Dude, driving up, I rousted a guy in a black SUV parked at one of the lower cemetery gates. Fucking sketchy. I took a pic of his plate. He's gone now."

"I'll be down in a minute. Meet you in the carriage house." The phone beeped as he hung up. El released his arm, and he sat up.

"I heard. Law firm asswipes, I bet," she said, sitting up cross-legged.

Jake was not self-conscious as he spoke while pulling on yesterday's jeans and socks. "I'll go out and get Rob started. Are you OK? Weird night."

"You gotta stop asking me that."

"I will stop asking that if you stop apologizing for everything. Deal?" And Jake held up a fist for her to bump.

Ryan hated fist bumps.

"Deal." She bumped it a bit too hard. His hand was like a rock. Jake grabbed the keys and headed out quickly through the unlocked door. "I'll make coffee!" she called after him wondering if she should mention the unlocked door.

El collected clothes from the dresser and went into the bathroom to pee and wash up. Her hair was wild. It always was as if she went to bed with wet hair.

Oh. My. God. I am sore, she realized.

She had not had the feeling of being sore after a good night of sex for years. Thanks to Ryan. She tossed the black lace panties into the hamper, reminding herself to ask Jake about laundry.

What was happening with Jake? What are you doing?

It was cargo shorts and a white tank top today. She put on white socks and tried to remember where she put her Timberlines.

She sped down the stairs. She tested the floor polish by sliding to stop just past the coffee maker.

Why do I always feel so rested here?

Coffee was ready when Jake came back in.

"Breakfast is almost ready."

"Oh?" was followed by a ding of the microwave. Jake poured coffee as she set down a plate with four Hot Pockets on it. He set a big colorful mug down in front of El and returned for his.

"I've never actually had a Hot Pocket before," Jake said.

"I lived on these in high school." She began and stopped when she saw Jake sip from a black ceramic mug.

El stood, took it from him, dumped the coffee into the sink like it had been poisoned, and smashed the mug in the sink. Without a word, she got a colorful mug from the cupboard. She refilled it and set it in front of Jake as he stared at her.

"Don't say it," she said.

"Great coffee, definitely better."

"Look, I'm not crazy. But I hate those mugs." She picked up a Hot Pocket and broke it in two. Super steam. Still too hot to eat. She set it back down. "See this scar?"

"I do now," Jake said, breaking another in half.

"Let's just say it was made by a mug just like that."
She pointed with a thumb over her shoulder. "If you
see any more of those mugs, trash them." Then, too
late, she added, "Please."

"Can do."

In an obvious ploy to change the subject, El asked,
"What is Rob doing today?"

"Mowing, trimming branches, cleanup in general.
He's going to come in later and help me with some
plumbing. If you talk to him, I'll bet you $5 he says the
words 'Wife Beater' within five minutes."

"Why would he do that?"

Jake just pointed at her tank top.

"Is this plumbing laundry related?" She thought of
her soaked panties in the hamper.

"Yes, it is." Jake was going to continue, but El cut
him off.

"Jake, about last night…."

"This sounds a lot like an apology starting." He
blew on the hot pocket and dramatically popped the
whole piece in his mouth. It was too soon. The hot
coffee didn't help.

"You obviously never had a hot pocket before."

"El, whatever is happening here, this thing," he
gestured back and forth between them, "whatever it is,
I kinda like it, weirdness and all. Because I genuinely
like you. Like who you are."

"The thing," she did the same gesture, "is even
weirder for me. But I'll admit, I kind of like it too. But
mostly, only because you are cool about it." El picked
up a piece of Hot Pocket and blew on it.

"To save an awkward discussion later, I'll stop at home today and get something better to sleep in. I was kinda warm last night."

I was super hot last night.

"We'll have Chinese again. That OK?" she asked.

"Suspiciously close to an apology." Jake smiled into the mug. "I'm going into town to get plumbing stuff and stop at the apartment. Need anything?" He stood.

"Besides lawyers, guns, and money. No," she joked.

"Well, you're in luck. Lillian had all those things." Jake emptied his mug and rinsed it out. "That reminds me. Besides the shotgun over the mantle in the library, Lillian had a revolver around here somewhere. Keep an eye out for it."

"We already found it," El mentioned casually.

***

El cleaned up the dishes from last night and today, then went back upstairs.

The screens were intact in the master bedroom windows on both sides of the dresser. The window opened smoothly. These screens were not new but newer than most of the ones in the house.

She went about making the bed. The four-poster bed was fresh and polished like the rest of the house now, with the added bonus of high thread count sheets and the smell of Jake.

She held a hand full of sheets up to her face and smelled sex.

That was some dream…

The bed was made in short order, and she wondered if she could air out the house a bit more. She stuffed the house keys in her pocket and went into the hall. She saw the transoms were open above all the doors already. Directly across the hall was her old room. The one she always stayed in as a kid.

She turned the knob and almost fell into the room, stopping short. She almost stepped into the thick layer of dust in her white socks. The room had not been cleaned or otherwise touched. It was the smallest bedroom on this level. It was the nursery at one time, directly across the hall from the master bedroom. It had a single-size canopy bed with curtains. They were closed. The ruffles were thick with cobwebs. A small dressing table with a stool had ruffles and was in the same condition. The round mirror she remembered was gone.

There were footprints.

Why didn't they clean it?

El slipped off her socks and looked at the bottom of her feet. They were dirty but not muddy.

She entered the room and tried the light switch. Nothing.

With a cloud of dust, she opened the drapes. The view looked to where Rob was zealously working while he wore headphones.

The cloud of dust she created, while dramatic, was overcome by the extra light. She decided not to open the windows because a breeze would send all this dust back into the clean house.

The prints went directly to the wall across the room

but not back with the new light she found. A strange arc was also there, drawn in the dust. She looked closely at the disturbed cobwebs and the white paint on the tall wainscoting. As if by muscle memory, she reached up and found the latch. The panel swung open.

She pulled out her phone and turned on the flashlight. There was a passage about thirty inches wide. It was the backs of the plaster and lath walls. Directly across from where she stood was another door. A pully and a weight were attached to keep it closed. She pulled the handle. A turnbuckle held it secure. She turned it and pulled. This secret door led into the back of the closet in the next bedroom.

My new house has secret passages. How cool is that!

She closed it but didn't lock the turnbuckle.

She moved farther in, and a similar weight drew that door closed.

She followed the passage and paced off how far to the wall. There was a ladder there. A dusty black velvet cloth was draped neatly over a rung.

Not draped, sewn there like a curtain.

She lifted it and gasped.

There was a hole about a foot square in the plaster and lath. It was a window that looked directly into the hall. It was a two-way mirror. Or was it one way?

She let the drape fall and shined the light back.

There were other six-inch squares of the same material tacked to the wall.

It looked into the next bedroom.

"Scooby-Doo, where the hell are you?" she said out

loud. Then she noticed there were no cobwebs in there. The only dust on the floor was at the edges.

After carefully testing the rungs, she decided to explore down first.

The next black curtain she found was through the mirror with a view across the main floor hall into the kitchen.

El had to stand on a shelf provided to see into the library. Through bricks that had been removed over the fireplace, the same was true over the mantle into the parlor.

Spy holes and one-way mirrors?

The doors were easy to find now that she knew what to look for inside.

The ladder to the basement level terminated in a claustrophobic space smaller than a phone booth. A box and empty mason jars provided some resistance to exiting. She had not been in the basement yet, but by her phone light, it looked like a root cellar. The walls were lined with shelves filled with empty canning jars and equipment.

She brushed off her clothes and then opened the door out of the root cellar. The lights were all on in the basement. It smelled of new concrete from the floor. She could walk without bashing her head, but it would hit any of the six light bulbs.

She saw the stairs that went up. A new light switch was there. At the far end were the unmistakable legs and jeans of Jake.

El heard a cordless drill as she approached.

"Whatcha doin?" she said in a sing-song voice.

Jake startled and bashed his head.

"Sorry," El said before she could stop herself.

"Dammit." Jake sounded angry. "Here, add this to your keyring." He tossed her a brass key that said, MASTER. "Dammit."

"I know, I know we had a deal." She almost said sorry again.

Jake slid down the concrete steps and sat up. "It's not that. I fucking bashed my head again. Pardon my language."

"I don't give a fuck." She smiled. "About the language, not your head. I usually save my fucks for when I bash my own head. So what are you doing?"

"I picked up a hasp and padlock this morning along with the plumbing fixtures." He touched his fingers to his scalp. They had a little blood on them. "This is now locked from the inside."

"Let's clean your scalp up, or you'll get it infected," she said. "Dumb ass."

Jake stood up but had to stoop over. He was so tall. "I see you're feeling better. How the hell did you get so dirty?"

"Mabel's Mops missed a room," she said as Jake reached the stairwell. And went upright. "Dust, windows, everything." She showed Jake the bottom of her feet.

"Show me." They climbed the stairs into the butler's pantry. At the top of the steps, brooms and mops hung on the walls. El grabbed a broom.

El led the way directly to the door. It swung inward, and she walked to the other side and began sweeping the dust up into a pile.

Starting with the dust that gave away the secret door.

Why are you not telling him?

"I could swear I checked every room. Showed him every room," Jake said. "I have never seen this room before."

"Did I mention earlier this is the room I stayed in as a kid?"

"Don't bother sweeping. Mabel's crew will come back." Jake took out his phone. "Smile." She did, and he snapped it. It was so dim his flash went off. "I'll send this to Mabel. He will come right back and clean it, but he will also owe me a favor."

She handed him the broom. "I'm going to wash my feet. That's what started this." She pulled out her still clean white socks.

She still didn't know why she didn't tell him.

***

El gave her feet a good scrub.

Now that they were scrubbed and dried, she put on her socks and boots. When she entered the kitchen, Jake was on the phone with Andrew at Mabel's. He was sure that he had not missed anything.

Jake said he had a photo but no Internet.

Finally, an agreement was met, and a smaller crew would be over right after lunch.

"Now sit down and let's have a look at your head," El said.

"That's what she said," Jake deadpanned.

"Oh boy." El slow blinked.

"That's what she said… next," Jake laughed.

"Don't start a war you can't win." And she pressed the alcohol-soaked pad on his head wound and held it there.

They heard the front door open, and Rob announced himself. "Is it OK if I leave my boots on?"

"That's what he said," El said beside Jake's ear. "It's fine if they're not tracking in mud."

Rob walked in a few seconds later in his socks. In time to see the blood-speckled gauze come off.

"So she had to tell you twice, eh?" His own joke highly amused Rob.

Rob walked to the fridge and helped himself to a Diet Coke.

"What she had to tell me twice, Rob, was that this is her fridge now. We will keep our lunches in the carriage house fridge."

Rob froze. Mid drink. El and Jake both tried to keep a straight face. And failed.

"Caught a branch on my bike last night riding down the mountain," Jake said.

"I'm putting some Neosporin on this. Stop touching it," El said.

"That's what she said." It was Rob's turn.

El and Jake groaned in unison.

"Hey, that was a good one," Rob protested. He chugged the rest and belched. "I need your help out by the hole. Rub a little dirt on it. Meet me out by the ice well."

The door shut behind Rob as he started singing "Sweet Home Alabama."

"So that you know, it's a law of nature that Rob will

take a run at you. He won't cross the line, but he likes to dance on it."

"You should see the lawyer scene in DC as a paralegal. They all made a run at me and danced right over that line like it was a cliff, and Ryan always gave a hand back up to those shit-stains." She started packing the first aid kit up again. "I swear I got my ass touched almost daily in that office. I had blinders on."

"I can't do big cities anymore. I can't understand why people live like that," Jake said.

El had been examining Jake's scalp before she let him up. She found another, even longer scar hidden in his hairline. "I take it that was not your first encounter with that tree?" She traced her finger along the scar. "The tree told you twice!" she laughed until she noticed Jake was not joining her. He stilled. She laid her hand on his shoulder in a silent apology she had promised to stop saying out loud.

"Iraq," was all he said.

"You OK?" El asked. How could she not?

"Hey, that's my line!" Jake came back, and the stillness evaporated. His chin ever so slightly turned toward her hand. Then, in a mirror, she saw him close his eyes for a moment.

"Not anymore, it isn't," she said.

Jake gathered himself and rose. "Will you be here when Mabel's crew returns? It's not required. I'll be here but working with the new laundry."

"I really need to take my laptop and find somewhere I can catch up on bills and stuff that I have been avoiding."

"You have several options there. Brian's Books has the fastest Internet if I must say so myself. The Bakery cafe has Brian beat, though, with coffee, pastries, and comfy chairs. Alan's Alley and pool hall also have it. The diner tried it. It didn't work out there. Peggy and Mike Brewer own the Bakery and Diner. It's why the diner has such great pie and bread."

"Stop talking about food!" she said. Jake started toward the hall.

"Speaking of food, I will show you where you can do laundry after dinner tonight." And he was gone.

Why didn't I tell him about the secret passages? Does he already know?

LAUNDRY

Felix sat at the top of the ruined bell tower. He had never smelled human up here before now. And it wasn't his humans…

***

Jake walked toward the sounds of the Bush Hog, the big mower. He really should have sharpened the blades on that thing.

The path to the ice well was now the width of a single-lane road. He walked the hundred yards and looked down into it. The tree had collapsed in farther as it burned. Fire was now climbing it, but the trunk was so thick it would still be days before it was gone.

Jake could see that tons of brush and branches had gone in as well. Six large logs were on the far side. Another path had been bush-hogged towards the ruins of the church foundation. The cemetery gates were also open, and a mowed path followed the old road down the center of the cemetery.

Rob dumped a load of branches into the well from the forks on the front of the old tractor. Then turned off the tractor and jumped down.

"I think she likes you," Rob said straight away. "Eleanore, I mean."

"Dude, we are not in high school," Jake replied.

"Someone needs to tell Sam that. She was very disappointed you didn't show up last night." Rob had a shit-eating grin. "We spent the night in your place. She wants to meet there again tonight. Is that cool? Please. Dude. Bro?"

"Rob, you are almost thirty years older than her." Jake smiled. "She'll wear you down like an old pencil."

"I'm willing to risk it. Can I just say she has the best tits I have ever seen? And she has access to drugs!" Rob said.

"Tell her that. She loves hearing stuff like that," Jake said. "But I am changing the locks tomorrow and washing the sheets. And by the way, she's an excellent pharmacist. Honest AND smart. The town is lucky to have her here."

"I'm outta here early today to go clean my house. And maybe take a nap. Just in case." Rob said.

"Dude, just don't be an asshole. Sam is a real person. Do not take advantage."

"I am allowing her to take advantage of me. I'm even going to the barber to humanize a bit. Don't fall over."

"OK, man. Why am I out here? I have plumbing to destroy inside."

"Were you saving these logs for your portable

sawmill?"

"I was, but getting them to The Cabin is a nonstarter. Besides, I already made the rafters. Don't need them," Jake said. "Then I was going to cut and split them for Lillian… I took my log splitter up there as well."

"I need to see this place when it's done," Rob said. "I'll bring beer."

"I think we can just roll these in the hole," Jake said. "But just small stuff after this. I want to keep it going until the tree is burned to ash. Plan to trim down the stump too?"

"Sure thing." The first log toppled with a crash, landing in the middle, end first. The others followed and landed in the same way, like battering rams compressing the decades of carcasses into the ash and ambers.

The final log was the biggest, and when it hit, the floor of the ice pit looked like it caved in ten feet with a shower of sparks.

"Yeah, only small stuff after that," Jake said, looking into the renewed inferno.

"Eleanore wants some paths cut. I will bush hog the old cemetery roads first, then go over it with the John Deer. Then I will focus on the area directly around the house. How far out do you want finish mowed?" said Rob.

"On this side to that hedge with the gate, and the other side to the line of boulders. Plus, the roadsides as far as the cemetery goes."

"You still taking weekends off to work on The

Cabin?" Rob asked as he climbed back up on the tractor.

"Don't know. Playing it by ear this week."

"Later, Dude." He started the tractor.

***

Andrew Rodriguez himself showed up and could not figure out how they had missed the room. The six cleaners had the room cleared in record time. Jake worked on the plumbing tie-in for hot and cold water first.

Mabel only interrupted him once, only 15 minutes after they started. Rosita wanted to wash and dry the curtains, bed ruffle, canopy, and stool cover because they were in good condition and would be difficult to replace. She left the site with the linens while the others continued working. Jake watched the old mattress get walked down the hall and to the dumpster.

Around 4 pm, Mabel came to get him with a question.

They were bringing the freshly cleaned and polished furniture back into the room. It was brighter now. Two new overhead bulbs made all the difference. The vanity dressing table and stool were placed, but there was no mirror—the wall where it should have been had a big conspicuous drywall patch he had not seen before.

"Do you have this mirror? So many mirrors in this house. Maybe one that would work. We could move in here."

Jake immediately thought of the oval mirror in his truck. "I'll take care of that. Thanks, man. Great job."

Rosita arrived just then. Not only did she have the freshly laundered linens, but two of the crew also carried in a new mattress. They quickly stripped off the plastic and placed it on the clean bedframe. But unfortunately, Rosita spoke in Spanish too fast for Jake to understand.

"She wants to know if she can make the bed. She cleaned the linen closet yesterday and knows the perfect sheets and quilt."

"Sure. Si, Si," he said to Rosita. Her smile was infectious.

"Pretty," she said in English as she adjusted the sunflower yellow bed ruffle and curtains.

Jake got out of their way. And went back to work.

Brian's Books

Felix finished eating the mouse and was grooming himself. He sat on the neck stump of his favorite statue. It faced the sun, and the white marble wings reflected the heat even more. He paused his cleaning to watch the black motorcycle go quietly by…

***

El pulled into a parking space downtown on Main Street under the shade of a giant oak tree that was disrupting the sidewalk in front of Brian's Books.

She was dreading the flood of emails she would get. With a sigh, she took her courier bag with her laptop and headed in.

All the shops in town had the same bell over the door. This building had deep bay windows on each side of the front door. Each side had displays of various used books that looked new. It was bigger than she first thought from the outside. Directly to her left were two leather wing-back chairs and a corner table between them with a lovely tulip-shaped reading lamp. There were also two small cafe tables with artfully mismatched wooden chairs. The walls in this small space were covered with framed old maps, newspaper front pages, and photographs. As she took out her laptop on one of the cafe tables, she noticed all were about Covington. It was a lovely setting.

The checkout desk was old oak and had a cash register that looked like it had been there for a hundred years.

The desk was vacant.

A hall made by the stacks to either side ran straight down the center of the store. Subtle lights illuminated a classic pointing finger sign that announced the contents of each alcove. SciFi and Fantasy held pride of place in the first two alcoves, left and right.

The wifi name she selected was BBooks. No password was required. Opening her email, it began downloading 611 emails.

"Oh, hello. I was out back. I didn't hear you come in." He had a tall armful of hardcover books he managed to set on the counter without incident. "I'm Brian. Can I help you find something?"

Brian had a mop of curly blond hair and round tortoiseshell glasses. He wore a black t-shirt that had a quote in a type-writer font. "It isn't hoarding if it's books!" He wore skinny jeans and penny loafers with actual pennies in them.

"I'm Eleanore," she said. "And I am here to steal your Internet."

"You must be Eleanore Wright. You must know

Jake."

"I do know Jake. He is the first person I met when I got here."

"I was just going to the Bakery to get a coffee. Can I bring you one?" Brian paused at the door.

El would normally decline the offer from a man she had just met, but Brian was ten years younger than her and gave off a strong gay vibe. "That would be nice. I can go for you if you need to watch the shop."

He waved her off with a gesture. "How do you like your coffee?"

"Black. Please. Thanks," she said.

"Jake will really like you," Brian said. "Watch the store, El." He said as if they had been lifelong friends.

27 of 611 emails so far. This is the fastest Internet?

El stood and wandered around the front of the store, gravitating to the wall of framed Covington memorabilia. A Covington's street photo was labeled '1933, CCC Crew plants trees'. The oaks were saplings, and the crowd of men stood in the street with their shovels and smiles.

There was a Front Royal paper, The Royal Examiner, with the headline "Covington Honors their sons lost in WWII with a new memorial." There were similar headlines about floods in the Seven Bends. The impact of I-81 bypassing the town. Photos of firefighters and Boy Scouts and blue ribbons at the county fair. Brian's first dollar was framed there, dated in 2014.

Then she saw a photo of Jake in front of the bookstore with his left arm around Brian's shoulder, shaking his hand with his right. Scaffolding covered the front of the building. The sign that said Brian's Books was being held by Brian. His smile beamed. Even though the photo was dated 2014, it was beautifully printed and framed 8x10 in black and white.

High up, she could see the faded newspaper headline, "East End Church Fire Kills 18. Arson suspected." There was no photo, and it was too high up to read. She was looking at a blank space and a single nail when the bell on the door rang behind her.

Brian handed her the coffee. "Peggy says you must go see her. She said you solved the math thing at Mike's Diner. Peggy is a dear. She's married to Mike. Her croissants are to die for."

"Thank you for the coffee." She sat at the table as Brian went to the counter and scanned the bar code on each book, and then looked at a laptop screen.

59 of 611. Does every email have a huge attachment?

She took her coffee and began to wander the stacks.

A radio back there was playing Frank Sinatra.

El found a book titled Birds of the Seven Bends, and a copy of the same cookbook her mom had when she was a kid. Then, closer to the front, she picked a SciFi novel by an author she loved, Harry Harrison.

By the time she got back to the counter, all the books Brian had picked out were in padded envelopes and packed for shipping. He began filling a post office bin on the floor behind the counter when he saw her. Then, without prompting, he said, "I don't know how any used bookstores existed without the web and a post office close by. For every book I sell in the store, I sell like 200 on the web. I love technology."

He rang up her purchases.

"Need a bag? Don't worry. They're recycled paper."

"No need," El said. "I have my satchel."

"So, is the rectory really haunted?" Brian asked with no shame.

An image of herself, naked in a mirror with glowing eyes, flashed into her mind for just an instant.

"Definitely," El said in a conspiratorial tone. "Ghosts, black cats, creepy cemetery and everything."

"Ace Alex said you started the midnight runs." Brian's eye flicked to the blank space on the wall for an instant.

"Brian, I need a spy in town. I think it's going to be you. What do you say?"

"You mean like a gossip spy? I'd love that."

"So, what have you got?"

"You mean besides the whole witch thing? You used witchcraft to murder your husband, your grandmother, and now bewitched Jake, made him ditch Sam to do your bidding stuff."

"Oh, Jeeze, really?" El rolled her eyes.

"Well, Sam is scorching hot. Even in a lab coat behind the pharmacy counter at the drug store. I don't go for women, but even I want to bury my face in between those beautiful boobies." Brian leaned across the counter. "No one could figure out what she saw in Jake. Or even why she stayed in this small town. Then

Lily died, and Jake was so upset, and Sam was out."

"Should I talk to her?"

"Don't do that. That bitch be crazy, and besides, you never mess with an alchemist," Brian said. "Plus, the diner math thing. More proof you're a witch."

"Oh boy."

Then Brian spoke with no affectation, "It's just in fun."

Her laptop beeped.

***

All 611 emails had finally been downloaded. Her filters still did a good job sorting them. Most she could ignore.

The correspondence from the Firm was most of it. Back and forth with requests to sign documents. Joyce replied with a polite, professional manner that must have driven the asswipes at the firm mad.

None of her replies said NO outright. But she teased around it and, at the same time, was making arrangements and laying the groundwork to sell the brownstone, the firm's building, plus two other properties El did not know existed. A condo in Crystal City and an empty warehouse in Arlington were recently purchased as an investment.

Joyce sent her two priority emails. The first had the subject in all caps, SIGN NOTHING REPLY TO NOTHING. The body just read, "See subject line."

The other email was a bit disturbing.

Subject: DO THIS ASAP

The sent time was 11 minutes ago.

The email had only an in-line image of a page from Ryan's will. Highlighted, the sub-paragraph read:

In the event that the recipient predeceases the appointment of an heir, all shares and assets in this codicil revert to equitable distribution among the partners of the firm founded by…

El's phone rang.

It was Joyce.

"Where are you?" Joyce demanded.

"Brian's Books," El said. "I just read your email."

"I tried the house before here. Can you come right to my office? It's important," Joyce said, calming a bit.

"You think I can finish my coffee before an assassin's bullet finds me?" El joked.

"Laugh now. Get your ass to my office after that coffee," Joyce said. "Say hi to Brian for me."

"Will do." El hung up. "Joyce says hi, Brian," El said.

"Joyce is my second biggest customer. She collects antique criminal law books. Only crime law. I hunt for them now. Super fun hobby, seeing she never does criminal law, except your occasional DWI."

"Who is your biggest customer?" she asked as she opened an email with the Subject: Invoice.

It was only an in-line image. A photo that she would have considered artfully done. It was a profiled silhouette of a woman arching her back in obvious release. Just the arms of the man below her showed—

her hands on his as they cupped her breasts.

She slammed her laptop closed.

The photo was her. She recognized Jake's wristwatch.

***

She was quickly packed and out the door with a wave to Brian, who was now on the phone.

El rolled her neck as she walked down the shaded street one block to Joyce's office. "Come on back," Joyce called out.

Not trusting herself to speak, she opened her bag, grabbed her laptop, and let the satchel drop to the floor. El placed the computer on Joyce's desk, and when the image was back, she spun it to Joyce.

Joyce was wearing glasses today. El had never seen her with glasses on before. "Is that Jake?"

"Well, yes. But nothing happened. I was dreaming," El stammered.

"Doesn't look like nothing," Joyce said. "They are just trying to rattle you."

"Well, it's fucking working."

"That's nothing. You're a grownup. You can do what you want. With the lights on, even. Forget that for now. You need to pick an heir before you leave this office. Pick a cousin, a friend, but now. We can always change it later after all the dust settles."

"Anyone?"

"I just need their name and address. Phone number if you have it."

El started looking through her phone contacts.

Joyce plopped a pad and pen on the desk in front of El.

El wrote a name, address, and phone number on the pad and, as an afterthought, added another name.

"This is the adopted daughter of a good friend I went to college with. That second name is her sister. She isn't old enough to have a phone yet."

Joyce was already typing fast. Two pages streamed out of the printer on the credenza behind her a minute later. Joyce pressed an intercom. "Amy, can you come in here, please." She was there instantly. "Sign here and then initial both pages at the bottom." Joyce also signed it.

Amy Bryant signed and dated it, adding her initials to each page, then pressed her notary seal on the papers.

"Thank you, Amy." Both pages were scanned then.

Joyce already had an email drafted and waiting for the attachments. It went to the lawyer that authored the will, a local judge, the county clerk, and El.

In a separate email, she sent a copy to Detective Tate.

"Now sign this." Next, Joyce slid over a standard DMV application for a driver's license.

"OK, but what's the rush here?" El said.

"It makes it easier to buy a gun in Virginia." She spun the laptop back to El. "What the fuck is this?"

Joyce pointed to the other window in the frame. The one without having dream sex on Jake.

There was a faint shadow shape of a man standing

in the corner in the other window as if he had been hiding behind the door. His eyes glowed like he was staring directly at the photographer.

"These are the biggest asswipes I have ever seen." Joyce had veins bulging in her neck and a V of them on her forehead. "To Photoshop shit like that just to scare the fuck out of a woman."

El looked up at Joyce. "Just make sure Ed never sees this."

***

El went to the Bakery for lunch and met Peggy Brewer. She was in her mid-fifties and probably just over six feet tall. She had short blond hair, cut in a stylish short cut that was both attractive and practical for a baker.

The shop smelled amazing and was another interior that was much bigger than first glance allowed. There were four bistro tables with umbrellas outside and about ten tables inside.

"I've heard a lot about you. Mike's trying to develop a better math problem for the diner. He was sure that one would last forever." They were chatting at the checkout when Peggy's teenage employee pulled a dozen of the legendary croissants and a baguette warm from the oven.

"I took a lot of math in college—a lot of math. I was good at it but didn't love it," El said. "I like your shop." It looked like most of the fixtures were original glass cases. The tin ceiling was perfectly restored and painted mint green.

"Jake Harris did all the work. I hear he's restoring the Wright House. How's it coming along?"

"Great, a few more weeks." Customers were lining up at the counter. "I won't keep you. Nice meeting you!"

***

Jake had not been to his apartment above the bookstore in over a week. It was mainly to avoid Sam. Avoid everyone if the truth be told. He parked his truck right in front of the door. He never scored that spot.

The door up to his apartment was between Brian's Books and the Pet Shop. There was a small alcove at the bottom of the stairs where four polished brass mailboxes were embedded in the wall. He grabbed his mail, looked it over as he walked up the long flight, and opened the door.

It wasn't locked.

"Hello, Jake." Sam was sitting on the foot of his bed. Her face made it was apparent she had been crying.

"Hello, Sam." He dropped his gym bag on a mid-century modern chair. It had new locksets in it.

She held out a key. More tears fell when Jake gently took it.

"Why were you so nice to me?"

"Why would I not be nice?" Jake slid an ottoman over and sat, so he wasn't towering over her.

"I realized a long time ago that you were nice to

everyone," she sobbed. "I saw you when you were with Joyce for a while. You guys were friends, too. More. Still friends. She still loves you. Even though…"

"What's this about, Sam?"

"When you were with me, you were kind, attentive, considerate, but you would have treated any woman like that. I'm not an idiot. I now realize I wasn't special to you in any way."

Jake said nothing because he knew she was right.

"I knew I was never smart enough for you." She held her hand up. "No. Let me finish."

Jake let her continue with what she had to say.

"I thought it was because I don't like to read the same books you do. I haven't read any fiction since high school, or I didn't like camping or hiking. It wasn't until I… I realized. I'm not a good person. I…"

Jake knew she needed to talk it out. He handed her a hanky and let her talk.

"I did a horrible thing to hurt you. To hurt myself. But something happened."

Jake wanted to hold her and comfort her, but he couldn't let himself.

"I slept with Rob. He told me last night that he had already told you. I realized then that Rob told me that because he was like you. So kind that he… The thing is. He looks at me like I always wished you would."

"Did you know he took the afternoon off to go to the barber and clean his house?"

"Really?" She looked up at him. "No."

"I'm always afraid, Jake. I think you know that. Better than anyone. Now I'm afraid Rob won't love me because I'm too young." Sam started sobbing again. "I fear what his kids will think."

At that Jake risked it. He sat next to her and pulled her into his embrace. "Can you keep a secret? Swear on a stack of mother's graves never to tell a soul?"

She looked up and nodded.

"Rob does not care what anyone thinks… Except you." Jake paused. "He's worried you will think he is too old. He's worried he'll fall deeply in love and get crushed horribly. But he is willing to risk it. Because it's you."

She began to cry even harder then. "Will you still be our friend?"

"I love you, Sam. I love Rob. How could I not?"

She cried as he held her for a while.

"I have to go, Jake. I have to find Rob."

"I'll walk you down."

Sam was completely changed. A weight was lifted. She was free. She held his hand as they descended the stairs. Out on the sidewalk, she threw her arms around his neck and kissed him on the mouth. Skipping away, Sam called back, "I love you, Jake Harris."

"I love you too, Sam Goodwin," Jake said just loud enough that Sam would hear.

***

El saw Jake walk out of the door just this side of the bookstore. She started to wave when she saw he held a beautiful woman's hand. Her face was flushed, and her smile was wide. The woman threw her arms around Jake's neck, and her feet left the ground as she kissed him full on the mouth. He playfully spun her a half circle and set her down, launching her in the direction of the diner.

She skipped away happily, saying, "I love you, Jake Harris."

"I love you too, Sam Goodwin," Jake said, barely audible to El but clear enough.

With a final wave, Jake went back inside.

El proceeded to her car. She had errands to run.

It's Jake's life. Why should I pry? Why should I care?

El took a deep breath.

Dammit, because… he made me… feel again.

Her chest tightened a notch. She had not known it had relaxed.

She got in her car and headed to the DMV.

***

By the time she got to the Front Royal DMV, she had eaten half of the croissants she had purchased. She was blank and numb. The perfect mood for DMV. Her face held the same expression as the people that worked there.

They had a good system in rural Virginia. El went through a fast triage line where they made sure she had the proper documents and gave her a number: E33.

She sat in the front row. The next thing she knew, the woman sitting next to her was nudging her with an elbow, saying, "Sweety, E33 is you. Bless your heart."

It took only 50 minutes to process the docs, take

the eye exam, and get her photo.

Super Walmart was next. She didn't find any curtains she liked. Her GPS located the nearest Target.

El got lost in shopping for curtains. It was an acquired skill she had learned from being married to Ryan, that asshole.

Was Jake going to one day be: Jake, that asshole?

El felt her eyes filling up. She blinked them away.

Target was the winner. She found curtains she liked.

It was dinner with Jake next. She could do it.

***

El had just finished hanging the new drapes in the master bedroom. She was looking at where the photographer had to be the night before. She was sure that the boulder outcropping just there would be it. The corner was blank—cold empty.

She heard the front door open and boots being kicked off.

"Honey, I'm home." There was unmistakable joy in his voice. Jake ascended the stairs two at a time.

El was busy adjusting the silk ropes with tassels that held back the drapes.

"Wow, those are perfect for this room. Warmer in the winter, too. I love the original historic windows, but they are drafty as hell."

"Why are you so chipper?" El asked.

"I got a present for you." He was digging in his gym bag.

"Handcuffs for the four-poster?"

"That's what she said," Jake slid in. "No, these. Your very own Solmate socks."

That is not what she said.

"Jake, you didn't have to do that," she said.

"Full disclosure, I didn't. I was packing my overnight bag and saw them in the dresser. They sent me the wrong size last time. They said to keep them and sent me another pair at no charge. I think they may be your size." It was then he saw her face. "What's wrong?"

She took the socks.

Dobby is free.

He was also murdered.

"The photographer was back last night. So I spent the afternoon at Jacobs and Associates. Then the DMV, then Walmart, and Target. It's not as much fun shopping when the reason is to stop peeping toms."

"Well, I think this will cheer you up." Jake held his hand out, the same hand. She took it, anyway.

He took her into the hall. She looked at her reflection in the two-way mirror. She wondered if someone was behind there. Was her real self behind there?

Jake opened the door and stepped aside.

She was instantly transported to another time. The yellow fabric was so cheerful. The ruffles on the bed skirt, canopy, curtains, and even the stool cover were so Matchy-Matchy that any HGTV designer would immediately change it.

El saw the quilt and pillow shams.

"How did you know?"

"We guessed," Jake said. Then he began talking about Mabel's reaction to finding the room.

"If you and Emma don't want to drive all the way up here, you can stay at my place above Brian's Books. Here's the key. Put it on your ring."

"I always thought the more keys on your keyring, the more complicated your life is. Some keys are good, some are fun, and some are sad or bad. Taken together, it gets complicated."

"We brought a mirror in from one of the other rooms for over the vanity," Jake said as he gestured to the Newly hung, ornate mirror. It matched perfectly.

"Things weren't complicated that last time I stayed in this room." El sat down on the bed and then lay down to look at the canopy from below. "Thanks, Jake."

El rolled over and faced the wall. The room was quiet for a full minute before she felt Jake sit on the edge and finally lie down and spoon her from behind. He wrapped his arm around both of hers over her sternum.

El sighed but didn't cry.

"It's not your job to make me feel better," El said.

"No. It's more of a hobby," Jake teased. El snorted. She was still embarrassed.

"I always dreamed of kissing a boy in this bed," El said. "I thought it was my fault we never came back."

"I hope you like the room. I'll paint it, and it's nearly done."

She rotated so she faced him.

She snuggled in, and they intertwined legs. Finally, he wrapped her up in his arms, their foreheads touching. Jake slowly caressed her back.

"Can I ask you a question?" she said.

"You know that's typically a trap. It usually comes with a 15-yard penalty and an automatic first down."

"You don't have to answer. But if you do, you have to be honest."

"OK, but that adds 25 yards."

"Do you still love Sam?" She was watching his eyes. Time stretched, measured in pounding heartbeats. He replied.

"Yes. I still love Sam."

El closed her eyes and kissed him…

***

Jake kissed her back.

It was slow and soft, and he had been hoping for it inwardly. The tiny single bed seemed vast because she clung so close to him.

She was the perfect fit.

She stopped only because she had to breathe.

El burrowed in under his chin in that place designed just for her. He felt her lightly kiss his neck.

"If this is a ploy to get out of microwaving the Chinese food for me, it's working." He lightly kissed the top of her head.

"Jake, I don't know what's happening." She squeezed. "All I do know is that when I am with you… I'm in this moment. There is inner peace."

Jake could feel her heart pounding. She continued.

"For so long, I have lived in the past, where there were only regrets and pain, or the future full of fears and uncertainty. Even the present was spent trying to self edit my words before I spoke, even my thoughts, averting my eyes from the truth. It was exhausting. I was so tired."

Both their stomachs growled.

"About that microwave…."

"OK.." She untangled from him but was smiling.

Jake got up and offered his hand. She took it. He had to slow this down a bit. He didn't want to lose control and mess it up.

In the hall, Jake stopped short, and his smile suddenly fell. He looked at the mirror beside the door to the sunflower room. He dropped her hand.

"What's wrong, Jake?" El asked as he began opening doors and sniffing.

"You smell that?" Jake cocked his head and sniffed.

"What?" El said as he returned to her side and sniffed again.

"Smoke." Jake came close to the mirror and saw the moment that El could smell it. He saw her look back to the sunflower room.

Jake followed El back in. She was sniffing like a dog. In the corner, she laid her hands on the freshly cleaned paneling.

"Smell that?" she asked. Jake didn't smell it.

Jake was tall enough to see where her finger found the knot that freed the panel with a click. When it opened toward her, the smell was stronger.

El reached in and grabbed a flashlight she had placed there. She didn't explain. Just went in.

The smell was stronger in the small passage. There was no smoke here. Dust created a wake behind El.

"This is why we could smell it at the mirror." She pushed the small curtain aside. She shined a flashlight down the shaft with the ladder. Far below, eyes shined back at them and then disappeared.

"Go. Go." Jake said, now more urgent. "You knew about these passages?"

"I just found that one this morning," El said. "I only went this far. I didn't have a flashlight. So I went out here."

El opened the door into the root cellar room but didn't go out.

"That's when I bashed my head."

"I didn't go any farther because I didn't have a real flashlight. Plus, I hate spiders." She moved to the other end and shined the light down a narrow spiral stone staircase at the end of the secret passage. It was filled with dusty cobwebs.

Eyes glowed back at them. Felix was on the stairs waiting. The smell was stronger still.

Jake took the flashlight and squeezed by El. Belly to belly, they barely fit. Jake raised his arms over his head, and El placed her hands on his ribs to squeeze by.

Holding up an arm to catch the webs, he descended. The steep, narrow, spiral stairs were so tight Jake disappeared around the curve in a mere moment.

"Wait." El followed down the awkward, too-tall steps. "Is any of this freaking you out?"

She placed one hand on his shoulder and one on the wall.

"Let's do the freaking out later. Fire is bad." He continued down for what seemed like forever. The smell of smoke was more pungent now as the air got cooler.

The stairs exited through a small doorway so narrow that Jake's shoulders touched each side, into a wide stone arched roof corridor. Plaster had fallen everywhere. The raw blocks were completely revealed above on the arch. The plaster on the walls was like peeling paint.

"Look. Smoke." Jake pointed the flashlight at the ceiling. A layer of smoke about a foot deep clung there. "It is rising like a chimney."

The cat's eyes were far down the hall. The beam was not bright enough to follow the cat as the hallway disappeared in a slow turn to the left.

Jake paused and shone the light between them. He was gray with dust and cobwebs.

"You OK?" he said before he could stop himself.

"I'm sorry," she said, on purpose. "A deal is a deal. Do you have your phone on you?"

"We'll never get a signal down here," Jake replied, but he still pulled his phone from his pocket.

"No, silly," she said. "It's for light when our flashlight inevitably dies. Have you never seen a movie?"

Jake took El's hand, and they started to jog down

the passage.

"Did you already know about this? From when you were a kid?" Jake asked as they loped along. The smoke was deeper here but not yet low enough to reach their eyes. Their movement stirred the still smoke. The walls were wet here, and lichen was growing.

"I wish," El said. "We would have Scooby Doo'd the hell out of this."

The hall abruptly ended in a collapsed pile of stone ahead.

"You need to know this was not included in the restoration budget." Jake was trying to relieve her fear. It was working until they almost stumbled over the skeletal remains of a corpse. El was crushing Jake's hand now. Felix sat on the steps of another doorway that led to spiral steps.

The skull still had hair. Its empty eye sockets stared at them accusingly—desiccated skin still clung in places. The jaw was frozen in what looked like a scream. A trickle of water flowed down the stairs. A gutter on the edge of the passage contained it.

The cat went up the spiral stairs. The smoke was low enough here that it was rising up it like a chimney.

"El, I want to turn off the light for a minute," Jake said, shining it through the smoke.

"Now you're just trying to freak me out. There are easier ways. If you want a hug, just ask me." She hugged his middle and pressed her cheek on his chest. "OK. Do it."

It was not the complete darkness Jake had expected. Sections of the rubble glowed red like magma.

"I think that is the bottom of the ice well. Rob and I saw it collapse today." The glow revealed the passage was not completely blocked. But the collapsed stones were keeping it open. "We are not risking that."

"Think we can get out up there? I think this is how Felix was getting inside the house," El said. "I don't think he'd mind." She released Jake but kept hold of his hand.

"We can try."

After two turns, it was apparent the smoke was too thick and dangerous. So they made an awkward retreat.

Backing down the corridor, they stopped and shined the light back at the corpse. His black suit was in rags. The style was pinstriped and had wide lapels. His shoes were gone. His socks were oddly intact.

"His socks match, at least." They laughed, and it turned to coughing.

"This corridor is wet enough. I don't think the house is at risk. We'll also stop tossing stuff in the ice well. The next rain will put this out. Let's head back to the house. It's a two-shower day."

***

"… a two shower day." El released his hand and turned back.

She walked back the way they had come as Jake examined the passage beside her with the light. On closer inspection, some of the walls were raw stone or maybe natural caves.

"There are lots of caves around here in Virginia.

They probably made this passage to get to the ice house. Ever been to Luray Caverns? It's huge."

While Jake wasn't touching her, her mind began to race again.

Their words echoed in her mind. I Love you, Jake Harris. I love you, Sam…

"There is a cave at The Cabin." It's deep but not big. "More like a shaft. I snaked a hundred and fifty feet of flexible drain pipe down the shaft. I can pump 56-degree air out of it year-round. It keeps the cabin cool in the summer and keeps my pipes from freezing in the winter. Primitive geothermal."

"Why do you do that?" El asked. Their pace was strolling like it wasn't odd to be walking alone with him there.

"Do what?"

"You start to carry the conversation and find stuff to say that makes me feel like you care what I think."

"You get this look. You're thinking about something painful, and I can't ask if you're OK because, you know, deals. So I just talk to you. With you. About things that matter to me. Otherwise, I'd just kiss that look off your face." They stopped walking. "You get this single wrinkle between your eyebrows."

He kissed her on that very spot. She felt it relax beneath his lips.

The flashlight winked out.

***

El found his hips with her hands in the dark and

said, "Not funny." Then, she heard click after click.

A crash echoed over them from around the bend, and a glow behind them became brighter. Then the echoing scream chilled their bones.

They ran by instinct. Jake had her hand held tight, he dropped the flashlight, and a dim light came on and then a brighter one. Jake had his phone out.

It illuminated glowing eyes.

It was Felix again. How did he get past them?

There was another blood-curdling scream from behind.

They kept running. When they got to the stairs, Jake just said, "Go."

He doesn't have to tell me twice.

They exited into the root cellar, and Jake immediately bashed his head on a pipe.

"Fuck," he growled through gritted teeth.

Stooping, they headed across the basement for the stairs. They coughed awkwardly in the butler's pantry but said nothing, catching their breath.

"Fuck."

Jake showed El bloody fingers. Again.

Something pounded on the front door. Hard.

They walked into the hall, and through the frosted glass, they could make out a man in a dark suit. Night had fallen while they were in the tunnels. He was backlit by the porch light.

"Who is it?" El called out.

"Detective Tate."

El went to the front door and was surprised to find it unlocked. She opened it but held the knob, making it clear he was not invited in.

The detective's eyes looked El up and down, then Jake.

"May I come in?" Tate said in a voice that didn't acknowledge their condition in any way.

"Do you like Chinese food, detective? Have you had dinner?" El let go of the knob. "This is Jake Harris. Jake, this is detective Tate. Frank Tate."

Jake simply nodded.

"It's been a long day, and no, I have not eaten." He stepped in but waited for El to lead the way.

"I'm going to wash up," Jake said and continued to the bathroom. El gestured for Tate to sit at the kitchen table.

"We have beer and Diet Coke. We are having a beer," El said, trying to calm herself.

"Beer would be fine." Tate unbuttoned his coat and loosened his tie before he sat. "I chased off a black SUV that was parked a ways down the mountain."

El set the three beers on the table and opened them. She slid one to Tate and took a long pull on one before setting it down and pulling out her phone. She clicked a few links and laid it down in front of Tate.

It was the photo of the SUV Rob had taken.

"That one was taken yesterday." She took up her beer and took another swallow. "There is probably an asshole out there with a camera right now. At least, I hope it's just a camera. I don't suppose you could go out there and arrest them for trespassing."

"Not my jurisdiction."

"I figured," El said as she washed her hands in the

sink.

Jake came out and started piling Chinese food containers on the table.

El got three plates.

"Fill a plate, and I'll warm it up in the microwave. My specialty."

"I like it cold. I can't begin to tell you how much cold Chinese food I have eaten." He loaded his plate with lo mein, Kung Pao chicken, and beef with broccoli.

"I see you are married, detective Tate. Got any kids?" Jake asked personably.

El put a plate in the microwave that sat on the counter nearby.

"No kids. Married 17 years. My wife is a forensic pathologist and is the only person I have ever met that hates people more than me. So, naturally, I had to marry her."

"Met on the job, I take," El asked as she pulled her food out and put Jake's in.

"Yep. I was still a beat cop securing crime scenes in DC. Daily murders on the night shift meant bagging and tagging evolved into coffee and breakfasts after our shifts. Someone that understood what it was I didn't want to talk about brought us closer where it kills most relationships."

El set the plate in front of Jake. She noticed a single line of blood running down behind his ear and down the back of his neck. "Why are you here, detective? It can't be my mad cooking skills," El said, using chopsticks like a pro and popping some General Tso chicken into her mouth.

"Just one thing. Eat first. It's no rush." He laid down his fork on an empty plate and took a paper napkin from the holder in the center of the table. He wiped his mouth and took up the beer as he sat back.

"You eat fast. Faster than Jake even," El noted.

"Habit I picked up in Iraq." He took a swig of beer. "Eat when you can…."

"Piss when you can." Jake finished the quote.

They just nodded. They both waited for El to finish eating as they nursed their beers.

"Can you call Ms. Jacobs? She left you several messages today," Tate asked.

"Yes, I can." El went to the cordless phone and the business card on the counter next to it.

"Do you think the house is haunted?" Tate asked.

As if on cue, a fox screamed its unnerving cry outside.

"More than you know…." She put the phone on speaker. Joyce answered on the first ring.

"Jacobs and Associates."

"Hi, Joyce. I'm here with Jake and Detective Tate. He recommended I call you."

"This call is being recorded," Joyce said. "Hello, detective. Ask your question. El, you can answer. Be completely honest."

"Do you know this man?" Tate slid her a photo of a man. He appeared to be asleep, resting on an ambulance gurney.

"I think I do," El said. "He was an investigator for my husband's law firm—Daniel something. I remember because my husband always called him Danny or Danny-boy, even though it was obvious he didn't like it. He was at the Christmas party every year, and, besides me, he was the only one that didn't drink. He never stayed long."

"El, he was found dead today in his car, at 4:11 am, on I-66. He was parked in a locked car under an overpass. Apparent suicide," Joyce said.

El looked at Jake. Jake said nothing.

"Why are you telling me this?" El said. "You know I am already scared here, barely keeping my shit together."

Detective Tate looked at Jake for a reaction.

"It's true. She has no shit," Jake said as he watched the crease between El's eyebrows fade.

It was Tate's turn to bring out his phone and open an image file.

"Daniel Manning had a high-quality digital SLR camera with him. This was the only photo on the SD card. Taken last night at 3:05 AM."

Tate turned the phone sideways so the image was displayed as large as possible. He slid it to them so El and Jake could both see.

It was the Wright House from a distance. The porch light was on. A man stood on the edge of the front porch. El used her fingers to zoom in. The figure was in complete silhouette, so there was almost no detail except his shape. His eyes glowed like a cat, or he wore round glasses that reflected something. A kind of black steam drifted from him.

She kept zooming.

Close in on his eyes, they could see details from the design in the frosted glass behind him. El zoomed out.

Jake raised his finger to the image and tracked it down.

The man had no shoes…

"Do you recognize him?" Tate asked.

El spoke first. "We have no idea who he is."

Jake shook his head in agreement. They all fell silent.

Joyce spoke. "Is there anything else, Detective?"

"Are you still recording, Ms. Jacobs?"

"Let it be known I am driving home directly from here. I expect to be home by midnight, and I am not suicidal at all. A bit creeped out. Not suicidal."

"Thank you, Detective. Likewise. Goodnight, everyone."

Joyce hung up, and El put the phone on the stand. Then, collecting dishes and cartons, they all stood. Tate snagged a fortune cookie. He cracked it open, and while chewing and reading the fortune, he said, "My advice. Stay somewhere else. Tonight at least."

He dropped the fortune on the table.

"I'll show myself out." They stood there until the front door closed.

Jake spoke first. "I'll clean this up. Go pack a bag, just for tonight and tomorrow."

"What about showers?"

"Fuck that. We leave in two minutes. I'll lock the doors." El ran upstairs.

Jake locked the front door, then came back and saw

Tate's fortune.

Things are not as they appear.

El was back in one minute. She had just stuffed things in Jake's gym bag. They were hanging out of it. He saw the MCR shirt as well as the Solmates socks. She passed him straight to the back door.

"We'll use my truck," Jake said as he locked it.

"Jesus," El said. "Are you freaked out yet?"

"Yes, and don't call me Jesus."

Jake didn't notice the mirror frame was gone.

The Cabin

Felix could see the anger drift off it like black steam. Restless anger. But this one didn't scream…

***

"Great. No seat belts," El said, but they were already moving. A pothole bounced them hard enough that the random tools behind the seat rattled, and the glove box popped open.

El had both hands on the dash but released one to close the glove compartment before it bounced the contents out. It wouldn't close.

She crushed the map and McDonald's napkins down hard, and her hand held the velvet box for a second. She looked at Jake, but he was intent on the road.

She slammed it closed as they reached the pavement.

"Now would be a good time to say that shit the way

you do, to de-fucking-stress me because I'm gonna crack. That guy on the porch… was the dead guy." She was still holding onto the dash like her life depended on it.

Without missing a beat, he began.

"You were asking about laundry. I thought we'd take a drive to my shed where I do laundry." He looked over at her for an instant. Her eyes were wide. "I still haven't figured out laundry at The Cabin because of how much electricity it takes, so I put my washer and dryer in the building where I park my truck when I go up the mountain. In the beginning, I thought it was going to be a pain in the ass. I got used to it."

"I found Lily's gun. It's in that small drawer at the end in the butler's pantry." El said.

Jake raised an eyebrow at the comment. The truck was slowing. He relaxed and sat back. Jake put his right arm out along the back of the bench seat as he continued. "I set it up with a chair and reading lamp, so on Sundays, I'd do laundry and read."

It was working. Her forehead crinkle relaxed and chased the potential migraine away.

She slid over under his arm and was rewarded with cobwebs and dust on her face instead of the smell of Jake she sought.

She didn't care as his arm closed around her. She relaxed.

It was only a minute more before he turned off the road, and motion sensors kicked on floodlights that revealed a rusty Quonset hut as an overhead garage door slid open. An old shipping container was beside the building.

The garage stayed open. And they parked the truck inside.

"Grab the bag," Jake said and climbed out.

"We're staying here?" El asked.

"No, this is where I do laundry."

Jake flicked on a switch, and fluorescent lights came on. The back eight feet of the room had a slightly raised platform that looked like a deck. There was a washer, dryer, freezer, a counter, an electric stove, and an incongruous tall tool chest along the wall. All the way to the left was a single bookcase packed with paperbacks. An overstuffed recliner had a mini-fridge as a side table with a lamp.

"We'll come and do laundry soon. But not tonight." Jake took the bag and stuffed the items in all the way, and bungee'd it on the front rack of his ATV.

He hopped on and started it up.

"Climb on." Jake hurried up, and she got on behind him. She wrapped her arms around his chest, holding him for dear life.

Smoothly the machine rolled out. She was impressed by how quiet it was. Jake pressed a button, and the garage door closed behind them, and they started up across a field.

The headlamps were super bright. They could talk in a normal voice.

"I'm sorry, we don't have helmets. They are all at The Cabin. They're just like umbrellas like that."

"Don't jinx us. Rain would really top this day off."

Slowly Jake drove the familiar narrow path. El could not see much but crowding pine trees. Several places were torn up as if by powerful wheels.

"You were up here last night and got to my house in like two minutes?" She thought about the neglected cut on his head. Jake made no reply.

They cleared the pines out onto a bluff and made a right. The path was only a few feet from the edge.

The ATV stopped.

"There it is." Jake pointed.

It was no cabin. It was a work of architectural art. It was a reminiscence of Frank Lloyd Wright. Subtle lighting was placed on paths, planters, landscaping, and even inside the glass-lined great room. "You built this, designed this? I thought Rob said you did it alone."

"I did." He pulled ahead and around the bluff. "Five years and counting."

They pulled the ATV into the massive, covered carport. And he shut down the motor.

She climbed off and stared at the massive iron-bound door.

"You made that?" She pointed at the door.

"Once I dragged the portable sawmill up here, it was easier to build things up here with local materials than to haul everything. The path is too narrow for even a 4x4 up here. At its narrowest, I can barely fit this ATV."

Jake freed the bag and said, "Showers first, then I'll show you the rest."

Jake opened the door for her. She moved slowly.

"The bath is through there. He pointed to the right. No internal door separated the bedroom. Instead, it was the width of the entire structure. A floating king-sized platform bed filled the middle of the room against a living rock headboard. The massive rock was varnished somehow, sealed with something that made it feel like glass.

Touching it, she saw how dirty her hand was.

Opposite the bed was a 16-foot wide wall of bookcases that went to the ceiling. Each dark-stained shelf looked strong enough to climb. It was full of books. She remembered her conversation with Brian.

Around the left end of the bookcase was a closet only a tenth filled. The other side had the master bath. The shower was the entire far end of the room. Mirrors covered the wall behind the sink bowls. She dropped the bag on a bench. Two doors to the right held a linen closet and a toilet. She snagged a bath towel and a washcloth. They were all mismatched but in earth tones.

She stripped and hung her filthy clothes on pegs. She started the shower and waited for the water to warm.

Relaxing piano music came across hidden speakers.

All the lighting was indirect and subtle. It was better than any hotel she had ever stayed in with Ryan.

The shower was steaming and too hot to use, but she quickly found an excellent temp. A little nook had Head & Shoulders shampoo, which was all she needed.

She washed her hair twice. She scrubbed her body

with no mercy. The enormous rainfall showerhead above and the handheld were excellent together. She shut off the water and stood on the rug in front of the bench.

Naked, she opened the bag. Unfortunately, in her haste, she had only packed one pair of her sports underwear, jeans, a black tank top, the MCR shirt, and her new socks.

She opted for the panties, MCR shirt, and socks that were not the same but sort of matched when she looked.

The XL-long t-shirt fit her like a loose dress. She wrapped her hair in a towel so it had a slight chance to dry. A basket on the counter had extra new toothbrushes, soaps, mouthwash, and deodorants.

Just like every swinging bachelor player I ever dated.

She padded out and down the hall to the great room. Short bookcases lined the room under the windows. The room was open, as were the kitchen, dining, and living room—almost spartan in the clean lines and uncluttered surfaces.

She didn't see Jake at first. Then he saw him holding a black ceramic coffee mug beyond the glass wall.

She tried to move her eyebrows up and down to divert the tension when a squirrel jumped up next to Jake like a person. They stood there together a moment, looking at lights far below. Jake poured out the cup of walnuts onto a small feeder, and the squirrel dug in. Then he threw the mug as hard as he could into the forest.

Jake gave Rocky's ear a scratch and turned to walk in.

He saw her.

He smiled and came through a door in the window wall that was all windows as well.

"Find everything, OK?"

"Yes. How is it so cool in here?" she said.

"Want some sweatpants?" He was moving toward the hall.

"Go ahead and explore. Make yourself at home. Help yourself to anything you like. Except for the walnuts. Rocky will get pissed."

"The squirrel is named Rocky?" El asked. She knew he was doing it again.

"Yes. Yes, he is."

It was Jake's turn to shower, and he disappeared down the hall. Soon she heard the water come on. She explored the kitchen, tried the gas stove, and then looked in the fridge. It was mostly stocked with breakfast items. The kitchen cupboards had everything. It all looked new—Scandinavian style.

She returned to the great room and out onto the patio.

Rocky was still eating. He looked at her but made no move to flee.

She looked a long time for the mug below the balcony. Then, finally, she said out loud, "Fuck you, Ryan."

You'll never hurt me again.

She turned back and opened the door in time to hear Jake calling to her.

She stepped into the bedroom and said, "I'm here."

"Can you come in here, please?" Jake said from the bathroom. "I need you to look at this."

El rounded the corner, and he was standing at the mirror. There was a rust-colored towel wrapped around his waist. He was trying to look at the cut in the mirror.

"I think a freezing shower stopped the bleeding. But when I hit my head on that pipe, ripped it open worse."

A red tackle box was open on the counter stenciled with TRAUMA KIT on all sides.

"This room has the best light," he said.

"Sit here," El directed. He sat on the bench opposite the sinks and wall mirrors as she brought the kit over. It had a penlight in the top tray. She clicked it on and had a look. "Jake, you should have said something."

"When?" he said.

"Oh, this is my washer and dryer, and by the way, I think my skull is showing. Fuck." She was already pulling on surgical gloves. "Hold these." She thrust two tongue depressors at him. She opened a small jar of Vaseline and put a dab on her finger, then buttered the edge of the tongue depressors.

"Now hold still, dumb ass." She twisted off the cap of the single-use tube of medical adhesive. She put a line in the open wound, set the tube down on a piece of gauze, took up the depressors and pressed the wound closed, and held it. "Now, don't move."

They waited.

El was suddenly aware of how close her breasts were to Jake's face. They betrayed her then by becoming more erect.

"Why do you call this The Cabin?" She set one depressor down on the gauze, still holding pressure with the other. "It needs a cool name like The Cantilever House or The Bluff." She laid her free hand on his shoulder.

He was freezing.

She lifted it and had a look. "Now, don't make me tell you three times." Then, she started packing the kit up. "Trash?" she asked.

"Middle door. Kit goes in the one to the right," he said. "Nice socks."

"Like 'em? They were a gift." She saw him shiver. "You get ready for bed."

She shook out her hair and hung the towel on a peg. She snagged a hairbrush from the counter and left.

She wanted nothing more than to climb in with him, to warm him.

***

"Today, I have seen a lot of weird stuff. But you know what the weirdest thing was?" El said as she sat upright in the bed with her legs under the covers. The quilt was a masterpiece of intricate designs and soft materials. The sheets were amazing.

"Weirder than old skeletons and ghosts that look just like them?" Jake said.

"That your bed is made," she said.

Jake came around the corner wearing loose gym shorts and a Motley Crüe t-shirt. He was about to touch his head.

"Don't touch that."

"That's what she said," Jake joked.

"Are you still cold?" she asked, drawing down the covers on his side.

"Kinda, it's just…." Jake said. "Look. Maybe I should sleep on the couch. The last two nights were… I mean…"

"What if I sleepwalk again?" El said as she hugged herself.

Jake looked toward the great room and was thinking. "Back in a sec."

El listened to odd sounds. Then, with the bolt thrown on the massive door, the sound of a giant terracotta planter being dragged on the flagstone. A minute later, he was back but still didn't climb in.

"Maybe I should take the couch." He said as he looked back. El had never seen him indecisive before.

"Don't be silly. Get in here. You're freezing," she said.

"It was the kiss," he said, looking everywhere but at her. "I liked it. A lot."

"Look, nothing's going to happen tonight, mister. Get in here. I'm getting cold, too." El had her arms crossed over her chest.

He decided.

He crawled in on his side and moved to the center, his back to El. She slid to him, like gravity, like magnets clicking together.

"Jesus, you are freezing!" She squeezed him closer instead of retreating.

"You are wearing socks, and don't call me Jesus," he said.

El still thought it was funny.

"Um… you plan to sleep with all the lights on?"

"Alexa, good night," Jake said, and all the lights faded. A quiet contemporary piano played softly from hidden speakers. Dim, indirect baseboard lights gave off enough light to find the way to the bathroom without a toe stub.

"I usually sleep to music. I can turn it off if you want."

"No. I like it."

"The Cabin doesn't lock that well. So I pulled a planter in front of the door. Moving it would wake me."

A clock on the shelf said: 11:11 pm.

"Good night, Eleanore Wright," Jake said. "Eleanore with three Es, beginning-middle-end."

"Goodnight, Jake Harris," El said. "Architect, engineer, builder." She kissed his spine through his shirt.

Warming a bit, Jake rolled to his back. "This is why I built The Cabin." He pointed up.

A skylight was roughly the same size as the huge bed was above. She had not noticed it until then. It was as clear as if it was not there.

El could see the Milky Way. She gasped.

"I build this home around this view, around this

bed," Jake said softly, "Four hundred and thirty-three bags of concrete. Nineteen pillars, forty-seven beams, and forty-one panels of glass. All so I could sleep beneath this view."

That is the most romantic thing I have ever heard.

El saw a shooting star, one brighter than she had ever seen before.

"Did you see that?" El said excitedly. She was lying on her back beside him, arms up behind her head.

"It's the Perseids meteor shower. It peaked about two weeks ago. November has the Leonid shower, which is also amazing. Dry, clearer skies."

Another falling star streaked by. This one even had an impressive tail.

"Watching and waiting for them quiets my mind," Jake said.

El imagined making love beneath that sky.

"I can see why you built The Cabin now. Total chick magnet."

Jake turned toward her before speaking. "I've never brought anyone else here. You're the first."

El looked at his eyes in the light of the Milky Way and saw no lies there.

But men always lie…

El's arms were still over her head. Her feet sought out his. "I love these socks."

Jake placed his hand on her belly. Her arm position had drawn the shirt up. Half of his cool hand was on her warm skin. El lowered her left hand to cover his.

"Warming up?" El asked, her heart rate increasing.

"Yes. Thank you," he said, and El noticed the

strong scent of mint and freshly brushed teeth.

She turned her face toward his. She pulled the shirt up just enough so his hand was completely on skin— her hand on top of his again.

"Jake…" she began in a whisper but was interrupted by his kiss. They intertwined their feet, drawing each other closer. El melted into the kiss, and the world narrowed to that moment, that feeling.

Hunger colored her kiss now. El slid Jake's hand up to cup her left breast. She felt him slow the pace. His gentle tongue retreated, and the kiss became teasing, brushing lips on lips. She pulled the shirt up farther, exposing both her breasts. His fingers drifted over one and then the other, just like his lips explored hers.

El opened her eyes for an instant to see Jake's were already open. It was like looking into his soul up close. She moaned as she felt the flood in her sex.

Jake closed his eyes then and kissed her hard and deep, and he kneaded her right breast, squeezing her nipple, and El wanted that moment to last forever.

Jake eased back and hovered his lips over hers as if the only air worth breathing came directly from her mouth. His hands began their drifting exploration again like he was blind and memorizing every square inch of her.

His hand explored her ribs and then her belly. Finally, he found the tiny ring in her navel.

His hand drifted over cotton onto her mound. El's hips automatically rose to his touch in welcome.

El was frozen in time as he explored the cotton. He mapped both edges along her thighs. She parted her legs slightly to extend and encourage the effort.

Briefly, the drifting paused as he applied a slight pressure over her very center, extracting another moan.

His hand retreated again, finding her breast. Another kiss, and she was lost again. Her hand joined his on her breast. Her want had never been this intense. She guided his hand down and under the leading edge of her panties and into her tidy trim. They explored her together.

His mouth left hers, and she wanted it back. But, instead, he was kissing her neck, and goose flesh blossomed on her whole body. El left his hand inside her panties to cup her own breast and pinch her own nipple. That's when his mouth found her right goosed bumped nipple.

He sucked on her as his fingers found her soaked. He didn't penetrate her. He teased, up and down between her folds. He barely touched her clit, but instead took laps around it, traversing the length of her.

El couldn't breathe. She put her left arm over her head again. She was trembling. Her right arm lowered between them and desperately sought access inside his shorts. The moment her hand closed around him, her climax slowly began.

When his finger entered her all the way to her G-spot, her vision burst into stars, and she came all at once. She felt the convulsions squeeze on his finger, and she cried out. His hand went back and forth, pressing her clit and entering her deep, over and over as the waves of orgasm arched her back.

The last wave was barely over when her left hand pushed off the soaked panties to be lost in the bed below.

In a guttural choking whisper, El said, "I want you inside me. Please. Need you inside me."

"El, not a good idea. I don't have any condoms."

"I'm on the pill." With the last wave barely over, she wiggled out of the soaked fabric that was keeping him from entering her fully. El was pushing down his shorts now with her feet, managing to kick off the covers.

El was drawing him on top of her. She didn't let go of him. The feel of his pulse there was about to make her come again with the hunger for him.

"Please…" She was rubbing the head of his cock at her threshold. "Just for a minute."

Jake had hands propping him up to either side of her shoulders. El began to strip his shirt off with her free hand. Jake helped with one of his.

He lowered his face to hers, leaving space between them to not crush her. She wrapped her legs around him.

"Please, Jake," she begged. She knew he was teasing her now.

He silenced her with a kiss. She had him at her threshold. She tried to raise her hips to take him, but he moved with her. She tried to draw him in with her heels.

Then the kiss stopped. Three bright shooting stars lit the sky. And he stopped resisting her pull, and he was all the way inside her.

She gasped and tried to say his name, but she couldn't. He began full-length thrusts, and the world disappeared in a flood of shooting stars. He stayed deep inside her. After the crescendo, El could hear her pulse thundering in her ears and feel him pulsing inside her.

He didn't move as she returned to reality. He stayed there a long while. He lowered to his elbows and let their bodies touch full length.

His movement drew out a whine.

"It's been more than a minute." He stifled any reply with a kiss. Jake withdrew as he kissed her. El tried to stop him with her heels to no avail. "Now it's my turn to do what I want."

El knew she could not deny him anything. Part of her longed for him to come inside her.

He began to kiss down her neck again. The sensation was too much, torture. She shrank away and pushed at him. He was made of stone and driftwood.

He kissed down her sternum and lingered on her breasts. Then lower.

First, one arm of Jake's arms and then another went under her thighs.

"I thought it was your turn," she whispered in the hush.

"It's about what *I want*." He drifted his lips back and forth in her soft ruff of hair.

Her head fell back. The Milky Way seemed brighter. Then, when his mouth found her swollen and already trembling down there, it got brighter still.

El was lost in the moment. His mouth was full on her, and only his tongue gently moved. The meteors burned and burst above, just for her. Twice more, the world melted away from El.

After a few minutes of lingering, Jake came back up to hold her. She said nothing but needed to taste this arcane magic from his lips.

Long kisses followed as she slowly stroked him.

She found herself draped over him as she kissed him. She was guiding him in again. "It's OK." His moan was the answer. Instead, she sat up and bore all her weight onto Jake. He completely filled her.

"How many strokes can I have before I finish you with my mouth?" El said in a breathless whisper.

"Ten" was his teasing answer.

When she drew up and then down, his rough voice said, "Nine."

She repeated at the exact angle to hit her G-spot every time. "Eight."

She exploded at the count of three. She collapsed on his chest with two strokes to go.

"My God, what have you done to me?" El whispered.

"Almost everything."

She slid on him and then back down. She was slick with sweat. "Two."

Again. "One."

He slid her off to the side by her hips. His hand reluctantly released her.

Her hand found him, then her mouth. He lasted less than a minute after he gave himself entirely to her.

***

They had fallen asleep in a great tangle clinging to each other, but when El's bladder woke her at 3:41 am, Jake had his back to her. His gravity wanted her to mold herself to him, but her need to pee won the debate.

She sat with her face in her hands.

What is happening to me? What did you do to me, Jake?

She had been married to Ryan for over five years, and he had never given her a single climax.

It was always about him.

El thought that was just how things were. All the bumbling high school and college boys she ever knew were that way, so Ryan seemed normal. All blond hair and expensive suits blinded her to reality.

She opened her eyes.

Perfect pools of light showed the way from under the bottom row of bookcases, the bed, and the bathroom vanity. When she left the bathroom, instead of coming straight to bed, she went in search of water.

Her socks were the only clothes the evening had allowed her to retain. She moved in silence on her mismatched stockinged feet. The night lighting was more impressive in the main room. The far wall was part of the living rock, and the illumination below accented it in light and shadow.

The planters in the room had lights that highlighted the plants there. The hearth wall was lit beautifully as well.

The setting quarter moon was bright enough to read by. She walked naked to the glass wall and could see the Milky Way.

Why had you never seen these things before?

Another shooting star punctuated the thought. El was feeling magical, happy, and daring. She had never been naked under the night stars in her entire life. She suddenly wanted to check that item off her bucket list. She tried the custom glass door. It was locked. She could not see a latch. She was locked in.

Then she saw the glowing eyes.

Her heart skipped. She couldn't breathe. Felix sat on the balcony wall, watching her.

A flood of images raced through her mind. The desiccated shoeless corpse, the overgrown headless statues, the burning ice well, the photo of the man on her porch.

Hands gently grasped her shoulders, and she started.

"El, wake up. You're sleepwalking again." It was Jake, not the shoeless corpse.

"How did Felix get here?" she said as he gently turned her away from the glass.

"You're dreaming, sleepwalking, Eleanore Wright. I am tempted just to let you. You are the most beautiful thing I've ever seen in the moonlight."

"I'm awake," she said. "I was thirsty."

"OK, let's get back to bed," Jake said calmly. He was clearly humoring her.

When El hesitated just for an instant, he swept her up and began gently carrying her.

"I must be dreaming," she whispered into his neck.

"Nice socks," Jake whispered back.

He lowered her into the bed, never releasing her,

except enough to draw up the covers. Finally, she fell asleep with her forehead tucked under his chin, thinking about the sky.

When El woke, he was gone.

Red in the Morning

She saw me. I didn't think they could see me if I wasn't really there...

***

Jake woke naturally to see red lines of clouds above through the sky.

El was beside him, softly snoring, spread-eagled beneath the covers. Comically, she looked like she had fallen from a great height in a Road Runner cartoon.

How could such a tiny woman take up so much bed space?

He used the facilities and put on fresh shorts and an AC/DC t-shirt.

Jake knew he was falling in love. It washed over him like a warm shower. So much for taking it slow. He had not even met her a week ago. He already felt more for El than he ever did for Sam.

Jake started a kettle of water and readied his large insulated French press. He preheated the oven. He was chopping peppers and onions when a small voice said, "Hey. You disappeared."

El was standing there in his t-shirt and socks.

Both had once been mine…

"Four minutes until coffee." He filled the French press with boiling water. "Omelets OK?"

Her hair was disheveled, and she didn't care. She hugged him around the middle. He now knew just how much taller he was than El. She kissed him. It almost ignited Jake again, except she let him go and began to leave the kitchen.

"Omelets are great. Give me five minutes. I need another shower, thank you very much…" and she disappeared around the corner.

Jake knew he needed another shower as well. Her scent was intoxicating, but he had work to do today— things to sort out.

Bacon was sizzling in the oven, and peppers, wild onions, and garlic were sautéing in a pan as he pressed the coffee.

He poured El a cup as she returned dressed in cargo shorts and a black tank top. Her socks were now pristine white.

"That was seven minutes, dammit," Jake said, sliding the steaming cup across the island to where she had sat on a stool.

"That's what she said," El added before her first sip.

Jake smiled wide and turned back to cooking.

"You were sleepwalking again last night," Jake said. "I didn't know whether to wake you or get my camera."

"No, I wasn't. I was awake," she said over her mug.

"You were totally naked, trying to get out, talking about Felix." He started whisking eggs in a large Pyrex measuring cup. "Do you remember any of that?"

"Yes. All of it. I saw Felix on the balcony. Seriously."

"Did I mention you were totally naked, just wearing socks? I approved."

"I aim to please." She laughed comfortably.

"That is an understatement." Jake's smile was brilliant. He poured his coffee and pushed his mug and the French press over to her. "We'll eat on the balcony. Please take these out, and I'll be out in a couple of minutes."

Jake had already set the table up with colorful placemats, silverware, and cloth napkins in antique, gothic napkin rings that had been a gift from Lillian. Matched salt and pepper shakers occupied the center of the table with a bottle of Matouk's Calypso hot sauce and a carafe of OJ.

Jake brought the plates with omelets, three slices of bacon each, and orange wedges.

El was watching the view. Three lines of clouds above were in the sunshine and glowed red. He poured juice and another cup of coffee for himself before he sat.

"This view is all about the sunsets," Jake said, sipping coffee. "On this side of the ridge, you can watch the sunlight rush this way across the Seven Bends plain below, though." He added hot sauce to his omelet and took a big bite, wondering what she was thinking.

"I never met a bachelor that could make his bed or an omelet this pretty." She took a bite.

"I love to cook," he said.

"Jake, oh my god. This is amazing," El said. "What is that?"

"Fresh ingredients, and practice," Jake said. "I love breakfast food."

"Is there anything you're not good at?" El asked, savoring a bit of bacon.

She was talking about last night…

"I suck at highway driving because I get sleepy. I suck at plumbing and have to go slow if I don't want leaks. I can't spell for shit. I somehow trip over stuff that isn't there all the time. I can't run because of a bad knee. I have a low tolerance for fools to my detriment. I suck at keeping in touch with family," Jake said rapid-fire. "And most recently, I keep bashing my head on shit."

"How is your head this morning?

"Itchy. I gotta wear a ball cap today to keep my hands off it," he said, touching it. It was hard, with a bit of a crusty feeling. He was surprised it didn't hurt. She batted his hand down.

She laid down her fork and took up her last piece of bacon. "Now the elephant in the room…."

Oh no. The friend zone speech.

He covered his heart sinking by raising the coffee mug.

"Elephant?"

"Is my house really haunted, or is the Firm just

messing with me?"

"Probably a bit of both." He tried to hide the relief in his voice as well. "It's Friday. Isn't your friend coming into town?"

"Oh shit. Where's my phone? She probably called." El said.

"You left it on the counter in the kitchen last night. So I put it on the charger." Jake said. "While she's in town, Emma, right?" Jake remembered her name. "Remembering names was another thing I am bad at. If there are private dicks sneaking around your house, the two of you can stay at my apartment in town," Jake said as he stood gathering empty plates. "I'll bring your phone out."

Jake put the dishes in the giant farm sink beside the pans, grabbed the phone, and took it back to El. "I'm going to jump in the shower. There is good cell reception here. Check your messages and come up with a plan. I have some trail cams I use for hunting I want to set up at the house."

He bent over and kissed her. When he began to rise, she followed him with her mouth, her arms around his neck. By the time he stood upright, her feet were not on the patio. The kiss was long, and he held her close.

"Want company in that shower?" El asked him breathlessly.

His phone rang. It was on DO-NOT-DISTURB mode. Only specific numbers would ring through. They both looked at it. It said: Jacobs and Associates.

"You should answer that. She doesn't call people

unless it's important. She emails," Jake said. "Want me to wait?"

"No. Go ahead," El said before she lifted the phone. "I'll be along if it's quick."

It wasn't quick. He took a long shower hoping she'd follow. Jake made the bed as he air-dried in case she followed. Glancing around the corner, El was still on the balcony talking on her phone.

He got dressed for the day in jeans and a random t-shirt. Even his socks and boots. All the dishes were done, and Jake risked going out to collect what remained. Before he could manage the French press and mugs, El spoke, "He's here. Yes. Soon." She held out her phone. "She needs to speak to you."

"Hey, Joyce," was all he said. The look on El's face alarmed him. The crease in her brow was back and deeper than ever.

"Jake, I need you to be in my office by 10 am sharp. The sheriff wants to talk to you. He was pissed because he was already at your apartment and up at the Wright house this morning. I have no idea why he knew to come here. I talked him down a bit with a no-service story, but they even pinged your phone. Somehow, they know El was with you. I smell the firm TMJL asswipes in this."

"We'll head down now. We can be there by 10 am," Jake said.

"Not WE," Joyce said. "Let's keep El out of this. It will be easier. If it is the Firm TMJL, I suspect they are doing it all to rattle her. They are going at you to distract her."

"OK, we will head down now," Jake said.

"You took her to that filthy dirt floor cabin?" Joyce said. "Did you cook for her? What did you make? Tell me it was your three-cheese omelet. The one with the wild onions you pick from the side of the mountain and heirloom green peppers you grow in terra cotta pots."

"Yes," he said deadpan.

"Oh. My. God," Joyce said. "Gotta go," There was a click.

"Thanks, Joyce," he said to dead air.

She's going to masturbate before I get there.

"We have to go," Jake said.

"I know," El said. "I'll need to get my car. Emma will get here around 11 am."

"Here is the key to my apartment right above Brian's Books." Jake gave her the key. It was on its own ring with an old leather and pewter fob. "It'll all be fine."

Jake kissed the crease on her forehead, but it didn't make it fade.

"I'm sorry, Jake," El said as she laid her forehead on his chest. "I didn't mean for you to get dragged into this."

"What did I say about apologizing?" Jake smiled as she looked up at him. Her eyes looked at him differently. He wanted El back. The real Eleanore.

She let him go and obviously rallied. "You're not the boss of me!"

***

El went to pack her things, trying to stop her mind from racing.

Joyce had summarized the latest flood of legal docs from TMJL. Their tone had shifted from trying to appear to be helpful to indignant that all the responses were from a 'hick' attorney. She found that she didn't care much about the TMJL anymore. Joyce would handle that. She'd sell the brownstone. She'd be fine until she figured it all out.

It was the texts that upset her.

She started folding the MCR shirt to take along and wondered if she should just toss it into the hamper.

This time there were multiple photos, the same photo of her, sleep fucking Jake on top of him. T-shirt pushed up—his hands on her breasts.

It was an exact mirror image but with better light. In one of Jake's t-shirts, it was Sam, her back arched. Like in the other photo, the man's face was not visible.

But she could see the Rolex watch on his muscled forearm.

The texts said:

- He's a player
- He's a conman
- He took all he could from your gramma
- You're next
- And that bitch lawyer knows it
- Ask him about Brooke

There was also an image of a cashier's check from Lillian Wright made out to Jake Harris Contracting for $250,000.

There was also an image of the tax assessment of Jake's 411 acre plot.

- He scammed it from her
- He climbs into bed fast
- That watch cost $30,000
- Player
- Lies to Sam
- Lies to you
- Lies lies lies

"You good to go?" Jake called out as she heard the giant planter scraping the floor.

What is wrong with me? Why would he even be interested in me?

El remembered being the new paralegal at the firm and thinking the same thing. Realization and denial about Ryan's character should have taught her.

Images filled her mind of Jake counting down,

"Nine...."

She shook her head and went out. Jake was by the ATV with two helmets.

"Here. Put this on and avoid the tree's wrath." He held one out.

She wordlessly exchanged the gym bag for the helmet. Jake set about securing the gym bag to the front rack.

Player. Conman. Dammit.

She was glad for the full-face helmet. The visor was tinted.

The bumps on the trail seemed to be specifically designed to remind her of last night.

Player. No condoms. Convenient. Ultimate bachelor pad. Locked in... Yeah, right.

Tears were threatening. She had them blinked away by the time they reached the bottom of the trail.

Before they parked, Jake's phone was ringing. He set the helmets on a shelf. "It's Rob," he said to El. "Rob, what's up?"

El was close enough to hear, "Dude, the cops were here looking for you. Answer your fucking phone."

To El, "I gotta take this."

El took the bag and went to the truck.

Did he hide the seatbelt so I'd slide over?

Player...

She dug the lap belts out and buckled up. Jake was listening to Rob with his back to the truck.

She opened the glove compartment. There was a velvet box there. She glanced up at Jake one more time before she opened it.

It was an engagement ring, a classic huge glass door knob diamond style she hated. The same kind she had in a jewelry box back in the brownstone.

Player.

She looked at him. He held the phone in his left hand. The watch was the same.

Her phone pinged—another text.

* He's fucking your lawyer

El blocked the number.

What did you do to me?

Her phone pinged again. It was from Emma.

* Be in Covington in about an hour. Meet where?

El texted back:

* The Bakery Cafe. Need more coffee!

* I love you, but not in that happenin lesbian way. Yet!

El barked a laugh, and a tear escaped her right eye.

* You wish.

Jake finished his call and climbed in. "That was Rob. He said the sheriff showed up looking for me. But don't worry, it's not about you."

"Are you going to mention the dead guy with no shoes?" El asked.

"Should I?"

"Don't if you can. The photo of the man on the porch makes it complicated."

They drove in uncomfortable silence.

"Who is Brooke?" El asked without looking over.

"Who… told you to ask me that?" he barked at her. Anger and accusation slipped into the comment before he could stop it. She saw Jake regret his reaction. The muscles in his forearms rippled as he squeezed the wheel.

She looked over, and Jake would not look at her. He visibly seethed. He remained silent.

He drove to the Wright house in silence.

He pulled in and stopped by the carriage house. Neither of them moved for a full minute.

"You like fish fry?" Jake said in a blatant attempt to change the subject. "Alan's Alley has the best tartar sauce in the known universe. Fish fry is tonight."

Stop apologizing.

"Yes."

"After five, you won't get a table."

"OK."

She got out and walked to her car parked in the carriage house.

***

El didn't bother even going into the house. But Jake didn't wait, and he knew he was driving too fast on the dirt road.

He took a deep breath and calmed himself. Guilt flooded in where the anger left.

She couldn't have known. Fucking small towns.

Jake was breathing in through his nose and out through his mouth. Finally, he rolled his neck and was rewarded with loud cracking sounds.

By the time he drove into town, he had decided that he would have to tell El about Brooke. He needed to tell her because it was obvious someone else would.

Most of the shops were not open yet, and Jake could park right in front of the law office.

"Morning, Amy Bryant," Jake said. Amy just pointed to the inner office.

"Morning, Joyce," Jake said and began to pour himself coffee from a carafe on a tray that held three tall mugs. Her back was to him as she typed furiously on her computer.

"Jesus," Joyce said. "These assholes are serious."

"What assholes, and don't call me Jesus," Jake said before sitting. "Is this about the dead guy?"

Joyce wore a phone headset, and she stripped it off and tossed it beside her monitor, rubbing her temples.

"The sheriff will be here in ten minutes. Dead guy? What the fuck?"

"An old skeleton, in a subbasement we found. Been there for like a hundred years."

"Do not mention that. This is what you need to know." Joyce got professional. "The TMJL Firm is going hard at El. There is a part that involves you. It's that they have been playing the helpful family attorney game, representing one of their own in need. They have managed in the last week to dig up every detail about Lillian, her estate, the renovations, and your involvement."

"It's all cool. I have receipts." Jake said.

"Just shut up and listen." Joyce held up a hand to stop him. "The 411 acres is assessed at $1.4 million. She also paid you a cash lump sum of $250,000. Yet, to look at the house, little has been done. NO, Jake, just listen." She stopped him from speaking. "You have been at it for two years, and it still looks haunted. The Firm has expressed concern that you have manipulated and taken advantage of Lillian. And will do the same to El."

"That's bullshit, and you know it," Jake interrupted.

"Jake, you need to listen. They are implying you may have been responsible for her death. That she found out you were ripping her off, and you killed her. They have requested the sheriff exhume Lillian's body to test for a drug overdose."

Joyce let that sink in.

"Yes. Like Brooke," Joyce said the name with great reluctance.

Jake's jaw clenched so tight his molars creaked.

The bell tinkled at the door. They heard low voices beyond the door. Amy closed the door.

"This is all because they are going at El. They have buried me in over 9,000 pages of shit to hide something. They are trying to upset and manipulate Eleanore. This is all part of that game."

"It's working," Jake said. "She asked me about Brooke this morning. So, of course, I reacted…

badly."

"Amy, send the sheriff in," she said over the intercom.

"Mornin', Joyce, Jake," Sheriff Jimmie Hanson greeted them. Joyce and Jake stood.

"Morning, Jimmie. How's Helen?" Jake asked as he shook his hand.

"On the mend. The new knee is already better than the old one," Sheriff Hanson said. "The handrails you installed in the bathroom last summer are holding up excellent."

Joyce shook his hand and offered coffee, but he waved it off.

"How can we help you, sheriff?" Joyce asked professionally.

The sheriff started with a sigh. "A bunch of suits from DC are 'Just asking questions' and looking to start all sorts of trouble round here. I don't know why, but they're good at it. They are looking to piss on Jake's picnic. I suspect they are really tryin' to upset Ms. Wright, Lillian's granddaughter."

"How can we help, Jimmie?" Joyce asked.

"They have inferred your representation of Ms. Wright is influenced by Jake here because you have a secret physical relationship and...." Joyce was about to interrupt. "Hear me out. And you are assisting Jake to dupe the new Ms. Wright of more money."

"Jimmie, you know I loved Lily like the grandmother I never had. The renovations were all her idea. I think she just wanted someone around...."

"Jake, he has not asked a question," Joyce inserted.

"The suits also implied you were growing weed on the mountain," Jimmie said. Jake opened his mouth, but Joyce stopped him with a gesture. "It was all the glass panels you purchased. Panels typically used for large greenhouses. And all the permit says is that there is a two-room, off-grid cabin. Dirt floor. Springwater fed."

"Is there a question, sheriff?" Joyce asked.

"If I take a plane up there, will I see a greenhouse?"

"All you will see is a two-room cabin with a stone chimney. It has a glass roof. All are made from fieldstone and timber. Well, maybe one room. Dirt floors now have flagstones on dirt. There are no doors inside anymore, even to the toilet," Jake said. "Totally off-grid. Lots of windows. That needed a lot of glass."

"Here is the part that made me suspect they were up to somethin'. They brought up Brooke Powell and 2002. I'm sorry even to mention it, Jake. They got a court order to exhume Lillian even though with everything else they knew, they must have known she was cremated. And that Jake handled the arrangements."

"Jake, the mistake these people make is that they think normal people are like them," Joyce said.

"Jimmie, hear me," Jake began, and it was his turn to hold up a hand to silence Joyce. "Lillian paid me $250K in advance because that's how she did things. So if I stay on budget and plan, I might clear $50k of that for myself. For two years of work. Two years."

"You can also expect a full project and IRS audit made on behalf of Ms. Eleanore Wright," Jimmie said.

"They want Jake to blame her?" Joyce asked.

"They are 'just asking questions' that are specifically designed to cause trouble," Jimmie said. "Can we drive up there so I can have a look at your progress? Not because I don't believe you, Jake. Because I want to tell these scumbags honestly, I looked into it, and they can go fuck themselves."

"They have been trespassing up there, watching. Taking pics and trying to scare Eleanore. Photoshopping, adding ghosts and such to scare El." Joyce was shaking her head. "They had to even be in the house. It's the only way they could have known about the dead guy."

"Dead guy?" The sheriff raised an eyebrow.

Emma Arrives

Felix sat on a tombstone above a collapsed slab. Smoke rose from the grave. Smoke and screams. Felix jumped lightly down and descended into the darkness.

***

Emma pulled into Covington at about 11 AM, and El was waiting in the Bakery Cafe. The Internet was good there, and El was unsure it was a good thing. The firm was still drowning her in emails, documents, and discussions with Joyce.

A new flood of emails was from the realtor she had contacted. This realtor was hungry for the listings—the brownstone, the law office, the condo, and the warehouse. Photos to be taken for the listing, packing, and storage were overwhelming.

Joyce could still handle most of it. She just wanted out and fast. She would have to go back real soon for a bit but hated the thought. All she could think about in her racing mind was Jake. Was he what she felt he was? Or was he another Ryan or worse? Ryan wasn't after her for her money. He wanted a show wife. He lied about wanting kids to get her to marry him.

Emma entered the cafe to a hug El knew was a bit too desperate.

"You drove the smart car all the way out here?" El teased.

"Hey! It can go 65 if there's not too much wind," Emma laughed. Her tiny car was canary yellow. "Plus, it's easy to park and find in a parking lot." Emma had a tall antenna on the roof with a yellow rubber duck that sported shades and a Mohawk at the top.

The teen waitress came to their table. "Are you serving lunch yet?" Emma asked.

"Yes, ma'am." The girl slid a couple of tri-folded paper menus out of her apron. "I'll come back for your drink order." She moved off to another table that was beckoning her.

"Did she just ma'am me?" Emma was incredulous. "Did she not see my hairstyle?"

"They're just polite here. Old school polite," El said.

"You're frowning, girl," Emma said. "You are supposed to be relaxing here."

"I think I upset Jake," El said. "I had a lotta things with Jake."

"Do tell," Emma said. "About what? Give me the dirt."

El sighed. "All I did was ask him about someone named Brooke."

The waitress was back. "Brooke? Suicide Brooke?

Know what you want to drink?"

El and Emma looked at each other and then at the waitress.

"I'll have the mango ice tea," El said.

"Make it two and a side of Brooke," Emma said.

"In my high school, she is like the poster child for suicide prevention. Happened a long time ago. I don't think any kid around here has been named Brooke since."

"What happened?" Emma probed.

"No idea. I was like three years old." She moved off.

"Think it's the same one?" Emma asked.

"I have no idea either. It really pissed him off."

"So, did you jump him yet, saucy one?" Emma asked, leaning across the small table.

"Emma!" El hushed her as she blushed all the way to her chest.

"You did!" Emma said too loud. "How was it? Tell me everything."

"Shhhh…" El said. "It was… unreal."

"This is getting good."

"I came like six times," El whispered and covered her face in her hands.

"What?!" Emma said, too loud. Then whispering, "I thought you said men never could bring you to... How?"

"With his hand, his mouth, and you know," El said. "Ryan never did once, ever."

"Excellent," Emma said, stopping as the drinks were delivered.

"Ready to order, or do you need another minute?" the waitress asked.

El saw Jake's truck drive by out the window, followed by the county sheriff's patrol car.

"Another minute," Emma answered.

They opened the menus and made quick decisions.

"What's the problem?"

"He has a girlfriend. I saw them together. She's beautiful."

"So? Perfect for the rebound boy-toy," Emma said.

"This is no boy. Maybe the first man I have ever known."

"A real man would not be messing with you if he had a girlfriend," Emma said. "You're hot, El. Not demon-hot, relationship-destroying hot, not corrupt a good guy hot. But hot."

The waitress was back.

"I'll have the Buffalo chicken wrap with the fruit cup," Emma said.

"Make it two," El followed.

"I still don't see a problem. So he can make you come? Just use him as a scratching post. You are an adult. Do whatever you want," Emma declared.

***

They stayed and talked through lunch. El told her everything. The house's condition, the sleepwalking, the engagement ring, the head wound, the skylight, the shooting stars, the fire, and the dead guy. The photos to scare her, the lawyers, the secret passages. The

Cabin, the cats, even the omelet.

"Jesus, you have not even been here a whole week," Emma said.

"Six days. And don't call me Jesus," El said. As Emma laughed, Eleanore thought of Jake and his TV and movie quotes.

He was many things, but what he wasn't was a boy-toy. Ryan hated TV and movies.

Even if he was a player, he never made any promises. She had, even if she had made most moves.

Magicians had you draw the card they wanted.

"Now what?" Emma asked.

"We are supposed to meet Jake for fish fry tonight at 5 pm," El said.

"Fish-fry? Are you serious?" Emma said. "Is this Mayberry?"

"I hear the tartar sauce is good," El said. Em was skeptical.

"Ooh… Sounds like fun." Emma said sarcastically. "Did I mention I have a half a gallon of Tequila that needs drinking?"

"Get your stuff. Wanna look at his apartment? He gave me the keys." El held up the key?

"Check, please!" Emma said instantly and too loud.

***

They paid the check and got Emma's carry-on bag from the smart car. El waved at Brian through the window as they walked by. Up the stairs and unlocking the door, they were in. The apartment was a modern industrial-style loft—a large great room was in the front.

The living room in the front had low bookcases that went all across beneath the front windows, making window seats on either side of a modern gas fireplace in the center. The kitchen in the center was C-shaped and shared its back wall with the bathroom. Only three stools were at the counter. Because it was an end unit, there was a window over the sink and a view of the diner down the hill that was like a Norman Rockwell painting. There was no dining table.

Past the kitchen was the bedroom. There was no door to the bedroom, but there was one to the bath on the right and one to the walk-in closet past the bathroom.

It was reminiscent of the layout at The Cabin but smaller.

El noticed that the queen bed was an early version of The Cabin's floating platform bed. It was not as big and had a thick, live edge, wood headboard. The bed was not made.

"It smells like sex in here. Are you trying to arouse me, El?" Emma turned on the bathroom light. "Jake uses a lot of hair products." The bench in the large shower had about 20 various bottles of shampoo, conditioner, body washes, and lotions. "He must really like his Honey Butter."

El told Emma about the photo. It had to be taken from a roof across the street. El showed it to her.

"Wow. Great rack," Emma said. "How do you know it's him?"

"The watch. The arm. They don't make many like that."

"The arm or the watch?"

"Plus, the date/time stamp fit. I don't know. It's not my business, really." El picked up one of his pillows and gave it a mighty sniff. "It's his."

"Who puts a full-size, stackable washer and dryer inside the big walk-in closet? That's brilliant!" Em said, snooping in the closet.

El started to unmake the bed. All the sheets, pillowcases, and towels went into the washer. Next to the washer and dryer, the shelves were neatly organized linens.

El made the bed with fresh sheets and pillowcases as Emma snooped.

"El, there's a tall wall safe in here behind his dress shirts," Emma called from his closet. "Are you sure he's not gay? I have never seen a closet this organized owned by a straight guy."

Emma came out and started going through his dresser drawers. "So much fun! How did you talk the keys out of him?" Emma said as she held up a YES t-shirt. "He's got a lot of t-shirts."

"Emma!" Eleanore called as Emma was checking out his boxers and socks.

"What's with the funky socks?" Emma held up a mostly matched pair of Solmate Socks. "He has to be gay."

"He is so not gay, Emma. Trust me," El said as she finished making the bed.

"Let me check his spice rack." Emma ran to the kitchen.

El could hear cabinets opening and closing.

"Holy shit…" El heard from the kitchen.

El walked around the corner, and Emma had slid a custom-made spice rack out from behind the far side of the fridge that had everything.

"I told you he was a great cook," El said. "He also built this loft. A total gut and custom-built."

"Do you know how much a knife set like this costs?" Emma said. "Sorry, El. I call dibs on Jake."

The expensive knives…

El shook her head to shake off the thoughts.

"Alexa. Good afternoon," El said, and the lighting changed. The Alan Parsons Project began to play "Try Anything Once."

"Alexa. Turn fireplace on," Emma said.

WOOF. The gas fireplace lit. And the lazy modern ceiling fan began to turn above.

"It's August, Emma," El said. "It's also 2 pm."

"Alexa, turn the fireplace off," Emma said. It went off. "It's magic."

Emma and El flopped onto the big L-shaped sectional sofa.

Both sidewalls of the room were floor-to-ceiling bookshelves that were full.

"When's the last time you read a real book? One made out of dead trees?" Emma asked as she looked at what had to be thousands of books.

"Last week, I read *Wings of Fire* by Stephanie Mirro.

What about you?" El said.

"*Turn of the Screw*. Well, the Cliff Notes for it, anyway. In 2001 right after 9/11. It was my only book report that ever got an A. I'm sure Mrs. Lang never read it. Everyone got As for that semester."

"You haven't read a book since high school?" El asked.

"Nope. I'll just see the movie," Emma said. "Did you know there was a movie of *Turn of the Screw*? I saw it like five years ago. Scared the shit out of me. You think he's read all these?"

"I don't know. Probably yes. Brian downstairs is now my spy. He says Jake is a big book buyer," El added.

"Oh my God. I just noticed there's no TV. Is he a psycho?" Emma looked around.

"Alexa, turn TV on," El said aloud, and the blinds closed in all the front windows. A screen began to deploy from behind the valence above the front windows. A high def projector is activated on a shelf in the kitchen. It was on the Netflix main menu.

"Who is this guy?" Emma said incredulously as she found the remote in a wooden tray. "He didn't make the bed?"

Wait… he always makes his bed…

The House is Open

Felix waited in the darkness. The screams were getting louder…

***

Jake and the sheriff drove up to the Rectory to find the front door wide open and Rob nowhere to be found. He gave Jimmie the full tour starting on the third floor and working down to the basement.

Jake explained the new roofing installed on the house, the outbuildings, the new floor in the basement, and foundation work, all of which were prerequisites for the cosmetic work. So why bother doing. drywall or painting if the roof leaks or the foundation fails?

The freshly cleaned rooms showed brightly in the midday light.

Armed with powerful flashlights, they descended into the sub-basement from the room they called the Root Cellar.

The smoke was worse when they got to the body.

"The smoke is from a fire still burning in the ice well. A tree was struck by lightning. Also, I think the guys from TMJL were even down here," Jake said, showing Jimmie the photo of the barefoot man on the porch. "They had to be. And did that just to scare Eleanore."

"Well, Jake. This body ain't a crime scene. It's an archaeological dig. I'd bet that guy is over a hundred years dead and been there the whole time," Jimmie said. "Where's that tunnel go?"

Jimmie shined his Mag light directly opposite the skeletal remains. Most of the smoke was drawn out in that direction.

Glowing eyes reflected in his beam. Felix sat still as a statue in the tunnel. Then, slowly he turned and retreated into the darkness.

"It looks like that body came from in there," Jimmie said and proceeded into the narrow tunnel without waiting for Jake. The tunnel went straight uphill for about fifty or sixty yards. Rough timbers held up some sections of the dry, narrow tunnel. Other sections were solid walls of roots or natural stone.

They found what looked like a window to the left side. Jake and the Sheriff didn't know what they were seeing at first.

This is the inside of an empty coffin. Someone cut into the end and…

Jake shined his light down.

They were standing on old bones and rotted cloth in the dust and dirt. Going in further, the story was the same. Old bones, empty coffins.

After about the tenth coffin, Felix waited there on the shelf. He followed the smoke out. Just beyond, the tunnel was blocked. The lower half of a statue had caved in from above. A carved skeletal hand on the figure revealed it to be a grim reaper.

"How far into the cemetery are we?" Jimmie asked.

"I have no idea. But, if we go out and look for the smoke, we'll know." Jake said.

"These graves were robbed long ago," Jimmie said. "A long time ago, and not all at once."

***

They made their way back out and up. Jake took the sheriff down the newly mowed path to the ice well.

"You can see where that old oak got struck by lightning. It fell right into the ice well. Been burning ever since," Jake said. "We were tossing brush and debris in there until it started a cave in below. That's when we started getting smoke in the house."

The sheriff was now looking into the cemetery. They noticed a bit of smoke rising about off to the left, sixty yards down the newly mowed path.

"Jake, this ain't got nothin' to do with Eleanore Wright or those suits from DC, but I am curious," Jimmie said as they both began to walk through the now open gate into the overgrown cemetery.

"These suits worry me, Jimmie," Jake said as they walked. "I'd bet money we're being watched even now. I'm getting an itch I haven't had since Iraq."

Finally, they paused at a monument that was missing its head.

"Now that's creepy." The sheriff said. Brushing the tall grass aside, the base was inscribed Saint Denis of Paris.

"All the missing heads have been gone as long as I can remember," Jake said, pointing to the spot where the smoke was emerging. "The one we saw in the tunnel must be just beyond."

The smoke rose from the burial vault, and the lid was fractured. The heavy stone lid had fallen into the vault box, crushing the empty plain pine coffin below. Just beyond, the headless shoulders of the grim reaper were barely visible in the weeds.

"It looks like the heavy point of that statue's scythe came down hard on that lid," Jake said, and Jimmie aimed his light into the hole. "Rain has been eroding the opening since."

Felix climbed out of the darkness and up the ramp made by the lid to jump in a single leap to the cross that marked the grave.

"So that's how you been getting in the house, buddy." Jake scratched that cat's ear. "I bet you could fit down there, sheriff."

"I ain't going down there," he replied. "I thought this place was haunted before. Damn, Jake. Now it's even worse. Please don't let Ed know about this."

****

Eyes followed Jake and the sheriff as they returned

to the house the way they had come. The ruins of the old bell tower were the perfect vantage point to watch through binoculars. The flooded basement below was like a moat on three sides. The stone of the tower walls survived the fire from decades ago. But even the ascending stairs were gone.

Vines had made the first climb easier but dangerous. A rope tied to the toppled bell fixed that.

He began setting up his tripod and long lens. The master bedroom window and bed had the perfect line of sight from there. Even the mirror above the headboard would be visible.

He aimed the camera, found the right window, and zoomed in. When he focused on it, a man was standing in the window. His eyes seemed to burn like fire from within. Eyes that looked directly into his lens.

No one heard the scream as he fell backward over the edge, bashing his head on the way down. His tactical vest weighed him down like an anchor made of stone.

The screen on the back of his camera displayed the final photo. It looked like black steam around burning eyes.

***

Emma and El got to the bowling alley at 4:45 and managed to snag the last table available. The place was getting packed and was filled with the sound of bowling. This was combined with the band Whitesnake on the sound system and the laughter of happy people.

Half a dozen young waitresses circulated, all wearing Alan's Alley t-shirts. Happy hour was between 4 pm and 6 pm with $5 pitchers of Miller Light, and almost every table held a pitcher or two.

El saw Joyce Jacobs enter the crowd and waved at her to come over. She weaved through the crowd, gladly took off her suit jacket, and draped it over the back of the tall stool before she climbed up.

"Joyce, this is my friend, Emma," El said, and they shook over the table.

"El's my best friend. So don't get any ideas. I'll fight you!" Emma said, smiling.

Before Joyce could reply, the waitress was there with bourbon in a cut crystal tumbler and another empty frosted mug.

"Hey! How do I get that kind of love?" Emma clowned to the waitress, looking closely at the bourbon glass.

"Emma, this is your new best friend, Ashley," Joyce said. "The best waitress in Covington. Ashley, this is Emma and the famous Eleanore Wright. Don't fuck with her, or she'll turn you into a newt."

"Ashley, ol' pal, ol' buddy, please bring me one of those. It looks like a triple: fancy glass and all. Please, O Queen of waitresses. Friend of the rich and powerful!"

"And for you, Ms. Wright?" Ashely was clearly and highly amused.

"Beer is just fine for me, and please call me El."

"You want to order food now or wait?"

"Three fish-fry specials and extra tartar sauce. And all of this goes on my tab, Ash. Thanks." Joyce said.

"Sorry, El," Emma said as she topped off all three mugs from the pitcher. "Joyce is now officially my BFF."

Ashley was back with the bourbon for Emma. "Sorry, Joyce. Someone beat you to buying Emma this round." Ashley looked over her shoulder, and Alex raised a glass from across the room.

"That's Ace-Hardware-Alex. I told you about him," El said.

"I don't think he knows how much that glass of bourbon costs that he just bought you," Joyce laughed.

"You dudes mind if I invite him over? I love thick full beards." Emma lowered her voice. They both nodded.

"Please, invite him over, Ash," Joyce said.

They watched Ashley speak to Alex, and they could see him blush from across the room. He casually wandered over.

"Hi, Joyce, El." He held out his hand to Emma, "I'm Alex."

"Alex, this is my friend Emma," Emma shook his hand and raised the glass in a toasting gesture.

"Thank you," Emma said, not letting go of his hand until they both sipped their drinks. "Oh my God, that's good."

"Hell of a way to buy the last open seat in the house, man. Well played." Joyce said as Alex sat.

"So you're Ace-Hardware-Alex," Emma said in a different tone from before, "El tells me you used to race in the cemetery with her back in the day."

"That is true. It's odd that you mention that. I was just thinking about it today." Alex said.

"Oh, why's that?" El asked and sipped her beer.

"I was talking to Rob. He told me he had just mowed the old cemetery road," Alex said.

"Oh really…" Emma was waggling her eyebrows as their food arrived.

"Don't get any bright ideas, you," Eleanore chastized Em.

"What?" Em said, still repeatedly raising an eyebrow at Alex conspiratorially.

***

Jake and Sheriff Hanson headed back up the newly mowed path toward the gate and ice well. Another crunching collapse sounded from the pit as they approached, and a cloud of sparks rose.

As they got to the stone edge and looked in, Jimmie asked, "What's the plan for this once the fires out? It's still wicked dangerous."

"We are planning to cap it at least. Maybe a picnic shelter even, if the budget is there and El wants it."

The sheriff went over to the ruins of the church. "What about this?" The foundation wall was only three feet high at that point. "Why did it fill with water?"

The foundation walls were thick. The black water below was actually crystal clear. It was the charred walls all around that were black.

"They had a cistern in the basement that was spring

fed. A hand pump above brought water up into the church. If it weren't for the basement window over there, this would probably be full up to here. And we could use it for a pool," Jake joked. His tone became serious then. "Lillian thought there would be time to discuss it later."

***

Felix watched them from the opposite wall. His black fur in the shade against the charred ruins hid him well. What Felix saw evaded them. The water that flowed out the small window in the basement wall had stopped. The small pool and stream below would be dry before long. It had been his colony's primary source of water for many lifetimes.

And Felix knew why…

***

Giving Jimmie the tour had made Jake feel good about how far the project had come and focused on the remaining items. He was looking forward to seeing Eleanore and figuring it out together.

Jake pulled into Ed's Texaco for his usual Friday fill up. Olivia was just pulling in from the opposite direction in her 1974 Vega station wagon. Jake knew she loved that car and was proud of being able to drive a stick. Ed kept it running and in beautiful shape.

He didn't even have to tell Ed what he wanted.

"Vega is looking good, Ed," Jake said as Olivia handed a brown paper bag to Hector and then left another on top of the gas pump for Ed. Then, waving, she took her bag inside.

"Thanks, Jake," he replied as he started the fuel and moved to check the oil. "Saw Jimmie go by four times today. Havin trouble with commies up there? Or are all them black SUVs deep state?"

"Those men in black, you mean?" Jake asked, looking at Hector, smiling. "I can't remember. But that fish fry sure smells good."

The closest garage bay was rolling up to reveal Olivia sitting at a patio table with three drinks on the table with her own fish fry bag. A broom handle was set where an umbrella would typically go. Instead, it held a roll of paper towels. Hector joined her with a 2 liter Mountain Dew.

"You feelin ok today, Jake?" Ed asked as he closed the hood. "Lots of chemtrails today, and I know they settle up there first."

The blue sky was crisscrossed with vapor trails from jets passing overhead.

"Feelin' fine, Ed," Jake replied. His mouth was watering at the smell, like a Pavlovian dog. "Hey, can you text me when you see those black SUVs again? Those jerks are bothering Miss Wright."

"Sure can. That includes the jerk on the black motorcycle?"

"Yes, please," Jake said. "Happy Friday, y'all!" Jake waved to them as he pulled away. They waved back with mouths full, as Ed complained about them not waiting.

***

El had been watching the door as she talked with Joyce. Emma was now taking turns talking into Alex's ear, encouraging him to speak into hers as well. It was one of her classic ploys. Light perfume only behind her ears.

Alex was doomed.

It looks like she might have Jake's place all to herself tonight.

Joyce was constantly texting on her phone while she kept up her side of the conversation.

"Yeah, Alan's parents purchased the lanes in the early '70s when Alan was not even a year old. So they named the Alley after him." The history amused Joyce. "He wore it like a badge of honor as a kid. He was very popular because of it, back before computer games. So his parents let him and his friends bowl for free. He even started an eight-team, Saturday after lunch league of kids. Four of those teams still play in the adult leagues now."

El saw Ashley then, moving through the dense crowd toward them. Instead of carrying their food, she was carrying another stool. It was one of the backless bar stools. She set the seat between El and Emma. Emma didn't even notice.

In El's ear, Ashley said, "Jake called. ETA 2 minutes. He knows where you are sitting."

"Thanks, Ash," El said while she was close.

"I already have Jake's order as well," Ashley said to her ear. "And Jake said it's his turn to buy dinner."

He must not be mad anymore.

Thinking of the likelihood of his apartment being

empty tonight, she poured herself another beer from the fresh pitcher Ash delivered. A minute later, she saw him enter. He was a head taller than most of the crowd.

His face could not hide how angry he was as he moved through the crowd.

Joyce had stopped talking and had focused intently on her phone at some point.

When he got to the table, he barely acknowledged her and began a conversation close to Joyce's ear. Then, when Ashely returned to the table with a frosted mug, Jake drew her in close for another long chat that made Ash uncomfortable.

Jake has her direct number so he can tell her his ETA?

Joyce was now deep into texting as he came around to his stool and poured a beer for himself.

"Hey, what's going on?" El asked with a bit of confusion, slipping past her forced smile.

Jake finally leaned into her ear as he brought up his phone in front of her. It was a chat session with Joyce.

"There is a black Escalade in the parking lot." It was all in the text message, including a Washington DC plate number photo. Joyce is chatting with the sheriff right now. "Ashely is looking for them in here. She knows everyone in town. So they will be easy to find."

Like a magic ninja-waitress, Ash returned carrying five platters through the crowd. As she was setting them down in front of everyone, Jake was topping off everyone's beer mugs as she brightly said, "At the bar, all the way to the left by the hall to the restrooms."

A man sat at the bar with his back to them. He was eating the fish-fry like everyone else, except that man was like no one else in the bar. He wore black jeans and a tropical shirt that, in one glance, was dark green palm leaves on black. It was almost camouflage. It was loose, but he could not hide his ripped muscles.

"When he pays, I'll take a photo of his credit card for you."

I have had enough of this shit.

El was on her feet, moving toward the man before Jake could stop her.

He saw her coming.

He's been watching us the whole time in the mirror.

The man had pulled a money clip out of his pocket, and he dropped a hundred-dollar bill onto the bar. When he turned toward El, he didn't expect the hard push she delivered. Instead, his head slammed into a Budweiser mirror on the wall, and it broke and fell.

The bar got quiet, but Eleanore got even softer. "You tell Thompson, if he wants a deal, I never want to see another one of you asswipes on this side of the Blue Ridge."

He just glared into her eyes.

She got closer, louder. "You got that?"

El was almost as tall as the man. She was so mad it was all she could do to control herself.

El heard a cellphone picture being taken as Joyce spoke. "Let him go, Eleanore. Alan would be distraught if you made a mess of him in here. Like last time…"

That humor was precisely what El needed to hear.

She turned away from him to a now quiet, staring crowd that was suddenly trying to look busy.

El's brain was catching up. Joyce would use it to leverage the negotiations. She got back to the table as the noise began to rise again. Through the windows, she could see the flashing lights of a police car out of view.

She got back to the table and said, "What?" She sat down and grabbed her full beer mug, and took a long pull.

"This tartar sauce is amazing," Emma said. "Careful, though. This shit's temp is hot!"

Emma was right. Best fish fry ever.

***

Four hours later, Eric Richardson was found dead. His Escalade was in a single-vehicle accident on northbound I-81. There were no witnesses. Mr. Richardson had not been wearing his seatbelt.

Two of the responding EMTs had had dinner that night at Alan's Alley. The whispers of witchcraft grew faster after that.

Pie and Coffee and Dreams

Felix watched from the roof across the street from where his favorite human lived.

***

The music got louder as the evening progressed. The playlist featured Molly Hatchet heavily. The Friday night bowling leagues began, and Joyce was the first to leave. Emma and Alex decided to "Go for a walk."

Emma gave Eleanore the 'don't wait up for me' sign and followed Alex out.

"Don't worry, Alex will treat her right," Jake said as he waved off Ash and another pitcher of beer.

"It's Alex I'm worried about," El said.

"You've been nursing that beer a long time." Then Jake said, "Can I interest you in some dessert? Maybe pie and coffee at Mike's?"

"Sure. We just need the check," El said.

"It's already taken care of," Jake said as he stood and carried his stool back to the bar.

Ash waved from where she was delivering long neck beers to the league bowlers. That entire team wore yellow bowling shirts that said MEDINA SOD on the back.

"Were you in Alan's bowling league back in the day?" El asked as they strolled along with the lengthening shadows.

"Wow. You heard about that?" Jake said with a smile that was somehow shy. "It's memories like that… that keep me here. You know he still has a Saturday Afternoon League that's free for kids."

"Does Alan have any children that are in the league?"

"No… not yet anyway," Jake said.

They walked in silence for a while. The diner wasn't far. It was about half full as they sat in the booth at the end. El intentionally took the far seat so she could see into the diner.

The tall black waitress who made her classic uniform seem stylish came up and set two paper placemats on the table and silverware bound in paper napkins. "Hey, Jake. How you doin'?" she asked with a wide smile and a questioning look at El.

"Sandy, this is Eleanore Wright," Jake introduced them. The waitress wiped her hands on her apron before offering to shake.

"I heard you are the math whiz." Sandy looked over her shoulder at the whiteboard. "Took him forever to devise that new evil thing. Want to give it a shot before you order?”

“We’re just getting pie and coffee, Sandy,” Jake said. “What’s the best pie today?”

“Crumble top peach,” she replied without hesitation. “Warm with vanilla ice cream.”

They both nodded approval.

As soon as Sandy turned away, El fished a new purple crayon from the napkin holder and turned over her placemat. She copied down the problem from the whiteboard, and before Sandy returned with the coffee, she wrote X=11705 in large letters.

Sandy set down the two coffees with a broad smile as El held up the placemat.

“Would you please give this to Mike tomorrow?” El said, “That was a good one!”

“He’s gonna have a stroke!” Sandy laughed, walking away.

“I always thought I was good at math. I haven’t been able to solve Mike’s problems for years,” Jake said. “I swear he makes up half the symbols.”

“I was a tutor for differential calculus for years,” El said, then sipped her coffee, “In calculus, the differential represents the principal part of the change in a function concerning changes in the independent variable….” She faded and stared into space.

“What are you thinking about?” Jake asked. “I can see the wheels turning.”

“Jake, what if it’s not the jerks from Thompson and Associates?” El said as she stared at the equation.

"What if the Rectory IS haunted? I mean, really haunted."

"El, when the sheriff and I were at your house, we discovered something." He sipped his coffee, clearly gathering his thoughts. "Someone was robbing graves. It kinda looks like the dead guy in the tunnel was the last victim before it stopped. They even stole his shoes. I think I may know who he is." Jake was hesitant.

"Who?"

"I think it's Everett Wright. Your great-grandfather," Jake said. "He died suddenly in the winter of 1945. He had been badly wounded on D-Day. Got a hero's welcome back to Covington. A few months later, he was found dead in the cemetery. He was a member of that church. The monument that's fallen over is his."

"How do you know all this?" El asked as Sandy returned with their pie and ice cream.

"Brian, bookstore Brian," Jake said. "He has this wall of Covington history. He is constantly on the lookout for interesting stuff. He showed me."

"What did he show you?"

Jake drew out his phone. After searching for a minute, he found a photo. It was a framed newspaper article.

El knew instantly which man it was. He was wearing the same suit.

"Something wrong with the pie?" Sandy startled Eleanore. She looked at the plate where her ice cream was melting.

"Not at all," El replied, lifting her fork as Sandy warmed up their coffee.

"We got distracted," Jake said and took a big bite.

"Wow. This is great," El added.

"Mike's wife Peggy makes them fresh every day," Sandy said. "After these two, there's only one slice left," she said, walking away. "Might have that one myself."

"Two months later, the church burned down. The minister and 17 people with it," Jake continued, not missing a beat.

El took a bite. It was delicious. She was beginning to enjoy the conversation as much as the pie.

"What if the minister discovered that someone was robbing the graves and called the congregation together to discuss what to do?" El speculated. "What if they were locked in and the church was set on fire… murdered?"

They ate in silence for a while. The pie disappeared quickly. Not a crumb remained on either plate.

"I saw your apartment today," El said awkwardly as she set down her fork on the empty plate and lifted the mug.

"What did you think?" Jake did the same.

"It's great. Very well done. Great bachelor pad," she said. "The laundry in the closet is a great idea. The layout is perfect. Did you build that bed before or after the bed at The Cabin?"

"Before," he answered.

"I even figured out the smart home stuff. The fireplace, even the TV," she said.

Jake looked at his watch. His Rolex. It was 10:35 pm.

"What are you doing tomorrow? For the house, I mean," El asked.

Ask him to spend the night. What's the problem? It's his place.

"Rob and I will finish up the hall bath and laundry plumbing. Then it's drywall, plaster repairs, and paint. One room at a time. Last will be the floors and trim."

"Want to give me the guided tour of your apartment?" El asked after screwing up the courage.

"Sure. I'll also give you that framed photo of your great-grandfather," Jake said.

El paid for the pie and coffee. She'd collect her free meal the next time.

***

The lights were already in night mode when they got to the apartment.

"The smart home knows when it's sunset. So it sets the lights accordingly." Jake took the framed newspaper article off one of the bookcases and handed it to her.

Everett Wright. He is even wearing the same suit.

Jake opened the wine and closed the front blinds. They turned on the TV and fell asleep watching *Barnwood Builders* with the volume low after half a glass of wine.

Jake woke at 12:35 am to find El soundly sleeping with her head in his lap.

"Alexa, turn all off," he said softly. The apartment went dark and quiet except for the nightlights. He was asleep soon after. Neither of them heard Emma and Alex stumble in.

***

Jake was startled awake to the sounds of screaming from the bedroom. Eleanore was gone. He had no idea how he got to his feet so fast. He was in the bedroom in an instant.

The first thing Jake saw was the glinting reflective profile of his best butcher knife rising. He clamped a hand on the wrist that held it.

Eleanore spun to face him, but somehow it wasn't Eleanore. Instead, her eyes were glowing like fire, and she was stronger than he believed possible.

The knife still came down, missing his face but finding his shoulder to slide down the side of his bicep to his elbow.

"Alexa, lights!"

Eleanore's mouth was as wide as if she was about to bite his face. Jake had a handful of her hair at the back of her head as they struggled and stumbled about. His grip had directed her face toward the wall mirror in the bathroom. The fire immediately extinguished in her eyes as she blinked awake.

As gently as he could muster, Jake said, "El, please wake up. I need you to give me the knife."

"What? Jake? Please stop… You're hurting me…"

Jake let go of her hair and took the knife from her hand.

"What the fuck is happening?" Alex said from the bedroom. It had been Alex screaming.

"Alex, get dressed. Wake Emma up." Jake was applying direct pressure with a bath towel to his arm. "You're driving me."

"Jake, what's happening?" El had her face in her hands.

"Emma will stay here with you. But you need to stay awake until I get back."

"Jake…" she sobbed. "I'm so sorry…"

Emma came into the bathroom. "What did you do?" she demanded from Jake.

Alex replied. "He just saved your life, Emma. That's what he did."

Jake made the mistake of lifting the towel for a look.

"Emma, listen. She was sleepwalking again. Make some coffee. Keep her awake until I get back. Can you do that?"

"Yes. Go. She told me about it." Emma sounded sober and awake.

"You sure you're OK?" Alex asked Emma.

"Oh, hey, Alex. Yeah," she said in a flirty tone, followed by, "GO!" like a drill sergeant.

***

"We'll take mine," Jake said to Alex, tossing him the keys and going back to applying direct pressure.

"It will take 30 minutes to get to the ER in Front Royal," Alex said. "And by then… What the fuck just happened?"

"We're not going to the ER. Head over to Rob's on River Road," Jake said in a tone not to be questioned.

Jake worked his phone out of his pocket and said, "Hey, Siri, call Rob Jensen, mobile, on speaker."

Rob answered on the second ring. "Better be good, man. It's 2:35 am."

"I need stitches. A lot of them. Have your trauma kit ready. Maybe put a shower curtain down like that time in Basrah."

"Oh shit. ETA?"

"Four minutes. Turning onto River Road now. I'll need to borrow a shirt when you're done," Jake said in a forced, calm voice.

"What the hell is Rob going to do?" Alex asked.

"He was a combat medic in Iraq. This is nothing compared to that. Why didn't you take Emma back to your place?"

"We went and played pool at the Covington Hotel. She got super hammered doing shots. Your place was closer, and she had a key. A good thing she passed out as soon as we got inside. Weirdest night in forever. Something made me wake up. El was standing at the foot of the bed, and I saw her eyes. Eyes like fire. I didn't even see the knife until YOU were there."

"Alex. You are not to mention this to a soul. You got that?" Jake winced as the road became bumpy. "Not a soul unless you want the town to know you scream like a little girl."

Alex looked over at Jake, who was smiling.

"Ok, ok, ok." They pulled into Rob's driveway. The lights were on in his kitchen.

"Just leave the keys in it," Jake said as he slid out.

Rob was holding open the screen door by the time he got there. Jake dropped the towel in the newly mulched bed. "Alex, you got a knife? Good. Cut the rest of this t-shirt off him here."

Alex's pocket knife was sharp, and he easily cut from the shirt's neck hole to the top of the sleeve that was already cut. Jake pulled the shirt off over his head and wiped the excess blood off before adding his shirt to the towel beside the steps.

Rob already had a large tackle box open on the kitchen table. A freshly torn-down shower curtain was on the floor under a chair.

Before sitting, Jake showed him the cut.

"Bah. Nothin'. Rub a little dirt on it," Rob said as Jake sat and dripped on the shower curtain. "Alex, there must be a story here, but first, you are on coffee duty." He gestured over his shoulder.

Rob put on a pair of glasses with no lenses but two lamps like headlights. Finally, he pulled on surgical gloves. After a quick exam, he said, "Sorry, bro. Gotta do stitches here in the middle. Gonna suck. No local."

"Just do it," Jake said as he thumbed his phone.

"Okay…" He started cleaning the wound.

"Jake?" El answered.

"This is me not asking because we have a deal." He smiled so she could hear it.

"Oh, Jake. What's wrong with me?" she said quietly.

"I think I figured out why there were so many mirrors," Jake said calmly. "It stops whatever it is… And Lillian must have known.…"

"The mirrors in the house?" Eleanore said. "I'm not in the house. How can this… follow me."

"We'll figure this out," Jake said.

Yawning and rubbing her eyes, Sam walked into the kitchen saying, "What's going on, Baby?" and then she froze at the sight of Jake and all the blood. She was only wearing one of Rob's white tank tops.

"I have to go. I'll be back soon," Jake said and hung up.

"Morning, Sam," Alex said as he raised his cup in salute. "Coffee?"

She pulled the shirt down in front a bit, holding it for modesty, making the top tighter. And more distracting for Alex.

"Jake got a scratch, and I'm fixing him up. Just like the old days."

Sam backed out and disappeared.

"Aren't you even going to ask what happened?" Alex asked as he set down two mugs of coffee for them. Jake took one right away as Rob worked.

"No," Rob answered. "If I needed to know, he'd tell me."

Sam returned wearing a pair of Rob's boxers and a light robe that remained open in front.

"Here is a piece of advice, Alex, just for you, whatever happened, one thing is for sure," Rob said.

"You have a chance to show how discreet you can be. Are you a stand-up guy, or just a gossip?"

"You can't be left alone for a minute, can you, Jake?" Sam said as she poured herself coffee and watched as Rob worked.

Eventually, Rob said, "That's it. Only 44 stitches. I'm going to add a quick clot dressing and bandage this up." Rob turned to Sam. "Babe, could you bring out one of my long-sleeved shirts, the one you like the least?"

Sam sauntered out, leaving Alex shaking his head.

***

On the phone, Eleanor heard a voice she recognized in the background, "What's going on, Baby?"

It was Sam.

"I have to go. I'll be back soon," Jake said and hung up.

El just stared at the phone.

"Come on, Emma. Get your stuff," Eleanore said. "We're going to my place. We can make breakfast."

"To be honest, I'm still drunk, so you'll have to drive," Emma said as she grabbed her duffle bag.

Fire and Water and Mirrors

Felix stood vigil on Kilroy's Rock. The car passed on the road revealing only his eyes. Tonight was the night. Eighteen sets of eyes glowed in the cemetery. They all knew this was the night…

***

Emma fell asleep in the passenger seat almost immediately. Eleanore's racing mind was more effective than coffee.

"What's going on, Baby?" Why did he go and see her?

The dirt road felt bumpier than ever like it was trying to stop her from getting to the house.

How could Emma sleep through this?

It happened when she looked over at Emma. A savage pothole almost tore her front wheel off, causing a blowout in both driver-side tires. Almost losing control, the car slid to a stop in a cloud of dust from

277

the dirt road. Her headlights shined down the tunnel of low branches.

Emma began to stir.

"El, are we there?" she asked sleepily.

Eleanore got out to see what she already knew. "Shit. Two flats and no flashlights."

"What?" Em was waking.

"Grab your bag. We're walking." El had her cell phone out, confirming she had no signal. However, she did use its flashlight to see that both her tires were flat and the rims were bent.

"Call Jake." Emma got out of the car. "He'll rescue us."

"Does your phone have a signal?" El asked.

"Fuck," Emma cursed. "No signal, no power, phones completely dead." Emma grabbed her bag and slammed the door.

"I'll leave the car running with the headlights and flashers on. That should light most of our way to the house. It has most of a tank of gas. It should keep running. We can call Ed's Texaco in the morning."

They started walking. The headlights provided enough light to avoid the potholes as they walked. The forest quickly swallowed the sound of the engine the farther they went.

"You walk like you're sober," El teased in a vain attempt to lighten the mood. "Damn, we left both doors open."

"Practice, O-pal-of-mine. Practice," she slurred.

The sound of the distant engine stopped.

The hush that descended felt oppressive as they turned to look simultaneously.

The flashers stopped.

Then the headlights turned off.

One of the car doors slammed like a gunshot in the silence.

They ran.

***

The moon was bright, but the trees' canopy allowed only small beams of its light through.

Emma fell. She opened her duffle bag and began rooting through it as El helped her up.

She discarded the duffle, and its contents went flying after finding what she wanted.

El turned on her phone's flashlight and took Emma's left hand. Emma's right hand held a small can of pepper spray.

They ran.

They got to the gate with the number 137 embedded in the brick column, and she turned off the light. El dragged Emma behind the pillar, between the short wall and the overgrown shrubs, whispering, "We have to be quiet. I think it's the Firm."

After thirty seconds, they managed to silence their breathing mostly. At the same time that they heard the jogging footsteps in the gravel, they noticed the towering flames in the distance on the other side of the road, across the vast lawn. El could even hear the fire.

He jogged past the gate and stopped only ten yards away from where they hid in the shadows.

It was Thompson himself, the Firm's chief asshole. El could see his profile, his white hair with the expensive cut. Even though it was a warm August night, he wore a black turtleneck, black jeans, and even gloves.

Is that a gun in his hand?

El saw motion beyond. A figure moved, briefly silhouetted by the fire in the ice well. The flames were more significant than ever, now above the edge. Thompson saw it, too. He moved to follow it.

After he was fifty yards away, Emma whispered, "What the hell is happening?"

"I don't know. But I know where we can hide until morning."

***

The real pain of Jake's injury was settling in: a dull ache that became sharp pain if anything touched it. Rob's ugly old white and yellow flannel shirt was too big for him, making it perfect. He still didn't know what he would say to El when he saw her. But he did know he'd play it down like nothing.

Jake followed Alex up the stairs to his apartment over the bookstore. They found the doors locked, lights off, and the apartment empty.

Jake tried calling Eleanore on her cell phone and got the standard out-of-service-area message that told him she went to the house.

He tried the number at the house next. No answer. He didn't leave a message.

"No answer. They must still be on the way."

"Jake, you should drink a lot of fluids and rest. You probably should also go get a tetanus shot tomorrow. Doc McCloud can do that. Have him take a quick look at the arm. You're all stitches and superglue, man."

"Thanks for your help, Alex," Jake said, moving toward the bedroom. "I'll call you tomorrow."

"Don't worry, Jake," Alex said as he opened the door to leave. "Not a word to anyone."

That is not what I am worried about.

Jake managed to untie his boots with one hand. He toed out of them and emptied his pockets on the bathroom counter. Then, going back to the closet, Jake took off the bloody jeans. He left them in the washer. He pulled on another pair of jeans and winced as he buttoned them up.

He consumed several Motrin tablets from the medicine cabinet and retrieved his wallet, keys, phone, and pocket knife. He looked at his watch, trying to decide what to do.

It was bloody.

Rinsing it under the faucet, he decided what to do.

He slid his left hand into his jeans pocket and looked at himself in the mirror.

The mirror he had forced her to look into.

Jake, you're hurting me.

He left the apartment, leaving all the lights on.

***

"Where are we going?" Emma whispered.

"The carriage house." They were walking in the freshly mowed grass to the right of the lane. It hushed their footsteps. The flames in the ice well had now completely engulfed the tree that had fallen into it.

They paused behind a massive oak beside the lane. They could see the form of Thompson moving toward the cemetery gate.

Emma gasped and slapped her hand over her mouth. She pointed, and Eleanor saw the dozens of glowing eyes moving toward them up the lane. The eyes disappeared one set at a time until Eleanore realized it was dozens of black cats turning to follow Thompson.

El dragged Emma away from the tree toward the house. Eleanore didn't cross the lane when they came even with the porch. Instead, she led them through the shadows to the carriage house. A single bare bulb illuminated the vast room. She dragged Emma to the stairs. Passing the workbench, she grabbed the cordless phone.

El pressed the button, and there was a dial tone.

"Dammit. I don't know Jake's number."

"Fuck that, dial 911," Emma said as they moved.

Halfway up the stairs, the power went out, surrounding them in complete darkness as they reached the top.

Screaming, tormented voices came from the phone. El pressed the button and hung up. Then, activating her cell phone's flashlight, she moved into the crowded attic. She had to release Emma's hand to do it.

"Follow me," El muttered as she entered the maze of the massive attic. Trunks and boxes were everywhere. A dress form startled her, but they kept moving.

Finally, she rounded a corner deep into the space, and her light fell on a dusty Victorian love seat.

"Sit here," El said with her light pointing to the floor. She set the cordless phone down on a trunk and slid a tall mirror to block the entrance to the small space.

El turned off the light and felt her way to sit on the oversized loveseat next to Emma. Neither of them had to say it was time to be quiet.

***

Jake stopped the truck at the start of the dirt road. He knew in a few hundred yards, there would be no signal.

He dialed the house number, and it was answered with static in one ring. No one said anything. The static and crosstalk voices were there.

"El, if you can hear me, I am on the way to the house," Jake said as he began to move.

"Jake, no." The call was terminated.

Jake felt every pothole in his injured arm. Because of that, he went slower than he wanted to.

His slow pace allowed him to notice the eyes.

A black cat sat on every pillar, rock, and tombstone he passed. He had never seen so many.

His headlights fell on the car up ahead. He stopped

behind it. The driver-side door was open. Forgetting about the pain in his arm, Jake grabbed his flashlight and got out.

"Eleanore?" he called out, almost stumbling as he rushed to the open door. It was empty. The keys were still in it. "El, where are you?"

His flashlight shined on the flat tires then. He closed the door and rushed back to his truck with his heart in his throat.

He saw clothes scattered on the road and then a duffle bag in his headlights. He sped that last quarter mile and skidded to a stop in front of the porch.

All the lights were out. The power was down. But there was a single light showing in a third-floor window.

***

Felix watched the man move through the cemetery and to the entrance grave. He lowered himself down and through the small opening despite the smoke.

Felix could smell panic and murder on the man's breath and knew he was heading for the locked house.

Felix followed…

***

Jake found that the door was locked. So he used his keys to enter.

"Eleanore?! Is anyone here?" he called out and began searching room to room by flashlight. He started with dread in the library. Then, dripping with memories of finding Lilly, he found it empty.

He began a systematic search of the house. Finally, Jake rushed up to the small third-floor room. Opening a heavy door, he found a silver serving tray in the center of the floor filled with black candles—all lit.

His flashlight flickered and failed.

A gust of wind in the room extinguished the candles and slammed the door shut. It sounded like a gunshot.

Jake was plunged into darkness.

***

"Did you hear that?" Emma whispered. It sounded like a gunshot in the house to El. "Come out to the country, and we'll have a few laughs…." Emma said sarcastically. "What am I sitting on?" She pulled a small book from under her and dropped it on the floor.

"Shhhh…" El hushed. The sound was not repeated. El stood up and was immediately unnerved. She had the sense that she was not alone. She felt that she was surrounded by many people standing still, just as she was.

El's phone lit just then. Not the flashlight but just the login screen. She shined it down, and Emma picked up the book from the floor.

It was just enough light to see the people on all sides that surrounded El. Men and women. Dressed in clothes from the past.

"El, you gotta see this," Emma whispered and

directed the book to El.

Tall mirrors on all sides surrounded them.

El could see it was herself in every mirror.

***

Thompson made his way through the tunnels and up into the house. The first peephole looked into the hallway on the main level. He turned off his penlight and drew aside the small curtain.

A pair of burning eyes stared in at him.

He screamed and fell backward onto the floor of the passage. He dropped his penlight and scrambled for it.

The apparition now loomed over Thompson.

He screamed.

***

Jake could not open the door. When it slammed, the doorknob fell out from the other side. The knob on this side was useless.

There was a blood-curdling scream. Then, a crashing so hard Jake felt the house shake.

That scream was not El—was not even a woman.

He was about to use his phone for a bit of light when he saw a crack of moving light in the wall. He ran his hand about the paneling like El had done in the bedroom below.

Directly below.

He found the latch, and the secret door swung

inward. It was the same kind of secret passage. Another door directly across opened inward in the back of the closet next door.

At the end of the short hall was a ladder. Light from a flashlight danced there briefly. He looked down into the ladder shaft and saw a man descending the ladder in a near panic.

Another crash informed Jake that he must have jumped or fallen below. Another scream followed a gunshot.

A gunshot?

Jake descended anyway.

When he reached the first-floor level, he heard what sounded like the radio. Again, static and voices whispered, but they were not screaming this time. They were laughing.

The laughing was worse.

He wanted to call out for Eleanore.

Another crash followed by breaking glass came from the basement.

Jars from the pantry shelves?

Jake left the passage into the library. He almost screamed, but it was only his reflection in one of the mirrors there. Stepping into the main floor hallway, he looked to the left, and the front door was wide open.

A Felix was silhouetted in the doorway.

Jake grabbed the gun from the butler's pantry and finished searching the house. He knew he had to go down to the tunnel next. But first, he would get a good flashlight.

Jake crossed the breezeway into the carriage house

to get the emergency flashlight in the shop. The single bulb over his head came back on as he reached for it. He grabbed the light and moved to the phone base station to call 911.

The phone was gone.

Jake ran back into the house, grabbed the cordless phone there, and immediately dialed 911.

Static screams and laughter blared from the phone.

***

Thompson ran.

Each time he looked behind, it was still there. Its eyes were small windows into hell. He kept tripping and falling in the long tunnel. The farther he went, the closer it got. The smoke was getting thicker. Then, finally, he ran headlong in panic.

A silent crowd of shadows filled the tunnel before him when he looked up. But these had open mouths filled with blood and flame as they silently screamed. An equal number of cats sat at the apparitions' feet with eyes that glowed just as bright.

He fled up the narrow tunnel that led to the grave exit, nearly blind from the smoke. The cats flooded into the cave behind him when he looked back.

Reaching the tiny access point, he climbed into the opening with blind panic, slamming his head hard on the marble slab above the entrance.

Disoriented, he crawled in on his belly to find a dead end. Rolling onto his back, he shined his light around and realized he was inside a coffin with the opening at his feet.

He turned off the light and covered his mouth to silence his breathing, hoping to hide there for a moment.

The burning eyes appeared between his feet.

Thompson screamed, and the tombstone above the opening gave way. It slid straight down like a blade on a guillotine, completely sealing him in.

He screamed.

***

There was a thick wooden door on the side of the ice well near the bottom. Years of spring water had soaked, swollen, and sealed the door tightly closed on the far side.

The spring that fed the church cistern had filled the basement and sub-basement of the church ruins. The tunnel to the ice well was the lowest point.

When the tombstone fell, the door gave way. It was like pulling the drain plug on a bathtub. Water flooded into the bottom of the ice well and into the massive bed of coals. Steam roared up and out, helping to extinguish the fire.

Felix sat in the bell tower, watching the cloud of steam fill the forest and cemetery as the foundation drained.

El Runs Home

They are all awake.

***

Emma showed Eleanore the first page of the open book. It was a handwritten diary or journal.

I buried Everett on March 1ˢᵗ.

On March 15ᵗʰ, I caught the priest wearing Everett's shoes.

"What is this?" El whispered as she turned to the last entry.

They had an altar in the sub-basement. Made of the heads of the statues. Saints and angels with the grim reaper's head at the top. Splattered blood from self-inflicted wounds. They've gone mad.

He watches through the walls, the mirrors.

The priest was evil—robbing graves.

He has Everett's shoes.

He lit the church on fire. He locked himself and all those people in that horrible room.

I was too late.

The entry stopped there.

"Where did you find this?" El asked in a hush. Sitting next to her.

"It was right here covered in dust," Emma replied. "I am still so drunk."

"Here, just put your head in my lap. I'll wake you once it's daylight." El said, drawing her over. She seemed so tiny. Emma was asleep in an instant.

El turned off her phone light. She listened to the silence of the darkness. Time passed by at a rate El could not guess. The wind in the trees grew discordant until it became a distant howl. Then rose the screams. They began like a baby crying and then insane laughter and finally screams of pain and turmoil.

Eleanore felt Emma's body tense in her lap.

Then she saw light on the floor. Dancing firelight. It moved as Emma turned her face upward to Eleanore.

Her eyes were pits of fire.

El was frozen and pinned down like a mouse beneath a cat's paw. Only the voice from the bottom of the stairs saved her.

"ELEANORE!" Jake yelled.

Springing like a pouncing cat, Emma was gone. She didn't slide a huge mirror aside. Instead, she crashed directly through it. Avalanching as she went, Emma moved in a straight line toward a window.

She dove through it without pause.

"Emma!" El screamed. She stumbled as she tried

to follow. When she got to the destroyed window, Emma stood on the grass below before a crowd of shadowy figures. All their eyes blazed.

El struggled toward the stairs. She heard more crashing, more eerie screams. She almost fell down the stairs. When she stumbled out onto the covered walkway, it was no longer Emma on the grass facing the cluster of shadows.

A barefoot, suited man with arms held wide created a gale-force wind the specters could not fight. Then, with an exhale of black steam, he turned his head and whispered, "Go…."

A crash drew El's attention as the fragments of the back door fell from the hinges. The power came back on just in time to see Jake slammed down onto the kitchen table, splintering it to pieces.

El began moving toward the house, watching Jake scramble to his feet. Emma came back into view with a butcher knife held high.

El saw it all in slow motion as she tried to move toward them. It was like her legs were in quicksand, like trying to run in a dream. She watched the knife come down, but Jake was ready. Somehow, he expertly deflected the knife and spun them both around until his left arm was wrapped around her neck, Jake was behind her, and the point of the blade was pointed at Emma's chest as they struggled into the hall and out of sight.

"Jake! NO!" El screamed.

When El rounded the corner, she saw the bloody knife on the floor. Jake's bloody left arm was tight around Emma, and his brutal grip on her hair looked like he was trying to break her neck. Her face was bloody.

He was forcing her to look directly into the mirror.

El saw the fire in her screaming mouth and eyes fade in the reflection. Then, when her eyes returned to normal, she began to struggle again.

"Jake, you gotta let her go," El commanded, noticing that she still held the journal.

Emma went limp, and she fell to the floor.

El dropped the book and went to Emma. She was sobbing, sitting up on the floor.

"Take my truck. It'll be dawn soon. Go to Ed's. Get cleaned up. Go to the hospital if you need to. Ed will get your car," Jake sounded angry.

"But, Jake…" El began.

"Go," he said.

"What happened?" Emma was waking up.

"Goddammit, Eleanore! Go. Now!" Jake pointed the way to Ed's with the gun, locking eyes with El. His burning anger, as well as his injuries, were evident.

Jake had a cut on the bridge of his nose. Emma had almost cost him his eyes. But, even though Emma had tried to kill him, he hadn't shot her. El thought they would talk later.

El was wrong.

***

Jake just sat in the rubble of the kitchen until the sun rose. Blood had stopped dripping from his nose.

Direct pressure had stopped the blood from his torn stitches.

Finally, he stood and started a pot of coffee.

Staring out the kitchen window across the lawn, he watched as the steam still rose from the ice well.

His mind emptied, and he poured coffee into a giant colorful mug.

"Must have been some party," a voice said from behind Jake. He turned his head. It was Detective Frank Tate, holding an old book.

Jake said casually without missing a beat, "Coffee?" holding up the pot.

"Please," Tate said and started leafing through the book.

Jake handed a steaming mug to the detective as if the kitchen wasn't in ruins. Then, holding an empty mug in one hand, he gestured with the carafe towards the dining room.

"And where is Ms. Wright this morning?" Tate asked, looking at the destroyed table and toppled chairs but saying nothing.

"Let's sit in the dining room," Jake said and walked through the butler's pantry to the dining room. Tate followed. Jake saw himself in the massive mirror there. It was worse than he thought. The cut on his nose had bled a lot.

"She had some car trouble and went down to Ed's to handle it."

"Ah, that was her car I saw on the flatbed tow truck I passed on the way up here. I thought I recognized her sitting in an old truck at Ed's." He took a long drink of coffee.

"You're here early. What time did you leave Fairfax to get here this early?" Jake asked.

"I have been staying in Front Royal for a few days," Tate said. "My wife joined me last night. We were planning a visit to Luray Caverns today when something came up. Have you ever been to Luray Caverns?"

"I have many times. It's lovely. Make sure you do the audio tour. They have headphones," Jake replied casually, even though he knew he was a bloody mess. The absurdity of the situation was beginning to amuse him.

"I saw a first aid kit in the pantry. I could fix you up a bit while we talk." Tate didn't wait for an answer.

Tate returned with the first aid kit and a roll of paper towels. "Pour me another cup of coffee."

While Jake poured, Tate returned from a trip to the kitchen. He found a clean soup bowl and half-filled it with water.

"The deeper I looked into the death of Ryan McKinley, the more it looked like murder. He was the king of the asshole lawyers in a town of asshole lawyers. Finally, we had the video of the motorcyclist shooting out the tire. No one knew that." He was scrubbing the dried blood from Jake's face. "Pressure began trickling down from above. Politicians, execs, and even judges. Leverage."

"Pressure to do what?" Jake asked. "Find who murdered him?"

"To close the case as an accident," Tate said. "In

the beginning, the pressure was to point at Ms. Wright. Then, after Joyce Jacobs started stirring the pot, the Chief started getting his chain yanked when that wasn't working out. Someone was panicking. Take the shirt off."

Jake took off the ugly white and yellow shirt. The left sleeve was soaked with blood. The arm bandages were also soaked.

"So why were you out here?" Jake asked as Tate cut off the bandages.

"Remember that guy at the Fish fry? He's dead, by the way. One-car accident on I-81 on Friday night." Next, he began cleaning, then closing up the spots that had torn open.

"Joyce being Eleanore's lawyer, she managed to leverage El's standing as a silent senior partner to find the name of the SUV driver with that plate number."

He wrapped the arm again.

"Oh, man. Joyce is good," Jake said.

"Of the four men assigned to that contract, two are dead. One is still missing. The last one was spooked. The security firm owner ordered him to cooperate with us in exchange for considerations," Tate said. "He said Thompson was harassing Ms. Wright. And you."

"So why are you here?" Jake asked.

"Thompson and another man from that security team are missing and are wanted for questioning. I'm worried they came here. Might still be here." Tate sat again and finished his coffee, looking at the destroyed table in the kitchen. "Jake, you don't seem like the type that would get wrapped up in shit like this. Get some rest."

***

Jake took the advice and went to The Cabin for rest. He decided to skip the shower and went straight to bed with his mind distracted by a million random thoughts. He knew he had to get it together before he saw El again.

Unfortunately, a fever arrived while he was sleeping. His mind clouded, and he lost track of time. He drank water and slept. He mostly didn't leave his bed for three days.

***

El woke with a start at the knock on the truck window. Emma didn't stir. Her feet were in El's lap this time.

It was Detective Tate.

"Good morning, Detective. What are you doing here?" El said.

"Good morning," Tate said. "Can we talk in private?"

"Sure," El slid out of the truck without waking Emma.

"I was up at the house this morning and saw Jake." Tate began. "Takes a lot to make a man like that angry."

"I know," El replied.

"You need to go see Ms. Jacobs today. This morning. There have been developments," Tate said in a lowered tone.

"What kind of developments?" El asked.

"Thompson is missing. He's not in DC. He is also wanted for questioning. He may be here in Covington. He may not be happy with you or Joyce."

"Jake is angry?"

"Ms. Wright, I don't know what's happening with you two. Just give him some space. And he is likely not the only one angry right now."

***

Jake didn't return her call that day. After a while, she could tell he had turned his phone off. She stopped calling.

On Sunday, both Eleanore and Emma returned to DC.

The Brownstone

Felix waited for a long time. She was finally here, for the last time…

***

It was after midnight when El pulled into the garage behind the brownstone. The one-way access lane behind the homes was now lined with trash cans.

The garage door slid up, and she pulled in at the angle she always did. It made her nauseous—a simple act reminding her of her old life. The garage was detached from the house, and a small walled courtyard was between the two. A professional gardener maintained that space, and she paused when she realized she didn't even know that man's name. She looked at how beautiful the flagstones, retaining walls, lush plantings, and stonework was.

A black cat watched her from the top of the wall.

It looked just like Felix. When it nodded and slowly blinked at her, her heart skipped a beat. She froze until it turned and disappeared into the shadows.

The house was sterile. She had never noticed it before. It was more than the smell of the Windex the maid service used. It was the modern, barren nature of it, a lack of life. She hated it. She had never hated it before.

El wandered through the main level looking for anything personal. She was looking for anything she wanted. She found only three things. She had purchased a piece of pre-Columbian art in Belize on a trip, a petrified skull of a saber-tooth tiger, and a painting by a local artist named Denis Goris. The picture was an abstract portrait of a woman. Ryan hated them all.

She looked into the fridge, and it was empty. Was that how she lived? The kitchen island had a full wine fridge, though. She poured herself a glass of wine and took it to the living room. She managed only half a glass before falling asleep on the sectional sofa.

Nightmares soon found her.

She was buried alive in a coffin, screaming and clawing. Then, it flashed to fire and smoke, and she was trapped with a cowering crowd. Then she was falling into the bottomless ice well. Then it was her wedding day again, except Ryan was bloody and his face ruined, and among the people in the church, a woman in the third row was also bloody.

El kept waking with a start. She could not bear to go upstairs to her bedroom. Not the bed where she slept with Ryan.

And then her dream turned.

Felix sat in the window seat. El somehow knew he stood guard. Was that black steam drifting up from him?

***

El finally woke up at dawn. She almost expected to find Felix there. Instead, she made coffee with the Keurig at 6:30 am. She made coffee directly into a travel mug. She'd never touch one of those black mugs again. The packers would be there at 8 am, and she needed to be awake.

She wandered through the house with a pad of Post-its and a marker, with coffee in hand. There was more than she thought. She'd take all the books, the wine in the cellar, and the expensive booze in the bar. That snowballed into the fine glassware.

The artwork she wanted to keep would need to be packed carefully. There was more of that than she realized as well.

By the time the crew had arrived, she had a good head start. They brought formal packing boxes and were really careful with everything. All her clothes from her walk-in closet were packed in garment boxes on the hangers.

All of Ryan's clothes were also packed but labeled for drop-off at the Salvation Army. His empty closet revealed a wall safe that El did not know existed.

The only woman on the crew was named Beth. She had impressive full sleeve tattoos. Beth handed her a long odd-looking key as they carried the last box out.

"This is the key to that safe. I found it on the shelf just above. It's supposed to be… In case you forget the combination." Beth had a lilting southern accent. "Pop this cover off, and that's where it goes." Beth left her alone.

El used the key to pop the cover off. It fit easily and turned with a heavy clunk. The safe contained two envelopes, a stainless steel .357 revolver, and a box of bullets. The thick envelope was full of $100 bills—the other envelope contained two concealed carry permits for Washington, DC. One was issued to Ryan McKinley and the other to Eleanore Wright. She checked the revolver. It was loaded. It was all a surprise to her, and it all went into her courier bag.

Only three pieces of furniture were packed. The biggest thing was a spinet piano she had learned to play when she was a child. She had dragged it around her whole life. And Ryan hated it. The next was an antique rocking chair that had been a gift from her parents. And last and most fragile was the antique mirror from the landing on the stairs. It was eight feet tall, and she had no idea what she'd do with it.

In all, it was one and a half PODs of boxes.

Carmen Burke, the realtor, arrived before the crew had left. The plan was that she would lead them to the warehouse and store the containers there. At the curb out front, Beth, the crew chief, handed El the keys to the new padlocks on the PODs. El tipped each crew member with a $100 bill from the envelope.

She thought of it as Ryan's money.

"Carmen, I will leave the house tomorrow," El said. "All that is left in there conveys. Stage it and list it for a quick sale. With my thanks."

"Still want to sell the warehouse?" Carmen asked as she made notes on her phone.

"Yes. Same deal, quick sale," El said.

The Firm

***

The law firm of Thompson, McKinley, Jones, and Levi occupied an entire floor in the historic Henderson building on M street in DC. The building was bigger than she remembered. The first-floor café was packed at 9 am. She was early and decided to get a coffee before she went up.

I'm not drinking ANYTHING they hand me.

The elevator was crowded. She went up, and four people got out on the same floor as El.

Clerks and interns like I once was... now I own this building.

She didn't recognize the attractive receptionist, but she recognized Eleanore.

"Good morning Ms. Wright. Please come straight back. Can I get you a coffee or water?" she said automatically, not noticing that El had a large coffee already.

"No thanks. I'm good." She held up the cup in explanation.

The main conference room was empty, and the receptionist pulled out the high-quality leather chair with a table setting of notepad with pens and pencils.

El ignored her and sat at the head of the table after laying her courier bag on the table.

Slightly flustered, she said, "I'll let Ms. Levi know you are here," and fled.

Eleanore had been prepared to wait. Power plays and all. She even had a book to read. *Rendezvous With Rama*. Two sips of coffee, and she had not even opened the book when Levi entered wearing a fake smile with her pearls.

She held out her hand. "Eleanore, how have you been..."

El didn't rise, just cut her off. "How do you think I've been, Helen?" She emphasized Helen, knowing she hated to be called that. She glanced at the hand like it was covered in spit. It probably was.

Levi wiped off her hand and sat, trying to regroup.

"Detective Tate tells me that Thompson and half your investigators have fled. As a senior partner interest in this firm, what can you tell me about that? And don't bullshit me because I probably know already."

"Well… Mr. Thompson, it seems has been…." Levi stalled.

"Embezzling," El interrupted. "And he is likely now out of the country. I don't care. I am here to discuss the terms of your offer. I believe Ms. Jacobs, my hick lawyer, was quite clear."

Levi slid a folder over to her.

El opened the folder and on top of the thick sheaf of paper was precisely what Joyce had specified. It was a summary sheet that was signed and notarized by all the remaining partners.

El closed the folder and placed it inside her courier bag. When she did, Levi saw the stainless steel revolver in the bag. Then, El stood and left the conference room, the offices, and the building without another word.

In the car, she took a photo of the summary page and texted it to Joyce, saying, *Almost done here.*

The offer was $18 million for her share in the law firm and the building. El knew it was half of what she should demand. She'd get another $3M for the brownstone. She didn't care. She was too tired. She was too angry. She was too disappointed.

I'd trade it all for…

She had to stop herself. She wasn't done. Then she'd drink wine and cry all she wanted.

No, you won't. None of this bullshit will ever make me cry again.

She knew she'd trade it all if Jake would be nice to her again and make her cry.

He just wants my money… He never called.

She literally shook her head and entered the condo's address in the GPS. It wasn't far, just over the river, in Virginia.

The Last Straw

Felix watched her from the wall. Yet another wall. So many walls…

***

El had dreaded the condo tour. She didn't need to know any more about the depth of Ryan's assholery. But, before meeting with the realtor this afternoon to turn over the keys, she needed to see the amount of work it was going to be.

The condo was on the 4th floor on North Meade street, overlooking the US Marine Corps War Memorial, the one where the soldiers were all pushing the flag up. She had never been to that monument before. So after parking at the curb right in front of the condo's address, El walked over to the small park.

The statue was far larger than she thought it would be. As she walked all the way around it, she knew she was avoiding the task. Stalling. She started back when she saw a black cat watching her from a perch on top of the marble wall beside the stairs up to the monument.

It was precisely like Felix.

The cat watched her exactly as Felix had watched her. She knew if she approached the cat, he would disappear. So she met his eyes and nodded.

The cat nodded back. She had the irrational feeling that it somehow said, *It's time.*

Time for what?

She looked at her watch, and it was 11:55 am, and when she glanced back, it was gone. It must have hopped down on the far side, and it was gone. El didn't bother looking for it. She knew she wouldn't find it.

She looked up at the 4th floor and the three large windows there. They all had arched tops and must have a spectacular view.

The foyer was clean and straightforward and on the elegant side. There were only seven brass mailboxes and only one on the 4th floor: unit 401, her unit.

The elevator opened onto a square foyer with a single door in the center of each wall. One was the elevator, one had a brass plate that said ROOF, another said UTILITY, and the one straight ahead said 401.

The key turned smoothly in the deadbolt. The door opened with a soft chime from inside the condo. A classic door chime from an alarm system that was thankfully not on.

The place was elegantly decorated in the Scandinavian style, and it instantly made her think of Jake. But, looking around, there was not a single book in sight.

The place was a mess.

Full ashtrays and half-eaten Chinese take-out cartons covered the coffee table, dining table, and even the hearth of the beautiful stone fireplace. Empty wine and Scotch bottles were everywhere.

Stained teak wood was the cohesive theme. The large coffee table was ruined with water rings from glasses. The low sofa and chairs were matched tan leather.

The tall windows drew her to the view. She could see over the trees to the memorial. The Lincoln Memorial, Washington Memorial, and even the Capitol building beyond were in line beyond the monument.

"About fucking time you show up," a woman's voice came from the loft above as she exited the double doors there. She had a slight Russian accent, heavily tinged with condescension. She didn't even look at El as she descended the black iron spiral stairs. She wore only a pink silk robe and black lace panties. The robe was untied and barely covered her fake boobs.

"Clean this level first," the woman said. "Master bedroom last. We'll be up in two hours." She entered the kitchen, opened the fridge, and took out a crystal carafe of OJ. When she turned, she saw El for the first time. She dropped the OJ and screamed.

"What did you do now?" came a man's voice from upstairs.

"It's her!" she yelled and backed away like El was a zombie there to eat her.

The man cursed, and after a minute, he came out on the loft balcony like a stormcloud. He wore jeans, but that was all.

He had a baseball bat in his hand.

He stormed down the stairs saying, "I suggest you get the fuck out and never come back."

"Funny, I was going to say the same to you." El had drawn the stainless steel .357 from her purse and held it with both hands, steady aim at his center mass. When he saw her, he dropped the bat and cowered. He began backing out.

I am so sick of everyone's shit. Joyce was right.

"It's her. Ryan wife. Please don't kill us, too!" She frantically put on a trench coat and grabbed an oversized Louis Vuitton purse from the hall table.

Really, Ryan? Could you be any bigger or more cliché an asswipe?

"Out," El barked. And they fled.

Gun still in hand, she took out her phone and called the realtor from recent contacts.

"If you still want these listings, get a locksmith and a professional cleaning crew over to the Meade Street condo in less than an hour," El said.

"I'm on it," Carmen said and hung up.

El opened the windows to begin airing the place out.

Carmen Burke was there in fourteen minutes. The locksmith was there in twenty-two minutes, and the cleaning crew forty-nine minutes.

The primarily cleaning crew of fifteen made El think of Mabel's Mops, Andrew Rodregiz and Jake. Again.

***

Two hours later, the cleaning crew was finishing up. El and Carmen were sitting at a table on the roof patio and talking about the sale of the brownstone townhouse. That would be an easy sale. But, for some reason, the brownstone, the condo, and the warehouse were all in Eleanore Wright's name alone. It was bothersome that she didn't remember signing anything regarding any of them.

One of the cleaners politely interrupted them. "Miss Wright, a Mrs. Petrov is here asking for Ekaterina's things. We collected all the personal items, like clothes and toiletries, into large trash bags. What would you like us to do?"

"We'll come down," El said and followed her to the stairs.

An elderly woman stood in the foyer wringing the handle of an old purse.

"May I help you? I'm Eleanore Wright." El said to the woman.

"I apologize for Ekaterina. My daughter. She told me everything. Even this. She stole this. I return." Her Russian accent was worse than Ryan's mistress. She took out car keys and a piece of paper from her purse and handed them to El with shaking hands.

It was a car title in Eleanore's name to an Audi R8 Coupe.

The cleaner carried out four large trash bags full of items, mostly clothes.

"Ekaterina not always bad girl. She come here, and bad men find her. Too beautiful, too weak. Needed the rug pulled. You puller. I thank."

"Carmen, have you got a pen?" El asked the realtor, knowing they always did. She took it, signed over the title, and handed it back to her with the keys and title.

"What this?" the old woman asked.

"Sell the car. Make a new start. I don't want it. Save her."

Two of the cleaners came out holding the four trash bags. They followed the old lady into the elevator as she was stoically trying not to cry.

"You do just want out," the realtor commented.

***

They toured the condo after the cleaners left. It was like a new place. Even the smell of cigarettes was gone. The condo was huge. It was a two-master suite, almost 3,000 square foot condo.

"I'm going to stay here tonight." El had made a decision. "Sell the rest. I'm going to take Levi's offer. I want a quick sale on the brownstone and the warehouse. If the warehouse sells fast, I will have the

PODS or whatever those containers are called moved. Hold off on this place, though."

The realtor left with a smile. El called Emma next.

"Em, you almost done for the day?" Eleanore asked as she collapsed on the sofa.

"Say the word, and there will be a cloud shaped like Emma in this cubical."

"I will text you the address. And do not dare show up without a case of good wine and a pile of Chinese takeout. The garage security code is 0666."

True to her word, Emma was there faster than the Roadrunner. She was kicking the door instead of knocking or ringing the bell because she carried a case of wine, a large paper takeout bag, and two grocery bags.

"Whhhaaattt???" Emma dragged out as she let El pile the bags on the counter and start stacking the wine in the now-empty fridge.

Emma rushed to the view. She ran from room to room as El related the morning experience. Finally, after seeing it all, they were back in the kitchen looking for a corkscrew to open the chilled white.

"I'm keeping it. We're sleeping here tonight," El said as Emma poured. "I call dibs on the main level master."

"It won't bother you that it's where he kept his mistress?" Emma asked as El grabbed another bottle of white and took Emma to the roof patio to eat.

"Hell, no. Nothing about this place reminds me of Ryan. The style is too modest and simple for him." El took a long pull on her wine as Emma deployed food containers. "Besides, all the bastard's come stains will be in your room in the loft."

"Stop trying to arouse me," Emma said. "When can I move in?" she joked, bringing an enormous amount of lo mein noodles to her mouth.

"Today," El said, deadpan. Emma froze with the lo mein poised in front of her mouth.

El tossed a brand new key onto the glass top.

"All this bullshit is finally about to be settled. I'll need to go back to Covington soon and figure out everything. But, on the other hand, I don't see you quitting your job anytime soon, so why not. Win-win."

"I'm not going to live here for free and be your maid-sex-slave-house-bitch! I'm paying rent and doing what I want! So you think there are come stains now? Just wait!"

"OK, but you will only pay what you pay now. And you will let me buy out your lease."

"Who gets the Escalade in the garage? The keys are in it," Emma said through a mouth full of noodles.

"Escalade?" El said.

The Return

We all sat vigil to witness her return.

***

El turned off the paved road onto a freshly graveled drive. Autumn was in full color. The driveway had been graveled, but it had also been regraded so well that her new Escalade's four-wheel-drive was unnecessary. The grass to either side of the road was neatly mowed, and the trees trimmed.

She slowed when she approached the first gate to the cemetery. The brick columns and the iron gate had been repaired and painted. The cemetery beyond had neatly mowed grass.

Further down the drive, Kilroy's Rock was neatly mowed, highlighted, and trimmed with fresh landscaping and mulch.

All three gates were the same. They were more beautiful than she had ever seen them. They now allowed views of the monuments beyond. Their heads had been restored.

The final columns were new. The only familiar part was the carved marble street number for the address.

137.

She remembered that first math problem at Mike's Diner then. As she passed through that final threshold, she saw the Rectory.

It was transformed.

The clean white of the siding and deep forest green of the shutters and trim dazzled in the dappled sunlight through the trees. New plants in artfully shaped beds around the old oaks took her breath away.

She stopped her SUV in the driveway and parked it just to get out and take it in.

The lawn to the left was perfect and as long as a football field and led to a sizeable screened-in gazebo that she knew must be over the ice well. She could see even from there the final gate had also been restored.

Eleanore Wright was thinking about the broken steps and ruined porch as she stepped up onto it. Her hand went to her mouth when she saw the oak porch swing.

She had to unlock the front door before entering. The antique furniture in the foyer gleamed with polish on the old oak. A vase of fresh wildflowers was on the side table next to the stained-glass Tiffany lamp. The fresh paint on the walls and ceiling was bright.

The lights were on in the house. Everything was clean new paint, and amazing. Several mirrors had been replaced with heirloom paintings found in the carriage house attic.

Room after room was beyond perfect. Every view from each window was like a beautiful photograph. The kitchen was the perfect mix of old and new.

When she opened the fridge, it was newly cleaned and only contained Oscar Mayer bologna, Kraft individually sliced cheese, a loaf of Wonder white sandwich bread, Hellman's squeeze mayo, and a pack of Diet Cokes.

She didn't know if it was a sob or laugh that slipped out as she closed the fridge door.

The hall bath was essentially the same with new fixtures. And the tiny bedroom was the same, but now pristine clean with new paint. The bed was perfectly made, with the same antique quilt. Before she knew what she was doing, she lay down on the bed. She buried her face in the pillow.

His scent wasn't there.

She sat up and gathered herself.

She started to exit the room but hesitated. Finally, she turned and went to the dresser and opened the top drawer.

Neatly folded, the only item it contained was the t-shirt. The MCR shirt. My Chemical Romance.

Gently she lifted it. She knew it was his.

***

She finished the tour holding the shirt. Even the secret passages had been cleaned and dusted. New flashlights were in there too. The tunnel into the cemetery had been walled up again. The body of her shoeless grandfather had been returned to its resting place next to her grandmother Lillian.

After touring the house, she took the spiral stairs that led to another cleaned tunnel. All the bodies that had been recovered now rested within the cemetery's consecrated grounds. The grave robber tunnel had been closed and sealed.

The passage now came out into the basement of the church ruins. It was no longer flooded, and the walls and flagstone floor had been power-washed.

An ornate patio table and four chairs were perfectly placed there.

Stairs to the ground level were inside the base of the bell tower. The new gazabo was near the exit. It looked like it had always been there.

The toppled tombstone was gone.

She approached the entrance to the cemetery and saw two new plots. The first held the toppled stone, now correctly installed.

It read:
Everett Wright
Beloved Husband
Proud Father

The new monument was there.

Lillian Wright
Beloved Wife
Loving Sentinel

Adjacent to it was a simple stone that listed eighteen names. Below were only the words REST IN PEACE.

***

El returned to the house. She was drying tears with the t-shirt when she entered the carriage house. All of Jake's tool chests were gone. It was tidy in there, and the only items in there were the riding mower, its little trailer, and her grandmother's light blue 1966 Impala station wagon.

Had someone washed and waxed it?

She turned to go back into the house via the breezeway when she saw a drawing titled Solarium Green House on the workbench.

A closer look showed a plan to convert the church's basement foundation into a glass-roofed solarium. The drawing and plans were not signed.

She carried the plans back into the house and laid them on the kitchen table, and when she reached for the old rotary phone, she noticed an invoice tacked to the bulletin board. Carl's Lawn and Garden services were paid through December 31st.

She called Emma.

Emma answered on the first ring. The connection was clear without a bit of static.

"Hey, girl. I got here," El said.

"So is it finished, or are you burning it down? If so, wait for me so you can have an alibi in town," Emma said quickly.

"It's done. It's more beautiful than I could have imagined," El said. "He…" she trailed off.

"You gonna sell it then? Two thousand one hundred acres and all will be worth a mint! So do what you want, go where you want. Leave all this bullshit behind!"

"I'll talk to Joyce. Let her handle it all," El said. "I'm too tired." She had not been sleeping well. No more sleep walking, though.

"I'm driving up to Covington tomorrow. Let Alex and me take you to Fish-Fry Day." Emma was trying to cheer her up. She knew it.

"I don't want to risk seeing Jake," El said in a monotone.

"Jake has not been to Alan's since you left. Alex says he is selling his place in town. Probably to Brian downstairs," Emma said. "Alex has not seen him, either. For a couple of months."

"Okay. I'll see you Friday," El said. "Say hi to Alex for me."

"You OK?" Emma asked.

El pressed her face into the t-shirt and sobbed. Rapidly gathering herself, she said, "I'm fine. Stop being nice to me, bitch."

"Fuck you, El. You're ugly, and you dress funny!"

"Eat shit, Emma."

"Now that's my girl," Em replied. "See you Friday." She hung up.

El hung the receiver up and noticed a collection of business cards stuck in the frame of the small bulletin board. She recognized Jacobs and Associates right next to Detective Tate's card. But there were new cards for plumbers, electricians, lawn service, and painters—even the funeral parlor in town.

He took her for all he could and moved on.

Selling his place in town.

I may be an asshole, but that doesn't mean I'm the only one.

Ask him what he did in Iraq.

We're getting married…

She left the lights on and locked the house. Felix was lying down on the porch swing. El could hear the cat purring from where she stood. She went over and sat next to him. He looked up at her and slow-blinked. Then, he rolled onto his back, closed his eyes, and purred even louder.

El sat and petted the cat's belly. Its fur was so clean and soft that she couldn't believe it was a feral cat.

El stayed there almost an hour before an old Ford Ranger pulled up behind her Escalade. Rob Jensen got out. She almost didn't recognize him. His hair and beard were neatly trimmed, and he wore a clean pair of jeans and a nice Tommy Bahama Hawaiian shirt.

"I've never seen anyone but Jake able to pet that cat," Rob said awkwardly.

"Hello, Rob," she said.

"I was just dropping off the rest of the keys. I won't bother you." Felix raised his head and gave him a death stare when he came up the stairs. El continued to pet him as Rob held the keyring out to her.

She noticed his watch.

A Rolex. Jake's Rolex?

"Thank you." After a pause, but before he could leave the porch, she asked, "Did Jake give you his watch?"

He looked at it then.

"No. We got these from a street vendor in Basera when we were in the service together. Jake and me and… Anyway, we knew they weren't genuine Rolex watches. Lasted pretty good, though. It still works. Looks nice."

"Rob, what did Jake do in Iraq?" El asked.

Rob was studying his new shoes as if he could find the answer there.

"He was a sniper." Rob glanced at her. "He almost got out clean. Only a week left on his tour…." He paused. "He was wounded, lost his partner. Not my story to tell."

El could see the discomfort on Rob's face. She instantly regretted asking him, putting him in an awkward position.

"Thanks for all your work here, Rob. It's beautiful."

Rob just nodded and went to his truck without another word.

Felix lowered his head and closed his eyes. His purring emptied El's mind.

El had lost track of time sitting on that porch swing. The leaves rustling in the breeze brought her back. Felix was gone, and she had not noticed his exit.

She got in her SUV and drove slowly to town.

***

Felix watched her go from Kilroy's Rock. El didn't see him sigh and dissolve into black steam.

Client Privilege

The Armies are gone. Peace has yet to be…

***

El marveled more at the state of her lane on the drive down to Covington. Her gas tank's warning chime came on as she turned onto the main road. She pulled into Ed's Texaco and waved to Hector.

Ed was at her window instantly.

"Miss Wright! You got a new SUV! I like to see folks buy American. Well done."

"Fill it up and check the oil, please," El said.

"Yes, ma'am."

El popped the hood release as she got out and headed inside. "Hi, Olivia."

"Miss Wright, you're back! House is done now, I expect. All them crews were stopping in here for breakfast, lunch, and fuel. Keeping my dad hoppin'."

"Crews?" she said as she set her Arizona Ice Tea

327

on the counter.

"That small army, working on your house," Olivia clarified.

"Yes. It's finished. It's lovely."

"My dad says they found the priest and his followers when they drained the old church foundation. Are they all gone now? The ghosts, I mean. Dad says they are. The good and bad ones."

"Everett Wright was my great-grandfather. He's at rest now, next to Lily."

I hope they can all rest now. Even the old grave robbing, peeping tom priest.

"Tell Jake I said hi!" Olivia added. "I haven't seen him in weeks."

El just nodded as she left the store, unable to speak past the lump in her throat.

Ed had finished. He was looking up at the sky. It was a rare, perfectly clear blue sky.

She held out her card, but Ed didn't notice. El looked up as well. "What is it, Ed?"

"Somethin's changed. No chemtrails. Ain't seen that since 9/11."

El paid for the gas and rolled toward Covington.

Maybe Ed was right this time…

The town appeared as it always had, with one notable exception. She slowed to a brief stop. Brian's Books had a For Sale sign displayed in the second-story window. It was marked SOLD. She looked through the window into the bookstore. Samantha Goodwin was in there showing her ring to Brian over the counter.

El's heart ached.

She parked directly in front of Jacobs and Associates. Then, after two minutes, she gathered her courage and went in.

The little bell rang. Amy Bryant looked up and smiled wide. "El, welcome back. She has a client in there right now, but she knows you're here. It'll just be a few minutes. Can I get you a coffee? Water?"

"No, thank you, Amy," El said as the phone rang, and Amy took it.

Instead of sitting, she admired Joyce's collection of books. It was mostly sets of leather-bound books on law. They were beautiful volumes. One book did not match the rest. It was a trade paperback titled *The Sniper in the Sand*.

On the cover was a photo of a man, a soldier. It was from behind, and he held a long rifle on his hip. He was overlooking an arid cityscape of lower buildings.

He wore a Rolex.

She opened the book, and on the title page, a handwritten inscription said, *No. It's not me. He was my friend.*

Joyce's door opened, and a smiling Ashley-the-Waitress came out first, saying goodbye to Joyce.

After her farewells, Joyce turned to El and froze. Then, finally speaking, she said, "I now do believe you are a witch."

"You mean this?" She held up the book.

"Yes. Please don't read that." Joyce gingerly took it from her hands, like it was a bomb, and gently slid it back onto the shelf.

"Why?"

"Because I wish someone had stopped me from reading it." Joyce turned and expected El to follow. Instead, El hesitated a moment looking at the book on the shelf.

Amy preceded her into Joyce's office and left a folder on the table.

The door clicked closed.

"Thompson is gone. There is a warrant out for his arrest. Probably fled the country. They did find his motorcycle in the back of the cemetery. The missing security guy was found drowned in the church basement."

"Tate told me. He fell from the bell tower. His gear was still up there," El said as she sat.

"Thompson had been embezzling from the firm for years. Tate thinks your husband found out. By the way, Levi signed the proposal, and the cash payout for your share in the firm and building has already been wired to your account. Just under $18 million. You add another $3.2 mil for the townhouse. The warehouse is listed. In the meantime, the contents of the brownstone have been professionally packed, moved, and stored there."

Joyce slid another page out for her to see.

"This is the new assessed value of the Rectory and land. Another $5.1 million after the renovations."

Jake knows your net worth. Why else would he want you?

"I wanted to start over where people didn't know me." El stood and paced. "I wanted people to treat me nice because of who I was, not because of the money."

"Has someone mistreated you?" Joyce asked, confused.

"Everyone has been way too nice." El couldn't look at Joyce because El counted her among those.

"Who did you tell you had money? I've only ever seen you wearing jeans or cargo shorts. That sure as shit isn't giving you away."

"Jake must know." Then she looked at Joyce. El thought the accusation was clear that Joyce had told him.

"How the hell would Jake find that out unless you told him?"

"Jake doesn't know about the money?" El's mind was reeling.

"Of course not. Not from me. Client privilege," Joyce said, stating the obvious. "What difference does that make? Jake doesn't care about money."

"What? But he is always…"

"He's always Jake."

"Are you sleeping with him?" El flat out asked her.

Joyce was surprised by the question.

"We were together for a while years ago. After he got out of the Army, he renovated this building, and we became friends, then more for a while. I'd like to think I helped him come back to the world. He was headed for hermithood. Because of Brooke."

"Who is Brooke?"

"I'm only telling you this because I think you need to know. Brooke was a girl he met in college. Jake was studying architecture, and she was an art student. Then

9/11 hit, and it kicked everyone in the guts… Everyone except for Brooke. She thought everyone's reactions were all stupid. Jake broke it off with her. She killed herself, an intentional opioid overdose, blaming him. Jake joined the Army to get away."

"He says he still loves Sam," El said, sorrow dripping from her voice.

"Here is a fundamental truth you need to know about Jake Harris. Once he cares about you, he always will. He still says I love you to me. And I know it's true. Even now, I could call him on the phone at 3 am to pick me up because I was drunk, and he would. No questions asked. He still makes people better somehow. You can tell a lot about a person by *What They Choose* to see in you."

"I saw him say "I love you" to Sam. I saw the engagement ring in his truck. She's wearing it."

Joyce smiled at that. "She's engaged to Rob. They've lived together since you were last here," Joyce said, trying not to laugh. "Now there is the perfect couple."

"What?" Things fell into place.

The Rolex in the photos. Rob's new look. The ring. Hearing Sam in the background.

"She lied to Jake just to get him in bed. He is magnificent in bed, by the way. She never wanted children and had already gotten her tubes tied. She lied by omission. All Jake ever wanted was a family, a woman to love. And love him back."

"What about you?" El asked.

"I was all about my career and his cooking. Food and fuck buddies. At least I was honest from the beginning with him about not wanting kids. Honesty, I guess, is what he wants."

"So he's not a player? A lady's man?"

"We have now discussed the sum total of Jake's conquests and heartbreaks. I don't know about his time overseas because he never talks about it."

"Why won't he see me?"

"This is just my opinion. He's afraid you will find out how much he loves you. And then know that he could deny you nothing," Joyce said. "You will never meet a kinder, more loving, or honorable man than Jake Harris." Joyce wiped a tear away. "You're a fool if you can't see that."

***

El parked in front of the Quonset hut and walked up to The Cabin. It had taken 90 minutes to get there, and she still didn't know what she'd say when she arrived.

She could see him on the balcony from the bluff view. He was just standing there like he was waiting for something. Waiting for her.

She let herself in and walked through The Cabin. It was just the same. She could see what he was looking at now. The leaves were changing colors. The sunset would be amazing soon.

"Jake, it's me," she said softly as the glass door slid open.

He spoke without looking at her. But Rocky looked. Rocky started tapping his hip like he was saying, "Dude, Dude, Dude, DUDE, she's here."

"I know, Joyce called," Jake said to the sunset.

"What did she say?"

"Don't fuck this up, asshole," is what she said."

"I saw the house. It's amazing. I'm keeping it. I'm staying."

"Me, too." Jake looked down at the squirrel. It held his index finger in both its hands as he stared at El. "Rocky talked me out of leaving."

"You're doing the thing," El said.

"Is it working?" he asked, still not looking back.

"You sold your place in town. I thought…" El said.

"Rob bought it. Well, we kind of traded. He and Sam already moved in," Jake said. "His old place is my next project. I've never seen Rob so happy."

"I'm sorry, Jake. About everything." She knew it was a clear violation of their rules.

"You OK?" Another violation of the balance rule.

"I am now…." She wrapped her arms around him from behind and laid her cheek on his back. She could feel his heart pounding.

"Red at night, sailor's delight," he said and laid his hands softly on top of hers.

"I saw the monuments. They are all at peace, thanks to you."

"Thanks to us," Jake said.

The evening sky was ablaze. Jake finally turned to her and gently kissed her smooth brow. Then he lifted her to stand on a rock. It was the monster's head from the cemetery. The height of it brought their faces to the same level. Her arms were around his neck. She probed his hair.

"All healed up?" she asked as her mouth got closer to his.

"I'm all healed up… now," he stated.

"I love you, Jake Harris."

"I love you, Eleanore Wright."

And he kissed her.

Rocky turned back to the view, trying to ignore the cat that wasn't there…

The END

Acknowledgments

Many people have helped and encouraged me with this book. I will list some here with my eternal thanks: Stephanie Mirro, Joe Kirk, Chris Schwartz, Lea Jones, Rachel Green, and my editor Donna Royston.

I also need to thank the Loudon Science Fiction and Fantasy Writers Group, aka The Hourlings, for helping me become a better writer and for the publishing side of the biz.

A special thanks to my Spouse, who wants to remain nameless, for all the help and support you bring me.

About the Author

Cora Baker was born in 1960, and she retired a year ago from her career as a computer programmer analyst. As a lifelong reader and lover of books, Cora has decided to try her hand at the craft of writing. Her love  of genealogy, history, romance, and travel will serve her well in her creative efforts. She has started on the path to greater things with the help of an encouraging group of local writers.

Cora is currently working on her next novel and several short stories. She lives in Fredericksburg, Virginia, with her handsome husband and two cats.